The Red Canary

by

Rachel Scott McDaniel

THE RED CANARY BY RACHEL SCOTT MCDANIEL
Smitten Historical Romance is an imprint of LPCBooks
a division of Iron Stream Media
100 Missionary Ridge, Birmingham, AL 35242

ISBN: 978-1-64526-281-7

Cover design by Hannah Linder
Interior design by Karthick Srinivasan

Available in print from your local bookstore, online, or from the publisher at:
ShopLPC.com

For more information on this book and the author visit:
https://rachelmcdaniel.net/

Brought to you by the creative team at LPCBooks:
John Herring, Shonda Savage, Denise Weimer, Steve Mathisen

Library of Congress Cataloging-in-Publication Data
McDaniel, Rachel Scott.
The Red Canary / Rachel Scott McDaniel 1st ed.

Printed in the United States of America

Praise for *The Red Canary*

What a fresh new read! The sassy heroine pops right off the page, perfectly fitting with all the color and energy of her Roaring '20s setting. *The Red Canary* is bursting with glamour and vintage music, and it feels like a visit to another time. With a beautifully authentic romance standing against a real force of evil and delicately woven faith elements, McDaniel's newest novel stands out in the historical fiction genre.

~Joanna Politano
Award-winning author of *The Love Note*

Nobody writes 1920s fiction like Rachel Scott McDaniel. From the smoky haze of historic Pittsburgh nightlife to the quiet beauty of the Allegheny National Forest, she truly transports her readers to another time and place, slowly drawing us in with vivid detail and expertly crafted phrasing. This book does a fantastic job of giving her readers a little bit of everything, romance, humor, mystery, and action, and all while making you feel like you've stepped into a classic movie! I honestly adore every single word she writes, and historical fiction lovers will not be disappointed by this beautiful story.

~Abbi Hart
Adventures of a Literary Nature

Rachel McDaniel once again gives readers a delightful romp into the Roaring '20s in her latest release, *The Red Canary*. This book will transport you to 1920s Pittsburgh with its vivid descriptions and quirky time period jargon. A straight-laced hero, rough-around-the-edges heroine, and an unsolved murder will keep readers turning the pages! Vera and Mick are an unlikely pair that will win readers' hearts as they learn to trust each other and unravel the mystery.

~Ashley Johnson
Bringing Up Books

The Red Canary features a dazzlingly intelligent heroine, an evocative sense of place, and a pitch-perfect historical narrative. Toss in a whiff of suspense expertly captured with a voice that makes the Roaring Twenties sing, and you have an unputdownable read. The whip-smart dialogue and shadows of danger nipping at the heels of our delightful protagonists is underscored by chemistry that snaps, crackles, and pops every time Mick and Vera share the page. Yet, deeper still, McDaniel has penned a treatise on finding ourselves and our value in a higher place beyond our human limitation. A delightful read from a stand-out talent.

~Rachel McMillan
Author of *The London Restoration*

Here's a book I could not put down. Rachel Scott McDaniel perfectly captured the glamorous 1920s in *The Red Canary,* from the sassy nightclub singer to the strong, silent detective determined to protect her. I smiled my way through this story, especially the scenes where Mick tried to help headstrong Vera endure hiding away in the Allegheny Forest. Great read!

~Karen Barnett
Author of the Vintage National Parks Novels

Acknowledgments

Writing is never a one-man show. Many have joined me on this journey, and I'm so grateful for the opportunity to brag on them. Rebekah Millet, yes, I dedicated this novel to you, but since I can't possibly thank you enough, I'm mentioning you here as well. I'm forever indebted to ACFW Scribes because that's where God paired us up! A special thanks to agent extraordinaire, Julie Gwinn, for never giving up on my stories. Your faith in me has been a huge encouragement. To Janyre Tromp, Amanda Wen, and Janine Rosche, I appreciate all your awesome input with this story and your sweet friendship.

A giant thank you to my editor, Denise Weimer. Your excellent guidance improved this story, taking it to a new level. To the entire Iron Stream team, thank you for all you do. I'm blessed to work with you. Amy, Joy, Crissy, thank you for reading this story and for all your sweet support. To my street team, you guys are rock stars! Your enthusiasm for my stories blesses me beyond words.

To my kids, Drew and Meg: I can't think of anything more rewarding than being your mom. Thank you for putting up with me during the crunch of deadlines. To my awesome husband: Not sure if I told you, but you're the inspiration behind Mick. Your quiet strength, fierce devotion, and solid faith inspires me daily. (P.S. Remember that song you wrote for me? I pay tribute to that sweet memory in the book.)

Most of all, thanks to my God. There was a time when I gave up on this dream, but You hadn't. Thank you for supplying me with courage to face hard things. You are forever the song of my heart.

Dedication

To one of my favorite redheads on the planet, Rebekah Millet. Thank you for all your guidance, not only with this story, but in life. I'm forever blessed to have you as a friend.

CHAPTER 1

May 29, 1928
Pittsburgh, Pennsylvania

"*From that day on, death was in my song.*" Vera's voice quivered as she ended her nightly number. Lying atop the worn piano, the length of her side hummed while the eager pianist, along with the rest of the band, punched the B-minor finale. The motley assortment of musicians had their eyes closed, absorbing the last few bars of musical euphoria, but not Vera. She wouldn't shut her lids for one count. Not when he was out there. Waiting.

Applause and whistles resounded from the crowd. The maestro scowled and motioned for her to bow. Did it even matter? This was a speakeasy, not the Royal Opera House.

Gut twisting, she slid her legs over the side of the piano's belly and allowed Angelo, her hired guard, to assist her to the spit-stained floor. Cigarette smoke crept like gnarled fingers into the shadowed rafters, burning her eyes. She offered a smile as diluted as the famous Pittsburgh Scotch which soured every breath in the joint.

The note tucked in her palm taunted her, daring her to reread its threat.

Sing pretty tonight, Red. I'll be watching.

How could innocent words harbor such a dangerous undertone? The memory ignited like a flash lamp—the cloaked man's hand grasping her elbow, pulling her from backstage into the night air, the screech from the neighboring rolling mill muffling her screams.

She stiffened against the tremble. She wouldn't allow it to happen tonight. Or ever again.

Her gaze swept over the sea of felt hats, searching for the marked feature—stony gray eyes. The hazy atmosphere prevented her from distinguishing profiles beyond the bar.

The mouse-faced bandleader tapped his baton on the music stand. She glanced over, and he winked. An encore? Any other evening, she would savor the request. Would seize any excuse to yield to the rich melody, warming the drafty corners of her soul, whisking her away from reality. From life. But she wouldn't—no, couldn't—indulge now.

She shook her head, her bobbed curls bouncing off her shoulders, but the clarinet players stuffed their reeds into their mouths for the start of "Lonely Madam." Did she have any say in this gig? She mouthed the word *no*. The conductor lifted his arms for the count off.

Not this time, Maestro.

A sudden heat pulsed her blood. "For the next song ..." She crumpled and tossed the note onto the piano where she'd found it. "We have a Kelly Club original. It's not listed to showcase until the start of summer, but"—she raised her voice and pointed at the stunned man behind the music stand—"Maestro insisted on it tonight!" She clapped her hands above her head, the throng following. "It was written by yours truly. I call it 'The Hideaway Heart.'"

Vera smiled, relishing the flustered expression on the baton-toter's mug. He clumsily leafed through sheet music, pages flying to the floor. With an exaggerated sigh, he arranged a single paper to the front of the stack.

Angelo leaned against the wall to her right. She blew a kiss, signaling him. *Creep in the joint.* He nodded and straightened to full height. With Angelo on her side and Maestro unknowingly obliging, the espionage could commence.

She tapped her hand on her hip with the beat, a flawless pace.

"*You say it's romance, but there's a mystery*," she sang and descended the splintered steps to the main floor, the fringe from her silver gown tickling her knees. "*Beneath your kiss. Behind your whispers to me.*" Vera weaved through the tables, inspecting the various patrons. Plenty of silly grins and faces buried in beer mugs, but no character with predatory eyes. Not yet. "*You live behind the mask of love. But I see what you're made of.*"

Spindly fingers seized her waist, pulling. She gasped. A man yanked her onto his lap.

"Hiya, gorgeous." A sloppy smile coated his weathered face.

The crowd laughed.

Her jaw gaped, then clenched. This string bean of a man was old enough to be her father. If his green asbestos uniform didn't identify him, then the soot in the cracks of his knuckles would. A steel worker. Her scowl softened. Factory men were served dangerous tasks but handed little appreciation.

While he pawed her locks, she composed herself to finish the first verse. "*I don't like the love you veil.*"

"Won't keep my love from you, sweetheart." His pungent breath stung her nostrils.

She glanced over his shoulder. Empty glasses cluttered the tabletop.

"Look, everybody!" He sprayed her with spit, his words slurring. "I caged the Red Canary!"

Cackles rose from all around.

Caged? Hardly. His hold was as loose as the lid to his whiskey. Angelo drew closer, and Vera waved him off. This drunk was innocent—his eyes held no danger.

"*You're gonna fail. For I never trust a hideaway heart.*" A musical interlude took over, and Vera twisted free from the man's grasp, being careful not to trip over the metal lunch-pail beside his chair. "Lay off the booze, mister." She whispered in his ear and flicked it.

Dodging grasps and pokes, she rounded the bar and pulled in air for the second verse. "*I'll invade your shadow. Shout your secrets.*" She projected her voice loud enough for the band to keep in beat with her. "*Give you sorrow and have no regrets.*"

Out the corner of her eye, Angelo lingered back, waiting to pounce. Why was this taking so long? Why wasn't she spotting him? The rapid pounding of her heart threatened to knock her off tempo.

A heavier man sat by the wall. His hat pulled low, hiding his eyes. Others around him swayed to the music, but he remained motionless. What kind of game was he playing? She worked her way to that side of the room, the crowd giving her courage.

Vera stood an arm's length from the suspect and stared at his straggly mustache. No smile. No scowl. If only she could see his eyes. She sang the bridge. "*You won't win this time. Not a chance.*" A shiver coursing down her spine, she lifted his homburg. For goodness' sake, he was asleep. "*Ignore the kisses. Forget the dance.*" She pinched his cheek, and startled blue eyes peered up at her. Vera plunked his hat back onto his bald head and stepped away.

One more chorus to go. The only thing obtained from this charade was a blister rubbing raw on her heel. She glanced down. Oh, and a shoe embellished with someone's chewing tobacco. Lovely.

A scuffle broke out in front of her. A man who could be Babe Ruth's twin yanked the collar of a man dressed like a lumberjack. Lumberjack shoved the Bambino's doppelganger, launching him toward her. With nowhere to go, she pulled her elbows into her sides, ducking her head, bracing for the hit.

It never came.

She cracked an eyelid, and her lungs allowed her to breathe again. A man had stepped between her and the human bullet, shielding her and taking the impact himself. The collision hadn't budged her rescuer, his massive build standing tall. He glanced at her as if making sure she was okay.

The trumpeter blared his overlong solo, and Vera's gaze locked on the mystery hero. Definitely not a regular. She would've remembered his striking jade eyes and sharp features. Plus, his pin-striped suit wasn't rumpled or frayed at the cuffs like every other man's who stumbled in the door.

"What's your name, stranger?" She spoke in a low tone.

"Mick." He tipped his hat to her and strode to some vacant tables, his confident manner capturing her stare.

The drummer struck the cymbals, and she blinked, forced her attention off his broad back, and started toward the band. How could she let herself get distracted?

A shaded outline lingered in the corner, snapping her back to the seriousness of the moment.

She stopped. "*I'll never trust your hideaway heart.*" The figure moved forward, and her muscles tightened. "*No, I'll never trust your hideaway heart.*"

A tall sailor emerged from the darkness with a blonde hanging around his neck. Vera's shoulders curled forward with an exhale. She tossed a wink his way and sashayed to the stage. Striking a pose, she belted out the finish with her jazz flare. "*Your hideaway heart.*"

Applause soared as high as her frustration. Everything looked clear. Wait. Offstage. She cut a quick glance to her left. Dottie, the cigarette girl, sat on a stool, counting her profits. Her heavily mascaraed eyes peered over, and Vera feigned a smile. Dottie grinned back, unreserved.

The horde cheered for another encore.

Not happening.

One bow. One wave. Done.

She hustled off stage, not granting Maestro another chance to tap his beloved music stand.

Mick tugged the hem of his sports coat, ensuring the concealment of his revolver. The holster had shifted during the scuffle he'd voluntarily stepped into. He shoved clenched hands into his pockets. The spectacle had drawn attention to himself. Foolish. But what was he to do? Let the lady get pummeled by a man twice her size?

Snaking through the crowd, his gaze shifted from the bouncer to the bartender. Nothing seemed out of the ordinary, except the blatant disregard of the Volstead Act. Tomorrow he'd contact the federal agents, but it wouldn't do any good. Pittsburgh was one of the wettest cities in a supposedly dry nation. And no matter what his badge read, there was not one thing he could do about it. His temple throbbed against his hat lining.

No sight of the manager or owner. He cataloged the entrances and exits. Perhaps they holed up in the offices. But unless he wanted to pose as a busboy, there was no procuring a clearance for that part of the building.

The familiar odor of men's perspiration and tobacco smoke seeped through his skin, leaking into the stale memories of his time in the Army. The boisterous camaraderie of men. The cramped space. Only then, they'd been protecting freedom. Here, they were breaking the law. Every single one of them.

Even the prima donna.

He scratched his neck. The disgraceful slop of words from the meandering drunks had clued him into her charm, but he wasn't prepared for breathtaking. Emerald eyes and satiny skin. A dangerous combination that screamed trouble.

"Care for a smoke, mister?" The cigarette girl's voice squeaked as she approached him.

The slight wiggle in her hips and generous flutter of her eyelashes suggested she was advertising more than the tray of Lucky Strikes hanging from her slim neck. Cosmetics slapped on like war paint couldn't mask her youthful visage, her chestnut waves reminding him of his sister.

A growl strove to break free in his chest. What appeal did

this establishment have that lured young women into its seedy boundaries?

She angled toward him, her neckline plunging deeper than the Monongahela River. The urge to shed his jacket and cover her stole through him, but that'd give him away. "No, thank you."

Brown eyes rounded and pink lips pursed. Was she surprised at his refusal or the politeness of his words? She blinked twice and strutted away.

He pulled off his hat and slapped it against his thigh as he walked to a less-crowded corner. The captain's words hedged his thoughts. *Look for any peculiar activity*. He'd seen degrading and reprehensible, but not peculiar.

A distinguishable cackle pulled his attention. Lieutenant Bolin wobbled on a barstool and then proceeded to chug a pint of ale. Another officer snared by the rumrunners. How much graft money was Bolin given to buy his silence? His protection?

Mick ground his teeth. Better call it a night. He couldn't risk his superior exposing him. Besides, too much prodding would incite suspicion, and he wasn't inclined to exchange punches with the bouncer. The empty stage attracted his gaze. If the Red Canary hid wrongdoings under her pretty wings, he'd be watching when she unfurled them.

CHAPTER 2

Vera's dressing room door burst open.

She gasped stale air, dropping her lipstick brush onto her lap.

"Good show tonight, kitten." Her manager slithered in, his gaze a lazy swagger across the small space before settling on her.

"Not havin' it, Artie." She scowled, first at the intruder and then at the red smudge on her tan skirt.

He shrugged. "Only makeup. It'll wash."

"That's not what I meant." She snatched the cosmetic brush and flung it onto the vanity tray. "This is my dressing room, not a social hall. Quit barging in on me." This marked the third time in a week. What was so difficult about knocking? She bit back a huff. Because that would suggest a note of consideration. And Arthur Cavenhalt's scope of courtesy was thinner than his hairline. "I want that door fixed. With a lock that works."

"It's in my office. A nickel-brushed knob just for my pretty canary." His languid perusal of her form made her joints stiffen. "Hey, you're all tense."

"I got the jumps."

His lips curled into a smile. "Who did Angelo throw out tonight?"

"No one. But it happened again. Found another note on the piano."

"This man's carrying quite the torch for you." He laughed, his hazel eyes squinting. "What'd it say this time? A proposal?"

"You can jab all you want, Artie, but you and I both know those notes are threats. Don't forget this past fall." She winced, not wanting to relive the memory which already had haunted her once this evening. "The creep dragged me out the door the minute I stepped off stage. What would've happened if Carson hadn't found me?" He'd packed some heavy punches to the attacker's jaw before the steely-eyed man dashed away. Vera had launched herself into Carson's arms and hadn't had the courage to step away since. Well, not until recently.

"But the boss handled it. Even hired a guard for you."

Angelo. Her thick defender took his protective role as seriously as he took his liquor.

"Those love letters aren't related to what happened last September. You're overreacting like a typical female."

She stood, her toes pinching in her shoes. "Typical females don't risk their necks each night. Don't commit crimes for a paycheck." Though legally she could only be arrested if she got caught with a drink in her hands—which would never happen.

"What's got into you, kitten? Not happy?"

Happiness was *not* serenading rowdies with their shirttails hanging out. Being trapped in a booze box where days melted into years. But then, what was it? Maybe when her voice reflected the strums of her heart, the song becoming as much a part of her as a vital organ—where she needed it to breathe, to survive. Happiness was music … and all she had left.

She snatched her gown previously draped over the dressing screen and slid a hanger through it. "This place has no class. And too many have itchy fingers." She hung the swanky garment on the metal pipe running across the ceiling.

Artie ran a knuckle down the side of the dangling dress with a brassy smile. "They're just showing their approval." He glanced over, and his eyebrows danced the Shimmy.

"Well, they can keep their *approval*"—she flashed her palms—"to themselves. That goes for you too."

"You bring such character to this place, Vera. It's beyond me how you fill each moment with surprise. Say, that's a pretty good lyric. Put it in your next song."

"No, you write it, Art-man. For all I care, you can sing it too. Then I could clear out for good." Would the blinding lights of New York City be enough to dim the memories of this place? Of her past? The hollow stirring in her chest begged for the chance to find out.

"You don't mean that."

She planted a hand on the curve of her waist and glared, hoping the flooding doubt in her heart didn't seep into her eyes.

"You're not thinking of abandoning me, are you?" He clucked his tongue and withdrew a cigarette case from his trouser pocket. "Don't go shooting for anything higher, because you might end up shooting yourself. If you get my meaning." He puffed out his chest as if Vera was supposed to bow to his philosophical superiority.

Why did narrow minds always have wide mouths? She slunk onto the vanity bench. "I don't remember askin' for your advice. And don't even think about lighting up in here. As if my lungs aren't charred enough." She couldn't escape the sorry fact she lived in a city known across the country as The Big Smoke, with its numerous factories belching ashen venom into the very air she breathed, but she could control the atmosphere of her dressing room.

He sighed and returned the case to his pocket. "Just trying to help, kid." He placed a hand on her shoulder, the sweat from his palm dampening her blouse. "I can't help but feel a particular concern for you. Especially after all we've been through, cousin."

"Don't start that again."

"Do you really want your little *mystery* to be revealed? Though some may call it a lie."

She swatted his fingers, chasing away his touch. If only she could smack free his words. Mystery. Lie. What about *struggling to exist*?

"Is the boss coming tonight?"

What else could she have done? The soot-tarnished streets of Pittsburgh hadn't been her planned destination, but after a string of failed typing tests and even more disastrous job assessments, her hopes for work had narrowed from slim to nothing. The only skill she'd mastered during her first eighteen years of life had been distinguishing a dime from a nickel. But that had been enough to pique Artie's interest. Being hired as the Kelly Club's cigarette girl had been a far cry from Vera's childhood dreams, but it'd saved her from starvation. Since then, she'd been promoted to leading canary.

"Vera?" He fingered her crimson locks. "Did you hear me, or is the Notox dye sinking in?"

She jerked away from his grasp. "I don't color my hair. And how am I supposed to know if Carson is comin'?"

His brow spiked. "He's your boyfriend, isn't he?"

"What about it?"

"Just thought he'd enjoy hearing a little story." He scratched his rounded middle and rocked back on his heels. "About a girl who'd been telling fibs about who she really was since the day she was hired. A girl who manipulated her way into becoming a bootlegger's girlfriend."

Her chin poked forward. "You had a nice racket going on, but I'm not afraid of him finding out. Not anymore."

He shrugged. "Then why not up and leave like you were belly-aching earlier?"

She tried—oh how she tried—to hold her sternum stiff, keep her chest from deflating, but Artie noticed, and his smile stretched longer.

"Because you know as much as I do how Carson Kelly is paranoid over the loyalty of his staff. Careful about his—"

"Can't tack all that on me." She gripped the edges of the seat, squeezing. "Don't forget you hired me. Forced me to pretend I was related to you so I could be accepted without question. Chiseled my pay because you knew you had me in a spot." How foolish she'd been, thinking Artie had rescued her from the gutter by offering her a job, introducing her to the handsome Carson. She'd believed he'd gathered her under his wing only to discover he'd pinned her beneath his thumb.

"I have a bigger bargaining chip with the boss-man. He won't touch me. But you ..." His mocking tone thickened with each word. "If he found out you've been deceiving him all this time, he'll start to wonder what else you've been lying to him about."

"Saying I was your cousin to get a job in this joint isn't earth-shattering." Not anymore. Now that she had a good standing with Carson. Maybe he would think nothing of it, especially since she'd been drawing in crowds. Considering the hundreds of speakeasies in the area, couldn't it be viewed as an accomplishment for the mob to linger at the Kelly Club, miles away from the famed Rum Row? "I'm telling Cars, tonight. So you might as well get it through your thick, blackmailing skull—your control over me is finished."

"Let's not be hasty." He helped himself to a stool.

"You've got *nothing* on me, Artie."

"Not on Vera Pembroke, but I have a whole lot on Collette Green."

Her throat went drier than an avid teetotaler's. *How could he—*

"I have eyes everywhere." He tapped his temple. "What would Carson think when I tell him his prized singer—his favorite girl—betrayed him?"

"Look, Artie, it was only—"

"Singing for the enemy. You know how much your boyfriend hates Tony Russo. That was no small thing when the whiskey king convinced all those bootleggers to quit selling their goods to Carson. Yet you go work for Russo using a fake name. And a wig. By the way, you look awful as a blonde."

She lowered her head, heart thudding dully in her chest. Maybe taking opportunity during Carson's business trips hadn't been a good idea. She'd crooned in the Moonlight Club only a handful of times over the past three months, and only because of rumors that Russo had connections with the Ziegfeld Follies. Yet the big shot hadn't shown up any of the times she'd been there. And now she was chained to Artie again. All because she wanted to escape.

"You stick with me, and everything will work out grand. You'll see." He gave a syrupy smile. "Don't know why you want to ditch the boss, anyway. He's a powerful man. Has *friends* in many places. And you know how loyal his friends can be."

Was Artie implying Carson was a gangster? Or was his threat cheaper than his fifty-cent toupee?

"Besides, you've been a lot more decorated since you two got together." His gaze slid to her bracelet. "That's a pretty trinket you got there."

She lifted her forearm, the diamond chain slipping under her sleeve.

"Looks like he has a lot of dough to hand around. It's a good thing Betsy got hungry."

Her brow wrinkled at the shift in conversation. "Who's Betsy?"

"Just another doll." He chuckled.

"I don't wanna hear about it." Poor woman. "Look, Artie, I'm off the clock. This time is my own."

He wiped his palms on his thighs and stood. "Sure thing, kitten. I have some business of my own to tend to."

"Club meeting?"

Both Vera and Artie turned toward the new voice.

Carson Kelly leaned against the doorjamb, his arms folded, his form occupying most of the frame. He removed his homburg and held it over his heart, the way he always did when he greeted Vera. A half smirk appeared on his face, his stare as blank as her high school diploma.

Her mind clouded. Was he irritated? In deep thought? "Come on in, Cars." She jumped to her feet, motioning with her hand. "Artie was just goin'." A trio in this overrated coat closet stifled the air, and tolerating any more of Artie's antics would suffocate what was left of her patience.

"See you tomorrow, Vera."

She mustered a smile, drawing pleasure as Artie skedaddled.

Carson pulled her to his side and kissed her cheek, the smell of aftershave filling her senses.

She rested her head on his lapel and felt his muscles tense. "Cavenhalt didn't acknowledge me. That louse."

Carson wasn't one to dish out approval, especially where Artie was concerned. She glanced up at Carson in time to catch his dark eyes narrowing on her.

"He giving you trouble? You know I only keep him around because he's your cousin."

Her chance arrived. What if she whined a couple of choice words and mixed in some tears? Could be the perfect recipe for kicking Artie out for good. She bit her lip, toying with temptation. But wrecking him came with the risk of sabotaging herself. Artie would squeal on her for sure. "Nothin' I can't handle."

"It's closing time." He squeezed her side and then released her. "Let's go."

"I don't mind walking, if you're busy." Regret spiraled through her. How could she say that? She hadn't forgotten about the note. And just because she hadn't spotted the creep didn't mean he wasn't there. He could still be around. Waiting. Yeah, she'd camp out on the dance floor before strutting home solo.

"No, I got some news you need to hear." His attention fixed on the mirror as he straightened his tie. "What do you have left to do here?"

She scanned the sparse surroundings. "Just grab my things."

"Don't be long. I'll be at the bar." With a nod, he strode out, his pompous gait entirely unlike the mystery hero's from earlier in the evening.

Staring at the empty doorway, her mind traveled to the swift moment of tonight's rescue. What intrigued her about that man? Sure, he'd taken the wallop for her, but something else had struck her. Had she seen him before? No. He had a face that would stamp any girl's memory. It was almost like a connection had been made. A silent linking.

She laughed.

Boy, she was getting batty.

Just because the man had shown a small dose of gallantry and had an appearance more brilliant than anything Hollywood could produce, she'd conjured up an instant bond. Could she be more pitiful? Or wrong? Chivalry only existed in fairy tales. And white knights didn't grace the soiled floors of the Kelly Club.

Pulling back a handful of wavy tresses, she leaned in, checking if Max Factor had done his job. Nope. No trace of the reputable greasepaint on her scar. Good thing her hair covered the side of her face, or the ugly thing would've been showcased to the world tonight.

She pressed her finger over the discolored skin, the thin line stretching from her temple to her upper cheek. *You aren't worth anything to anyone.* Her breath caught. Why hadn't his growling voice faded from her head years ago? She snatched her powder and smeared her face with an ivory sheen, careful not to get any in her eye, until the marking was no longer visible. If only she could erase the memories.

She shot her arms through the sleeves of her coat, shoved a handkerchief into her pocket in case the dust and smoke in the air made her nose drip, and pulled the overhead string to shut off the light.

With the grace of a blind elephant, Vera plodded into the main room where Carson chatted with Angelo. Her poise had clocked out after her last number. Vera's rubbery legs weren't up for the labyrinth of tables barricading the bar. Instead, she crossed the empty dance floor, her heels a choppy cadence against the wooden slats.

Both men turned, but her brawny guard spoke first. "Hey, there."

She joined them. "Still hanging around, Angelo? Don't ya split at closing?" Or had Carson paid him overtime to babysit her? Usually, those schemes annoyed her, but not tonight. The idea of Steely-Eye being outside made her spine rigid.

"Yeah." He palmed the back of his neck. "I'm just waiting for Artie to come out of his office. He had some sort of job for me."

Carson downed the final drops of amber liquid in his glass. "You ready, baby?"

"Sure." She flashed a smile like the three painted girls on the Iron City Lager sign collecting dust behind the rows of long-necked bottles. If Carson was as enthralled with her as this area was devoted to their hometown brew, then all her problems would disappear. Well, most of them, anyway.

Carson only nodded. "So am I. See you, Vinelli."

"Later, boss." Angelo nodded, then slid his gaze to Vera. "Have a good night."

Vera waved. "Catch you tomorrow."

"Nope. Leonard's covering." The guard rinsed out Carson's cup, mildly surprising Vera. Angelo wasn't a busboy, but then the boss of the club demanded his workers wear several hats. "I'm here in the morning."

"Dust don't stir in this place until the evening." Her stomach twisted at the thought of Leonard being her personal guard. She'd welcome Angelo's oppressive vigilance over Leo's negligence. The man had a penchant for escaping into the storage room with his flask, leaving her vulnerable.

Angelo stacked the glass with the others and tossed the dishtowel over his shoulder. "It's the last Wednesday of the month. I'm needed in the offices."

Her mouth formed an *O*. She hadn't the faintest notion why Angelo was needed on that particular day each month, but she knew better than to ask. The business office of Carson Kelly Enterprises had stood here before the club's existence and had since acted as a buffer should any government man come around snooping. Though now, feds, as well as cops, were some of their best customers.

Carson's hand wrapped her elbow, and they stepped out into the night air.

"Where's your car?" Artie's beat-up Ford was the only vehicle sullying the lot.

He withdrew his touch. "I parked around the side. Wait here."

Vera opened her mouth, but words wouldn't come. That gut feeling prickled her insides. Carson walked into the shadows. She was alone.

CHAPTER 3

The chill of the night air smacked Vera's face, along with a couple of sprinkles.

With the club being stuffed between a blast furnace and a steel plant that worked longer hours than she, noises resounded, unyielding. Clinks and clanks. Whooshes and hisses. And just like those steel men who tirelessly pounded at hot metal, creating sparks which burnt the hair off their arms, the familiar sounds relentlessly thrashed her spiked nerves, searing her throat dry.

Movement to her left pulled her gaze.

A figure with a crooked profile crept into the streetlamp's weak glow.

She relaxed. "Hey there, Grimby."

Same pants. No hat. Day after day. Boots looking as worn out as the man who filled them. A trench coat swallowed his feeble frame, the tattered edges looking like a giant windsock that'd been dragged through the dirt.

"It's kinda late to be out, old man." Vera spoke above the muted hum of the factories and stepped closer to the guy who was as much a mystery as he was a vagrant.

He clung to a rickety vendor's cart. Where he'd discovered it, she hadn't a clue, but he employed it as a cane. The bed of the basket housed his furry creature, Fred. Boy, that Pomeranian was as loyal as they came. She wished she could say the same about Grimby's other dog, Peppin.

"Peppin's gone," Grimby said. "I set food out. She didn't come. Peppin's gone."

"Don't worry about Peppin. She'll be back. Just like I said last week." And last month. And the month before that.

Grimby smiled and patted Fred's ginger coat.

Poor guy.

"The light's on," he muttered and gazed toward the river. "The light's on and the boat comes."

Had he been a sailor? A fisherman? Rumors had spread that, years ago, Grimby had suffered a fall while mining along Pittsburgh's coal seam. Others blabbed he'd lost his sweetheart to tuberculosis and had never been the same since. All Vera knew was the man's anchor was out of the water, and he'd been drifting for years. If only she could find a way to draw him back to the shores of reason.

"Did you used to work on boats? What about the lights?" One would think she'd understand the meaning after hearing it for the thousandth time.

"The light's on and the boat comes." Make that a thousand and one.

"Sure, sure, Grimby." Her smile fell. The man hunched over the cart more than usual. She squinted, focusing on his aged face. How old was he? Seventy-five, eighty? He had all his hair, though grayed, and deep lines framed his mouth. "You doing okay?"

Dull eyes blinked back at her.

She withdrew her handkerchief and dabbed away the dirt striping his cheek.

Carson's car rounded the corner, its headlights cutting the black mist.

Vera reached for Grimby's hand and pressed the handkerchief to his callused palm. How long had it been since he had something fresh and clean? "Take care of yourself and Fred." She lightly squeezed his fingers and then joined Carson in his Rolls Royce.

"Grimby?" Carson asked as Vera settled in.

"Yeah, old man Grimby."

"What makes you want to speak to him?" He yanked the gear shift, jerking the car forward. "The man won't remember. Says the same thing over and over. If you ask me, he's a nutcase."

"He's gentle." And wholesome. She'd rather listen to Grimby's ramblings than the vulgar drivel thrown at her a hatful of times a night.

Carson drummed the steering wheel with his thumbs. "Vinelli told me there were a decent amount of customers this evening."

"Yeah."

The car lurched over train tracks leading to the rail yard, which whistled more than a Saturday night crowd.

"Was it mostly the regulars?"

"Some. People off the riverboat too." Though she couldn't understand why anyone enjoyed boating in the three rivers framing the city. Factories fed their waste to the watery bellies, the filmy sludge earning nothing from her except a disgusted glance.

"It's time to make some changes, Vera."

The whip of his words lashed her heart with a sting. Had he overheard her conversation with Artie? Was he aware of her visits to the Moonlight Club?

"It'll be uncomfortable for a while, but it's for the best."

Her mind tangled with excuses she could prattle, but all would crumble against the grinding reality. If she got tossed out, where could she go? It didn't matter that her heart hummed along to the melody of her dreams because the tip jars she'd emptied last month for rent lamented the truth—affording New York was beyond her means. "What'll be for the best?"

"The club. It could stand some improvements."

She swallowed and willed her queasy stomach to behave.

"You know I've been bored with my real estate businesses. And as lucrative as they are, I found where the real dough lies. The club started as a way to turn a dime into a dollar, but it's really taking off." Pride filled his voice. "Must be the entertainment." He smirked but kept his eyes on the road. "The crowd is enthralled with you, baby."

Yet she couldn't sing her way into Carson's locked heart. Not that she'd been entirely open with hers either. The gamble wasn't worth the consequences.

"Best thing I ever did was let you sing."

The words, though spoken smoothly, scraped her ears, peeling the raw truth from the swell of doubt—she'd become more of a business asset than his girlfriend.

"I'm moving my offices to Forbes Avenue."

Her brow scrunched. She had never been sure why he'd chosen a sooty old building along the factory-lined river for his real estate headquarters, but after all these years, why move it now?

"As for the club, I have big plans. Gut it out and refine it." Carson's deep voice invaded her ears. "I need it to rival Moonlight's joint or even the speakeasy inside the William Penn. But my place will gleam brighter because of the gem that's inside." He tossed a wink her way.

How could Carson speak so casually about breaking the law? Her fingers fidgeted the chain necklace her grandmother had given her.

"Just wait until my men are done. We'll see where the hoity-toity flock to. Without the offices acting as a smokescreen, it's gonna cost me more to get the club safeguarded, but everything will be worth it."

Safeguarded. More like bribing cops and city officials to turn a blind eye. Oh, how did she ever get caught up in all this? She clenched her teeth.

To survive.

To make it through the cold winter. But had she lost her soul in the process?

He dropped one hand from the wheel to grab hers. "I need you, Vera. I'll do whatever it takes to keep you happy. A raise. A new wardrobe. You name it."

His offers flitted through her mind. As much as her vanity admired newer gowns, her instincts prized the raise. She'd have to finagle a way to get her pay directly from Carson, or Artie would sink his grimy fingers into it. Perhaps it'd be enough to fill her escape-to-New-York jar to the brim. That way, she wouldn't have to sneak away to the Moonlight Club in search of Tony Russo's assistance. She could finance herself.

"It's gonna be a natural, baby. Your golden throat'll draw 'em all in."

And there it was. His smile. She'd bet he could charm a whole fleet of ladies with his broad grin and crinkly eyes.

Carson put the car in neutral but let the motor purr. Her apartment building at nighttime seemed almost passable. She couldn't spot the flaking paint or the bowed balusters. No signs of the neighbors drying their undergarments on the support beams. Yep, viewing her world through the slant of darkness allowed her creativity to brighten what was sallow. Good thing she had a vivid imagination.

"I'm not coming up. I gotta scoot to Ward's place. All that legal stuff."

Oh, the irony. He cared to be upstanding with his rental properties yet ran a whiskey dive. "At three a.m.? Strange time to be going to an attorney's house."

He lifted his hand, and she shrank against the door. Why couldn't she just keep her mouth shut?

"You make me feel like a heel when you cower like that." Carson rested his hand on her knee. "I told you I wouldn't hit you again."

Because he regretted it? Or because her ears had rung for two days and she had sung poorly? A dull ache stretched behind her eyes.

"Besides, I think I overcompensated with that string of rocks around your wrist."

"Yeah, guess so."

"Did you know I got that when Ward and I went to Belmont

Stakes? Went to check out a new trainer for Thundering Gallop and came back with a genuine Tiffany's."

"It's beautiful, Cars."

"So are you." He hooked an arm around her and smiled. "I'll be here tomorrow around seven to pick you up. We'll have dinner at the club."

"I'll be ready."

He gathered her closer and kissed her. The taste of alcohol on his lips soured her stomach. She could never become immune to that putrid odor—memories speared her every time.

She waved as Carson drove away and then walked to the flight of stairs leading to her apartment.

A realization hit her like ice water in the face. "Rats. My bag." She glared at empty hands. "No bag. No key."

Too late to hail down Carson. His car disappeared into the night's blackness. She scrunched her nose. Had she brought it in the car? No. Must be in her dressing room.

Was Artie still at the club? She groaned. No choice but to check. All that stress to keep from being unguarded, to avoid walking alone, and yet here she was. Her stomach twisted in a hundred corkscrews. She hustled down the street, passing Winston's Drugstore and several other shops, all dark and locked tight.

Sporadic drops of moisture, which had teased her face earlier, returned, but this time they allowed no mercy, showering fat beads of rain.

"Why?" She shook her fists at the sky that had been blanketed gray all day. Figured it'd wait until now to come spitting down. She slipped her arms out of her jacket sleeves and pulled the collar over her head, her makeshift umbrella tunneling her vision. Three more blocks.

A car horn blared. She flinched. A taxi pulled up beside her, spraying her ankles.

"Need a ride?"

"I've got no money." She ducked under a barbershop awning.

"Where ya headed?"

Rain cascaded off the thinned canopy, a watery sheet, misting her. "Harold Avenue."

"Harold Avenue. The Kelly Club, by any chance?" Understanding registered in his tone as the orange circle of his lighted cigar bobbed with his words.

"Yeah." She huffed and adjusted her grip on her overcoat. The longer she remained chatting with the cabby, the less of a chance she'd find anyone at the club.

He jerked a thumb to the rear of the car. "Well, jump in."

She took a step toward him, then stilled. Offers like this had been made before.

"I accept other forms of payment, angel-face."

Knew it. She bit the inside of her cheek and walked on, hastening her pace.

"Hey, where you going?"

"Get lost."

"Go ahead and catch a cold." He sped away, tires screeching.

The kitchen door was unlocked. About time she caught a break. Easy in. Easy out.

Rain pelted the tin roof, grating her ears, like somebody shaking a can full of rocks. She hit a slick spot, her feet slipped out from under her, and she smacked her backside on the hard floor. *Could this get any worse?* Time to nix the wet shoes.

Evading a few puddles caused by the leaky roof, she walked with brisk steps. Maybe she could dodge Artie. Keeping the lights off seemed the best plan.

She felt her way to the dressing room door, brushing the wood and then scaling her fingers down until she reached the cool metal knob. Voila! She grasped the air a couple times, hoping to pull the string for the light, but couldn't find it. Never mind. She stretched out her hand in the direction her vanity tray should be.

Aha, gotcha.

She snatched the troublesome bag and cleared out.

Curious, she peeked down the side hall. A sliver of pale gold shone under the door to the front offices. She crept farther.

"Your way isn't my way, Cavenhalt. It's yellow-bellied."

"Carson," Vera whispered. Hadn't he told her he was going to Ward's? Check the box next to liar on the *terrible boyfriend* list.

"It's your choice." Artie's grumbly voice sounded. "Pay up because I know the exact people who I can squeal to."

Her blood froze. Was this the bargaining chip he'd mentioned earlier? Her fingers fumbled. Down went her shoe.

Clunk.

"What was that?" Carson's voice crashed through the door.

She plucked up her shoe by its satin strap and sidestepped into the storage room.

The hallway light flicked on. She sunk her teeth into her lower lip, squeezing her elbows into her ribs.

"It's nothing." Artie shut the door.

Her chest expanded with much-needed air. Fingers clenched around her belongings, she braved her way into the hall, footfalls quiet.

"I know about Steubenville, Artie."

Vera's heart launched into her stomach. She recognized that tone. Her cheek tingled as if reminding her of his wrath.

Artie cussed. "How did—"

A shot pierced. Thunder cracked. All fell silent except for the rain's fury.

CHAPTER 4

Vera clamped her lips together, imprisoning the rising scream in her throat. Legs trembling, she dashed out the hall and through the nearest exit, clutching her shoes and bag to her chest.

Rain pellets stung her face as she raced toward her apartment, each thunder crash rattling her marrow. Had Carson spotted her? Was she being chased? She ran harder.

Her wet clothes hung like sandbags tied to her shoulders. The cement terrain stabbed her insoles, ripping her stockings. A dark chant echoed through her. *Carson killed him! Carson killed him!*

Vera forced herself up the stairs under the porch's protection. Lightning struck, allowing a glimpse of her door. Her foot caught on the uneven floorboard, but she managed to keep from falling. She fished the key from her bag, opened the door, and locked it behind her. Pressing her back against its solid surface, she slithered to the floor.

A violent shiver overtook her.

Her gaze darted to the phone. The one the murderer had installed for her. *No. Couldn't call the police.* Or anyone. She pulled her knees into her chest and rocked back and forth. In this crooked city, it was hard to know who would be friend or foe. And even if she found people to trust, no one would believe her. Especially if word broke that Artie had been blackmailing her. She pushed herself to stand, water pooling under her stocking-clad feet.

In her bedroom, she exchanged her dripping dress for a terrycloth robe. She pressed her fingers to her temple. Where should she begin? What did she need to do? Pack. Run. Leap into oblivion. Her tears blended with the rainwater spilling down her cheeks.

She couldn't return to that club. Couldn't. Once away, she'd change her name. Cut her hair. Dye it. Speak with a foreign accent if she had to.

Her attention flashed to her open closet, the highest shelf. A wall of hatboxes—all purchased by a killer—barricaded her luggage. She groaned. Agile or not, she had to get her suitcase, stuff it full, and be on her way. As her brain caught up with her panic, she realized her getaway was impossible. The bus terminal didn't open until morning.

She collapsed her arms to her sides and sank onto the bed.

She was trapped.

The trembling intensified. Her teeth chattered, making her jaw ache. She pulled a blanket around her, but it didn't soothe the ferocious chill. No, it deepened, rooting in her bones.

What was that? Her head jerked.

Knock, knock, pound.

There it was again. Someone with a sledgehammer for a fist assaulted her door. Her gritty eyes burned as if she'd rubbed salt in them. Several long blinks swept in the tide of her vision. The light streaming through her window wasn't bright, indicating another bleak morning.

She bolted up.

Morning!

She swallowed hard, a fiery sensation blazing her throat. When had she fallen asleep?

With a deep breath, she stood, teetering forward before stabilizing herself on the nightstand. She paused until the dizziness subsided. Wait. Who knocked? Carson? Last night's events cut through her. She slid her eyes shut, the fogginess in her mind clearing. Couldn't be Carson. His nightly sleeping powder held him in a trance until noon. So then … who was it?

Tiptoeing proved challenging, considering half her muscles were still asleep and the other half shook in trepidation.

She peeked through the skinny gap between the curtain's edge and the window.

Her heart skittered into her stomach.

A cop!

A support beam for the patio roof obstructed the sight of his head, but his navy threads and the gun holstered on his hip exposed his identity.

She twisted, pressing her back against the wall, and pushed the palm of her hand on her forehead. This couldn't be happening. She couldn't talk to a cop. Not now. But then … who said she had to? Just keep silent. For all he knew, she wasn't home.

Hunkering, she padded to the bedroom. Her foot landed on something—her shoe from last night. She toppled over it, sending the ridiculous thing back, thudding against the door. She gritted her teeth. So much for her not being home.

Knock, knock, pound.

"Yeah. Yeah. I hear ya. Give me a minute." More like a lifetime. She moaned, picking up the shoe. Ruined. The silver satin had shriveled from the rainwater. She grabbed its mate and shoved them under the couch cushion. No one was going to know how those heels got damaged. No one.

Knock, knock, pound.

Her breath snagged in her chest as she unlocked the bolt and yanked the door open. Squeezing the knob, her knuckles drained white.

Her mystery hero.

The man who had shielded her from the tussle. The man who had mirrored a page out of *Vanity Fair*. The man who now stared at her as though she had three heads.

"Are you Vera Lynn Pembroke?"

She opened her mouth, but her voice wouldn't budge. Clamping her lips shut, she gave a tight nod.

His uniform stretched across broad shoulders and an expansive chest. "I'm from the Allegheny Police. May I speak with you?"

Didn't he recognize her from last night? Was he trying to trick her? His gold-toned badge read SERGEANT, but where exactly did his loyalty lie? Since he had been at the club, did that mean he was in cahoots with Carson? Her heart stalled and then took on a rapid pace.

But no one—not even her murderous boyfriend—knew she'd returned to the speakeasy last evening. At least, that was what she hoped. She pushed back all emotion and smoothed her hair with a trembling hand. Above all else, she had to appear collected. "I'm … uh … not dressed. It's pretty early."

If he was aware of her shaking, he didn't show it. He didn't show anything except a straight face and stern eyes. "It's nearly two o'clock, ma'am."

She'd missed the bus. Lost her chance of escape. Her gut churned as her mind scrambled to her next move. What about Union Station? Hadn't she heard they ran several departures a day? A perfect Plan B, except for the pricey train fare. She fought against a groan.

"Can I come in?"

Did she have a choice? She opened the door wider.

He shuffled his feet on the door mat and removed his hat, revealing wavy, dark-blond hair she'd swoon over if he were anybody but a cop. The fixed slope of his nose, the slight dip under his lip, the sharp turn of his jaw all a gorgeous combination. But again, the badge spoiled it.

Mouth pressed into a tight line, he glanced around the room. One brow arched.

Was he surprised to find the inside of her apartment wasn't as dilapidated as the outside? Or was his sharp stare inspecting something other than the condition of her tufted chair?

His gaze landed on her, and her tongue cemented to the roof of her mouth. "Are you alone?"

"Yeah."

"Seems like you had a rough night last night."

"Yeah." Was that all she could say? A single look at the sergeant's chiseled face and her vocabulary diminished to one word.

He raised his chin, exposing his thick, corded neck. "I'm sorry to be the one to inform you, but someone you're acquainted with had it rougher. Have you heard?"

No, no, no. She folded her hands behind her back to hide their shaking. "Heard what?" She averted her gaze from his stare, looking at her feet, digging her big toe in the carpet.

"Arthur Cavenhalt is dead."

Dead. The word sliced her soul like a dagger, ripping her courage to shreds. Tiny bumps developed from her neck to her ankles. Couldn't mistake it for a nightmare. The truth numbed her. Artie was dead by the same hands that had held her.

"An employee found him this morning at the Carson Kelly Enterprise building. Shot."

"Shot?" The backs of her eyes stung, tears threatening. The blast of the gun echoed in the hollow of her gut. Flickers from years back ignited in her mind—the first time she'd heard gunfire, running from her home, stowing away on a westbound train toward Pittsburgh. What irony—one shooting had brought her here, and another was forcing her away. How much trauma could her heart take before it imploded?

He cleared his throat. "Looked to be a suicide."

His words bit into her thoughts with an abrupt sting, turning her breath shallow. How could they think it was a … "Suicide?"

His lips pressed together in a slight grimace, brows pulling in. "Yes."

Carson must've staged it. A lump hardened in the back of her throat. The only other person who knew the truth besides Carson … was her. A mental tennis match volleyed uncontrollably. *Tell the cop. Don't tell the cop. Tell the cop.*

"Does that surprise you?"

"It's … not …" *Don't tell the cop.* "I'm shocked."

His rigid gaze locked on hers. "I need you to come with me to headquarters, Miss Pembroke."

A gasp catapulted up her throat, and she swallowed it back. "What?"

"To headquarters," he repeated in the same low tone. "I need you to come with me."

"Why?" The police station—buzzing with people she'd hid from as a kid.

He slapped his hat on his head with a finesse that revealed he'd done it a million times. Not skewed in the least. "For questioning."

"I don't get it. Why talk to me?" Breathe in. Breathe out. She clutched the back of her tufted chair, bracing herself. "Can't you talk to me here?"

"Just routine, ma'am. The captain wants to meet with you." He motioned to the door. "We've talked with most of the employees at the offices, plus Mr. Kelly."

"Carson … was down at headquarters?" Had he been answering questions for the police or paying them off? Murder was a way more serious offense than owning a speakeasy. Though, she hadn't yet seen an officer turn down an easy grand or two.

"Yes." He studied her face, then glanced at her hand strangling the seatback. "Are you all right?"

"What if I choose not to go?" Time for a staring match with the man, but her competitor held the advantage, his face natural and confident, while she struggled to keep her features calm. And why all of a sudden was her eye twitching?

"It wouldn't be wise." His gaze swayed faintly to the left of her face.

Was he staring at her scar? She untucked the hair from behind her ear, letting the locks fall across her temple. What exactly did she look like right now? She hadn't taken her makeup off from yesterday, and no doubt it had smeared during the jaunt in the rain.

The phone rang. She jumped.

"Go ahead and answer that." The sergeant sat on the same cushion she'd shoved her heels under. He grimaced.

Oh, rats. She should've left them where they were. The man probably wouldn't have noticed. But this looked a million times more suspicious.

The sergeant shifted to the left and relaxed.

Her shoulders eased, and she picked up the receiver. "H-hello."

"Baby?"

Carson! Her grip tightened on the receiver's neck.

"How are you?" His voice pounded against her skull, making her wish she'd left town the moment she had returned to her apartment. But what had she done? Slept. Now she had a murderer on the phone and a cop lazing in her living room.

"I have bad news, Vera. Still trying to understand it myself."

She couldn't detect any suspicion in his tone. But maybe this was a trap—lure her into thinking everything was on the up and up, only to dispose of her down the laundry chute.

"You there?"

"Yeah, I'm here." She bounced her weight from foot to foot, keeping her ankles from caving.

"It's hard to say over the telephone." His tone wobbled. What a faker. "It's about Artie. He committed suicide last night."

This morning a killer, this afternoon a liar. No way she'd be sticking around to see what he'd transform into this evening. Was running from violent men her lot in life? A remote convent looked mighty appealing.

"Did you hear me, Vera?"

"Uh-huh."

"I'm sorry, baby. I know he was your only relation. Do you need me to come over?"

"No." Her voice squeaked, and she winced. Had she given herself away? A large hand pressed her shoulder.

"Make it short, Miss Pembroke." The sergeant's deep timbre brushed her ears.

"Vera, is someone with you?

"No, it's just the noise box. Hold on, I'll turn it off." Vera held the phone against her chest and turned to the sergeant, pressing a finger to her lips.

He made a grave look and returned to the sofa.

"I'm coming over," Carson said. "I'll be there in twenty minutes."

"No, Carson. I'm, uh … I'm not feelin' so well." She faked a cough. A terrible delivery, but hopefully, it sounded more believable on his end. "I caught somethin'. It's fierce. Plus, I'd rather grieve alone."

"You sure?"

She twisted the receiver cord around her finger, pulling. "It'll be better that way."

"As long as you're okay for tonight. Catch ya later, baby."

Not if she could help it. "Bye." Her shaky hand returned the receiver into the cradle, making the candlestick base dance a wobbly jig. Her breathing steadied, but her heart beat wildly against her ribs.

"Who was that, Miss Pembroke?" The sergeant stood.

"A sharp note that turned flat."

"Excuse me, ma'am?"

"Nothin', forget it." She grabbed her purse off the coffee table. "Let's go and get this done." There were bags to pack and murderers to escape from.

His eyes pinched at the corners. "Wouldn't you like to … get more decent?"

Her gaze shifted downward and then to the sergeant. How could she have forgotten her state of dress? Something in her stirred. Could be from the sergeant's pointed look, the frustration mingled with adrenaline over her conversation with Carson, or, she hated to admit, the slight twinge of disappointment for having discovered her handsome rescuer had turned out to be a cop. Most likely, the blend of all three prompted her sarcastic smirk and jutted chin. "Perhaps I should change." She headed for her bedroom and glanced over her shoulder. "I save sauntering around town in my bathrobe for the weekends."

The lock on her bedroom door clicked, and Mick exhaled, the tightness in his chest unraveling. Why he'd felt tense around a woman a head shorter and over a hundred pounds lighter than him, he couldn't pinpoint. What he did know was last evening the prima donna, even with her layers of cosmetics and flashy gown, couldn't mask the fear marking her entrancing eyes. He'd identified it the moment they'd held gazes. Stark terror. This afternoon the same thing, only with some confusion tossed in.

Her appearance when she had opened the door had caught him off guard. Gone was the stylish nightclub singer. Instead, there stood a vulnerable young lady with wild curly hair and black makeup smearing her face. He preferred her messy, natural face to a painted one. Her mannerisms had reminded him of the first time he'd gone hunting with his pap. When they'd stumbled upon a doe, her wide eyes and panicky movements had poked his conscience. He hadn't wanted to harm her but rather to protect her.

Mick glanced around, assessing the small space. The kitchenette bore no semblance of use. The furnishings weren't lavish like a Shadyside home, but they weren't poverty-grade like a few of the apartments he'd seen in this very complex.

He didn't expect a picture of Mother Mary or a cross, but there should be something here of a personal effect. Instead of pictures and photo albums, shellac records lined the bookshelf. On the coffee table and counters where most women had knick-knacks, she had sheet music. As if music was her only love, her entire world.

Didn't she have family? Anyone who loved her? His heart clenched, and he chided himself. Hadn't he learned his lesson five years ago? Most likely, the duchess of the gin joint wasn't as vulnerable as she appeared to be. Her powers of performance, no doubt, stretched beyond the stage. Mick wouldn't be taken as the fool again.

Stick to the rules. Adhere to guidelines. If you don't, then people … died.

Sinking onto the sofa, he pushed the demons of his past back into the caves of his soul. He'd accepted the promotion to sergeant as a sign from God to get on with his life, but … the screeching brakes, the blood on her collar stark against her porcelain skin. If only he'd chosen differently, not been blinded by the betrayal. He pressed the heels of his palms to his eyes, shutting out the memory, the painful reminder he needed to look beyond Miss Pembroke's pretty face and defenseless eyes.

The woman could possess more trick plays than the Pitt Panthers at Forbes Field. But soon she'd be in his arena, and he was trained at anticipating his opponent's move. A skill gained from failure.

He leaned back, the couch cushion poking his thigh again. A loose spring? Maybe he could fix it before she came out. He lifted the cushion.

Shoes?

He bent low, examining the pair of heels which looked as though they'd been left out in the rain. Or maybe … a thunderstorm. He scrubbed his jaw, eyeing the door she'd fled behind.

Perhaps the Red Canary would fly right into his plan.

CHAPTER 5

Alone.

Vera figured this as some kind of police tactic. Leave the lady by herself in a dismal interrogation room so she could feel the pressure. Man, she was feeling something. Why was this room so hot? Another strategy? Bake her insides so the information would come spilling out.

She tugged her collar and frowned. How could lace be this constricting? Of course, she wasn't used to being so covered. It had taken a good deal of time to find a dress with a higher neckline and lower hem. While some of the officers would appreciate her rolled-down stockings, she'd chosen the *respectable* look and employed the granny garter though it choked the life out of her thighs.

Looking around, she had her choice of about twenty chairs arranged around a large rectangular table almost as long as the room itself. Vera skidded back the seat closest to the exit and sank onto it. Maybe this wouldn't take long. She'd answer a few questions, smile, and then shake Pittsburgh's sooty dust off her heels.

But what if this was more than just a routine questioning like the sarge had said? If the badge bozos got nosy, what would she tell them? The truth? She drew in the stuffy air and released it. No. Couldn't let them know she was there last night.

If by some slim chance these cops were honest, they wouldn't believe her. If they were as tainted as a shot of White Mule moonshine, then the truth could land her at the bottom of the

Ohio River.

The short drive to the station had her nerves tangled and raw. Though the sergeant's voice had been silent, his sharp eyes had spoken loudly, assessing her with every glance in the rearview mirror, making her wince as if he knew something she hadn't. She rubbed the small links of her necklace between her thumb and index finger.

The dimmed ceiling lights left the corners of the room shadowed. The edges of her mind were just as bleak and twice as dark. *The entrance of His words giveth light.* Oh, if she could only hear her grandmother's feeble voice in her ears rather than in her head. The light. When they had closed her casket, the windows to Vera's soul had locked, shutting out the light from that moment on. She was careful not to touch the festering memory long, or it would burst through her heart, bringing fresh pain.

Men's voices split the tortuous silence. The sergeant returned, striding in with the same magnetic gait as last night. An older man, who looked more like a grandpop than a law enforcer, trailed behind him. The sergeant's searing gaze leveled on her even as Grandpop's—or maybe just Pops—had landed on her with a gentle appraisal.

"Hello, Miss Pembroke." Pops extended his hand, his eyes crimped with a smile.

She eased forward for the quick handshake. Her bracelet caught on her sleeve, and her breath hitched with the blossoming idea. Her bracelet. Why didn't she think of this before? A trip to the pawn shop could cure her financial issues. A train ticket. Lodging. All of it now within reach. A renewed determination flowed through her.

"I'm Captain Harpshire." His grin faltered, stumbling into a frown. "Blazes, it's warm in here." He craned his neck, looking at the sergeant who stood by the door. "Ace, get a fan in here. This pretty young lady doesn't need to be perspiring." He glanced back at Vera and winked.

The sergeant dipped his finely shaped chin in acknowledgment and exited. The captain sat across from her.

"That's the nice thing about being captain. You don't have to get off your backside unless you want to." He laughed. His jowls extended past a rounded chin, flapping with each chuckle, like a basset hound. "I'm going to ask you a few questions. Do you mind?"

Why ask if she had no voice in the matter? She pushed past the invisible steel grip around her throat. "Go ahead."

"Tell me exactly your role at Carson Kelly Enterprises." Pops schooled his features better than any poker player she knew. But she held the bluff. Would he call her on it? She didn't have much to wager.

"Umm … what do you mean?"

His head tilted and his gaze hooked on hers. "Young lady, I think you're too smart to play silly parlor games, and really, that's not how I operate. So I'm just gonna cut the fluff and bring it all in the open."

She shifted in her seat.

"To start with, I know you're a canary at the speakeasy held secretly behind the walls of the office building. Though I wouldn't exactly label it a secret since everyone in Pittsburgh is aware of the Kelly Club."

She stiffened against a wince. What was the old man driving at? Was he going to arrest her for being part of that racket? She'd always been under the assumption she'd have to be caught in the act of drinking to get arrested, but now, with the suspicious tones in Pop's voice and the niggle in her gut, she wasn't so sure.

"Don't knit those brows, darlin'. You aren't in trouble for crooning in a gin joint. I need you on my side."

The question sat like fire on her tongue, but voicing it could get her burned. She pressed her spine against the seat's back. "Which side is that?"

His eyes registered her meaning. "The one of justice. Do you suppose you could sing me a song?"

"What would you like to hear?" The captain didn't strike her as one who'd like to hear her rendition of "Sweet Georgia Brown."

"Let's see. Let's see." He bounced a curled knuckled on his chin. "How 'bout we start out with what you were doing at the Kelly Club last night?"

Dread sluiced her veins. "I had to work."

"No, I mean after Mr. Kelly dropped you off. You returned, why?"

Grabbing fistfuls of leather, Vera pulled her bag into her stomach, something snapping beneath the pressure of her fingers. "W-what gives you that idea?"

The sergeant walked back into the room, a fan in hand. He placed the small metal mechanism on the table and plugged it in.

Vera angled toward it, the cool breeze kissing her face and neck.

"Anything else, sir?" The sergeant angled toward the older man.

So *now* he was polite. Figures.

"Stick around, Ace. I was just asking Miss Pembroke why she was at the club at the time of the murder."

"Murder?" She shrank, watching both men nod their heads. "Y-you knew … all along it was murder."

"Didn't you?" Two gray brows arched.

The twinge of betrayal returned, igniting fire in her blood and heat in her cheeks. Sergeant Stiff the double-crosser. She sliced her finger through the air, pointing. "You lied to me!"

His jade eyes sparked. "I said that it *looked* like Cavenhalt committed suicide."

"It was ruled that way at first, darlin'"—Pops put in—"but the more we investigated, the more we saw it was staged."

The sergeant stepped forward, stealing her stare away from the blank space on the wall. "Your fingerprints are on the door, Miss Pembroke."

The sting of the accusation launched her to her feet, sending her handbag to the tiled floor. "How do ya have my finger pri—" Understanding kicked her in the gut. "Hey, listen here, fellas, I was cleared of that break-in." What a crummy way to get her on file. They'd got her prints along with the rest of the renters in her complex the day the maintenance man had decided to crowbar his way into the landlord's safe.

"You can sit down. We didn't forget." The captain replied with a much cooler tone than Vera's fiery one. "We're aware you had nothing to do with the incident two months ago. We—"

"Then why are you picking on me?" She shoved aside her bag with her foot and sat. A quiver ran down her calves, invading her toes. "My prints are all over that joint. It's where I work." Too bad for her Pittsburgh had succumbed to the nationwide craze for identification using ink and an index finger.

"I have the proof right here." His title indicated Sergeant, but his tone labeled him Judge. He'd judged her guilty before he'd knocked on her door. He'd fooled her into thinking this was a routine questioning. Surely, a dank cell awaited her. Men like him could stand tall to shake the mayor's hand but couldn't stoop to accept truth from the likes of her. Or … this place was so shady that it needed to cast its shadow on someone else. A someone who needed to pay for Artie's death. Carson no doubt escaped through his bank account. She, on the other hand, wouldn't be so lucky. The sergeant waved the small notepad he'd clutched for the past five minutes. "Would you care to see it, sir?"

Pops motioned with his fingers. "Read it out loud, Dinelo."

He flipped through the pages and cleared his throat. "We spoke with the bouncer this morning." He read from the pad, his eyes methodically moving from left to right. "His name was Angelo Vinelli." The sergeant's gaze met Vera's, and she narrowed her eyes. "Vinelli gave me the whole account of his last dealings with the deceased." He returned to the paper. "Mr. Kelly and Miss Pembroke left. Cavenhalt came from his office, told Vinelli to change a doorknob and then go home." The sergeant closed the notepad.

The captain tilted his head and pressed his fingertips together, forming a steeple. "Do you happen to know what doorknob he changed?"

She could almost hear "Taps" playing in the background. Her plan of pretense had been buried.

"It was the doorknob to your dressing room," the captain said. "We found two sets of fingerprints on the knob. One being Vinelli's and the other yours, sweetheart."

All her strength depleted, defeat gripped her heart. "I-I was there." She drew in a ragged breath. "I heard Artie … get shot."

"Miss Pembroke." His silvery stare pinned her to her seat. "You now have center stage. Tell us everything you know from the time you entered the Kelly Club until you left." He leaned forward. "Start singing."

She encountered the most important performance of her life. But instead of wowing the rowdies with fluid octaves, she needed to persuade the boys in blue. She couldn't offer them thousands like Carson, but perhaps, she could appeal to their hearts. It was the only option left. *Curtains for sure.* "I'd left my bag. It had my apartment key in it." She motioned to the brown leather handbag on the floor. "I went back to get it."

"Did you see the deceased?"

Deceased. Bile filled her mouth. She pressed her lips together.

The clock above the door filled the stretch of silence.

The captain furrowed his brow. "You okay, Miss Pembroke?"

Vera shook her head.

"Need water?"

She nodded and was surprised when the captain stood. Wasn't the sergeant supposed to do his bidding? Pops walked out, leaving her alone with the double-crosser. Vera folded her arms on the table and rested her head, closing her eyes to the surroundings.

She should probably use this time to think. To plan her next move. But snatching a logical thought was harder than holding a sixteen-count finale.

Hushed voices snagged her attention, popping her lids open.

The sergeant directed his glower to the huddle of officers gathering outside the door. He angled toward them and used his broad form as a barrier, blocking their views into the room. Was he protecting her privacy? The thought bounced across her chest and pushed out a snort. No one protected her.

"All right, boys, clear out." Shouldering past them, the captain adopted a stern tone, but the amusement shone in his eyes as he ambled into the room. "You're creating a stir around here, missy." A smile broke free, and he handed her a cold glass. "Got this from the pitcher in my office. It's the freshest."

Drawn-out sips bought Vera more time. What should she tell them? How much did they already know?

The door clicked shut and she jumped, the water in her cup splashing against her lips. The sergeant stood, his arms folded and his chin poked forward in a way she'd seen Angelo do when he'd been challenged. Only, the sergeant's penetrating stare had a direct effect on her blood pressure.

"Go on, when you're ready." The captain leaned back in his chair, calm and relaxed as though he was listening to the noise box.

She jittered her foot against the chair's leg, her rapid pulse pounding in her ears. "I heard Artie and Carson in Carson's office. They were arguing."

"About what?"

Vera tightened, sliding both hands under her thighs. "Not sure."

"What happened next?"

"Then I heard Artie … he yelled. Then … shot."

"How many shots fired?" The sergeant widened his stance, his pen poised above his notepad to write. When had he started logging her responses?

"One." She scratched her neck, averting eye contact by staring at a groove in the table. "One shot." The piercing noise still rang in her head, haunting.

The captain glanced at the sergeant and then back to her. "Did you see Mr. Kelly at any time during this?"

"No. I heard him. I know his voice."

The captain pressed his lips together and nodded slowly. "That storm was pretty loud last night. The Kelly Club's metal roof probably made it tough to hear. Do you think you could have mistaken his voice for somebody else's?"

"I know what I heard. It was Carson."

"What about the deceased? Did you hear him identify Mr. Kelly?" The captain scooted the glass of water closer to her, as a father would to a small child. "Call him by name or anything of that nature?"

She forced out a *no*. What was the use? They didn't believe her. Or *wouldn't* believe if Carson had gotten to them first. Fire itched under her skin. "See. That's why I didn't buzz you."

"Pardon me, Miss Pembroke?" The older man's eyes revealed not a teaspoon of agitation, but a whole gallon of curiosity.

"I wasn't keen on giving whispers to the police." She exhaled with enough force to cause the lace on her dress to tremble.

"Why?" He shoved his glasses farther up the bridge of his nose.

Because she'd heard stories. Tales of police shielding the bad guys and sticking it to the innocent. She inclined her chin, refusing to answer.

"Someone died, Miss Pembroke," the captain said. "Don't you want justice done?"

"A dandy of a line, but here's the thing. Ya say you're on the side of *justice*, but you and I both know the boundaries of that line are slanted by who's shelling out the dough."

Double brackets furrowed between his gray brows. "You're right, young lady. I've been a part of this police force for thirty years, and for most of it, I've been proud of our division. But now." He rubbed the creases in his forehead. "Now I'm not certain of anything." His frank admission seemed to deepen the lines framing his downturned mouth, and the silvery spark that highlighted his soft blue eyes extinguished.

Was Pops the best actor never to grace the stage? Or was he telling the truth?

He blinked as if shirking away from the sadness. “One thing I am sure of, missy, is that we can’t stop the corruption unless we’re brave enough to step out from the shadows.” He raised his flappy chin with a determined gaze which made Vera squirm. “Your testimony could trigger the light to be shed on this city again. Help clear out the wrong-doers.”

“Who do you guys think I am, little red ridin’ hood? I’m a nightclub singer.”

“You’re our only witness.” The captain was nodding while Vera was shaking her head no.

“How could I be sure you flatfoots aren’t tricking me? Everyone around knew I couldn’t stand Artie. He and I were always sparring about things.” One major thing. “I’m not gonna be left holding the bag for murder.”

She could’ve sung three encores to fill the gap of awkward silence. Finally, Pops shrugged and said, “You couldn’t have done it.”

A thread of hope tugged her eyebrows, lifting. But this could be another ploy, enticing her to drop her defenses.

Pops studied his fingernails as if gleaning advice from them. “I won’t cloud your mind with the details.”

“I’m a big girl.” She tossed her hair over her shoulder and sat taller, attempting to enforce her argument that she was a capable woman and not just a scatting moll girl.

He motioned to his underling. “Ace, send a dispatch to pick up Kelly on the suspicion of murder.”

“Yes sir.” The sergeant flicked a glance her way before exiting.

She bit the inside of her cheek. *They’re corralling Carson.* She’d either accomplished her first virtuous act since fleeing Redding or made the biggest mistake of her life.

“Ready to get down to the nitty-gritty?” The captain laced his fingers together and stretched, cracking his knuckles.

She nodded.

"We couldn't buy the suicide theory for several reasons, but let me just say all that concerns you. All right?"

"Yeah."

"First off, it was clear that the body had been moved. Scuffmarks from the victim's shoes left a trail in the hallway. That rules you out as a suspect due to your size."

Her head tilted. "My size?"

"You're a tall cookie, but other than that, there's nothing to you."

Was that a compliment? Or an insult? She glanced down her frame. She had some padding, where it needed to be, anyway. "I don't understand."

"Arthur Cavenhalt was a large man. There is no way you could have drug him around like that. And even if you could have, you couldn't have hoisted him into his office chair."

"Was that where he was?"

"Yes ma'am. Face down on the desk, his hand over a pistol."

She shuddered at the mental image. "So I'm not a suspect?"

"No."

Got it. But understanding and trusting were two very different things. And if she confessed the part about Artie blackmailing her, then the big guy might think differently. She tapped the sides of her chair, trying to chase away the numbness. "What's left for me to do?"

He offered a sympathetic smile. "You have to give a written statement."

Her shoulders slumped. And here she thought she would stroll on out of here, having at least one problem dealt with. "Do I have to?" She whined like a three-year-old but didn't care. She had other issues to face—well, run away from. The longer she waited in policeland, the more trains she missed to NYC. "The rest of the world thinks it's a suicide. Why do I have—"

"Not for long. The district attorney is leaking it to the press"—

he glanced at his watch—"even as we speak."

She'd never been able to bargain well. In second grade, she'd lost all her jacks in exchange for a paper doll that ripped even with her careful handling. And now her heart felt torn in two. She should comply as much as possible to keep suspicion away, but the spotlight of attention shining over her might expose everything. And then the blame would be on her again. "Am I really the only witness here? Can't you nab your man without me?"

"Right now, you're all we have. Without your testimony, there is no case."

So simple for him to spout off like that. It wasn't his name on the witness paper. "I'm not flyin' with the idea of crossin' swords with Carson. It's a snap to see he won't like it. Look at Artie."

"Listen. Only me, the sergeant, and the D.A. know you were there last night, no one else. Yes, the defense will know we have an eyewitness, more like an earwitness." He laughed at his own joke. "But they'll be clueless as to who it is."

"What am I supposed to do until the trial comes? Sit around and knit?"

"We'll cover that in a bit." He shot a glance toward the door, the heavy look on his face making her leery.

What had she gotten herself into?

CHAPTER 6

Mick refilled the dinky paper cup and emptied it in one swig.

"How's it coming?" Officer Hundley joined him in the tiny breakroom, clutching a paper sack from the delicatessen.

"Captain's talking with her." Better his superior than him. His chest still burned from her explosive remarks. *You lied to me.* Smoldering under the flames of anger in her eyes were embers of hurt. A hurt he'd stoked, unintentionally. He crumpled the pathetic cup in his hand. Maybe he'd been deceptive, but what else could he have done? His job required confidentiality.

"Is she as dishy as the rumors say?"

He grunted and tossed the trash into the wastebasket.

"That's not an answer, my friend." Hundley bit into his sandwich, lips smacking as he chewed. "If you would've let us get a quick glimpse of her, then I wouldn't have to ask."

"You guys looked like a bunch of ogling schoolboys." And Miss Pembroke looked one breath away from an emotional breakdown. The woman probably hadn't been aware of the bright red rash stretching across her neck, but what concerned him was her glassy, blank stare. Was she in a mild form of shock?

Hundley's throaty chuckle ripped into his thoughts. "What can I say, we're a desperate lot." His thick brow rose, disappearing under the brim of his patrolman hat. "Well?"

"Yeah. She's attractive." Gorgeous, really. He'd be blind not to notice her hourglass frame and full lips. But alluring eyes often veiled danger. And her being Carson Kelly's girlfriend placed her in the hazard zone. He jerked down a cuff. Not that he was interested.

"Don't worry, Dinelo." Hundley clapped his shoulder. "You'll be on vacation tomorrow, and this case will be dropped into someone else's lap."

But whose? The good cop to bad cop ratio dwindled every time another speakeasy opened its doors. And while the feisty nightclub singer appeared to be harboring secrets, Mick wouldn't place her under the protection of a crooked officer. But it was getting harder and harder to determine which ones were on the level.

Mick eyed the man before him. Hundley may get distracted by anyone in a skirt, but he was trustworthy. "I'm going to put a good word in about you to the captain."

The other officer stopped mid-chew. "About what?"

"Taking over while I'm gone."

Hundley swallowed and wiped the mayonnaise from his mouth with the back of his hand. "I'd be honored, sir. Enjoy your time away."

Mick inhaled a calming breath. His parents had begged him for months to visit them in their new home, and frankly, the skyline of the Virginia mountains enticed him as much as his mother's fried chicken and apple pie. "It's been a long time coming." Yes, the anticipation of the following weeks gave him the stamina to finish the day.

Even tolerate the fury of a certain redhead.

Two hours and counting.

"How much longer 'til I can leave?"

The sides of her mouth cracked, dry from all that blabbing to the district attorney. Man, did he like to ask questions. "I think it would've been better to record my story on a gramophone." Then there were the written statements. She massaged the tops of her hands, lessening the cramps. If she had to chronicle her entire testimony one more time, she was certain her fingers would fall off. Her signature had become less and less legible.

"Not too much longer." The captain offered a sympathetic smile.

"Good."

"Captain?" The sergeant returned, and like a magnet, Vera's gaze was drawn to him.

She shook off the strange reaction to his presence, blaming it on fatigue. Because really, who wanted to stare at a man with a muscular build and ruggedly gorgeous face? She steadied her sights on his badge, a glaring reminder of his deception. How could she have fallen for his little trick at the apartment? He'd known it wasn't suicide, and he'd played her for a dope. She bet he'd been inwardly laughing at her ridiculous state of anxiety. She allowed the ugly force of that thought to drive away any attraction. However small it was.

The captain stood. "Excuse me, darlin'."

He and the sergeant lingered in the hallway, remaining in Vera's view. The men conversed back and forth, the captain using his hands as he spoke and the sergeant nodding. Vera scooted back her chair, giving her a better glimpse of the sergeant. He curled his fingers into fists behind his back and then slowly unclenched. What were they talking about? A scowl appeared on the sergeant's clean-shaven face, and the captain shrugged. This was worse than watching a silent film. At least with those you had title cards. Finally, the sergeant retreated down the hall, and the captain retreated the other way. Once again, Vera was alone.

In a handful of breaths, the captain rejoined the interrogation room, his hands loaded with a tray of food.

"Miss Pembroke, do you have any family you could stay with?" He set the food on the table, the Dr. Pepper nearly tipping, and he claimed the chair beside her.

"No."

"How about a friend? Anyone you could trust?"

"No."

"Anybody at all?"

As if this wasn't depressing enough. Not a big deal, right? A little jab here. A little jab there. Like poking toothpicks into her heart. "Nope. I sing solo." Not all by choice, but he didn't need to know that. She needed to appear tough and confident, a colossal—but necessary—venture.

Pops crossed his arms, a frown rippling his forehead. "Miss Pembroke, do you think you could do me a favor?"

She hated favors. "Depends."

"I want you to eat."

Her nose wrinkled. "Why?"

"You look too pale for my liking. Eat and then you'll be on your way."

When was the last time she'd eaten? Yesterday morning? She couldn't remember. One thing about not having a working stove in her apartment was the reliance on Woolworth's roast beef for a dime. "That's it? Okay, Pops, you're on." Vera sugared her words with her best smile and straightened in her chair.

He chuckled at her nickname for him, and she was relieved. Her mouth had often gotten the best of her, but this time her slip-up seemed to warm his countenance.

"Eat up." He slid the tray toward her, stood, and patted her shoulder. "I'll be back in a little bit."

"Sure."

He disappeared and she now had the task of making this food vanish.

She grabbed the knife and plastered the mayo over the bread. Egg sandwiches weren't her favorite, the texture of the yellow fluff strange to her palate. No matter. She'd eat chicken gizzards if that were the ticket out of there. Potato chips. Perfect. She grabbed a few and shoved them into the sandwich to give it a crunch. Much better.

After a few minutes, Pops walked into the room with the

sergeant in tow. "All set?" The captain reached for her empty plate.

"Yeah." Vera snatched a napkin and wiped the corners of her mouth. A swig of soda washed it all down.

"You're going with Ace." He jerked a thumb toward the giant subordinate. "Goodbye, Miss Pembroke."

A frown escaped. She'd have to endure ten more minutes with Sergeant Mean Eye. "Bye, Captain. Can't say it's been a pleasure."

"Remember, Ace," the captain said, "you have your orders."

"Yes, sir." He all but saluted and led Vera out the room and down an unfamiliar hall.

She stilled, her brow wrinkling. "This isn't how I came in."

"No, we're taking my car." A muscle ticked in his cheek. His annoyance evident.

The feeling was mutual.

They descended a flight of steps with a steel door at its base. The sergeant unlocked the deadbolt and gestured for Vera to pass through first. She tightened her grip on her bag and stepped out, her elbow skimming his arm in the process.

"Which jalopy is yours?" Her heels clipped against the Belgian block lot, and a steady breeze lifted her collar against her neck.

He pointed straight ahead. "The one parked closest to us."

"Keen ride." It wasn't as if his pale-yellow convertible was beyond anything she'd seen. Goodness, Carson's car had to be at least double the cost of Sergeant Stiff's Lincoln. But the Rolls Royce, with its sharp contoured body and dark interior, held the same persona as its owner—intimidating, cold. Which was why she internally dubbed it *The Steel Phantom*. The sergeant's, however, had the feel of an afternoon drive on a sunny day. "Can we put the top down?"

"No."

Rinky-dink. "What's the point of having a breezer if you're gonna keep her locked up?"

He grunted as he opened the door.

She lifted her foot to climb in but was stopped by a large hand on her right shoulder.

"Wait." The sergeant leaned inside and pulled out a towel from under the seat. He spread it across the plush bench.

"Sarge, if you think I'm going to soil up your precious Lincoln, then why not take the cop car? No, better yet, strap me to the roof." She patted the canvas top of his car, and his jaw tensed.

"Get in, Miss Pembroke."

Vera stuck her tongue out at him. Childish, maybe, but so deserved. Home couldn't come soon enough.

The sergeant shut her door, weeded out a leaf embedded in the radiator's grill, and with a determined expression, he strode to the driver's side. Normal-sized people would've had plenty of room in the car's cabin, but when he settled behind the wheel, his stature instantly shrunk the space in half, making her wish she'd volunteered for the backseat. She pinched her arms to her sides, trying to ignore his hulking presence less than a foot away and the pleasant woodsy scent coating the air.

"Pardon me." He reached across, his hand dangerously close to her knees, and adjusted something under the dash. The fuel line, maybe? He straightened and fussed with the levers on either side of the steering wheel before pushing the starter.

Ah, the hum of an engine. The sweet sound that told her that she was leaving this establishment. So long, suspicious flatfoots, daunting interrogation rooms, and sweaty palms. The glimmer of diamonds on her bracelet promised a new life. Yeah, she was on her way. She glanced out and clutched the fabric of her skirt. *No, no, no. Wrong way!* "Sergeant, you need to take a right." She tapped the window.

"Please don't do that. The glass is sensitive."

What? "We're going the wrong way."

Nothing. Not even a glance. Okay, he needed to get his hearing checked or maybe acquire a new brain. She snapped her fingers in his ears. "Sergeant, are you listening? Turn around!" Her voice squeaked. "You were supposed to take a right back there!"

"I know where I'm going, Miss Pembroke."

Vera dug her fingernails into the armrest. Yeah, she knew where they were going too.

The county jail.

CHAPTER 7

Vera's breath stopped in her throat, suffocating her composure. "You're goin' to throw me in the jug!"

"No, I'm not." He braked for a traffic sign. "Please keep your feet on the floor mat."

"Oh yeah, you are. You're picking on me for not coming forward."

He shot a look as transparent as a mud puddle. "You're not going to jail."

"If you aren't takin' me there, then where are we going?" Every block they passed inflicted slow torture, like pulling out her hair one strand at a time.

"Just following orders, Miss Pembroke. Following orders." His brows lowered, and his steely stare never left the road.

What kind of orders? And from who? Dread snaked through her. Expensive clothes last night, nice car today. He was a sell-out. And she was a key witness. "If you even try to get rid of me by—"

"Turns out, you had a friend."

No doubt, a friend who told him taking her life would be worth the compensation. "What are you talkin' about?" She inched toward the door and eyed the handle. Everything within her balked at the thought of jumping from a moving vehicle, but she'd risk bruises and scrapes to keep air in her chest.

"Jerry Gredinger."

She stilled. "Don't know him."

He gave a quick sidelong glance. "His name has been broadcasted all over the radio news hour. He's a cabdriver."

"Oh." She slid her eyes closed with a wince. "I forgot."

"Why didn't you tell us you talked to a cabdriver on your way back to the club?" He'd gotten on her for tapping the window frame, and *he* was strangling the steering wheel. "You put yourself in more danger."

So maybe the sergeant wasn't a bribe-taking weasel, but he definitely was a grating badger. "Didn't you hear me? I said I forgot."

He grunted, a scathing noise she'd begun to loathe.

"The chump tried to pick me up."

He scowled. "Did you take the ride?"

"No." She blew out a noisy breath and slouched against the seatback. "There were strings attached." So because of a slimy cabby's nosiness, she was getting kidnapped by the Allegheny Police Department? Her mind swirled, keeping her from snatching a logical thought.

"The plan was to shield your identity as long as possible. Now, all of Pittsburgh knows you were at the Kelly Club around the time of the murder."

Over the past hours, the idea of Carson being aware—and after her—danced around the edges of her sanity, but now it was a fact. He knew. She pushed her palm into her stomach, a feeble effort to control the swelling queasiness. Yesterday at this time, she'd been slipping into her gown for her nightly show, a loose hairpin her only concern. How could this—

"Your apartment was ransacked."

Her gaze swung to his grimacing profile. "What?"

"Your apartment. There was forced entry. It wasn't even forty-five minutes after the news came out with the cabdriver that the janitor of your complex called with the complaint." He inclined his head to the backseat. "There's what's left of your belongings."

Don't look. Don't look. But her stare pulled in that direction. Her shoulder blades locked together. "Two bags? That's it?"

"Sofa cushions were ripped. Mattresses slashed." He spared her a look, a trace of sympathy in his eyes. "The reporting officer said the place was demolished. Someone was on a search."

"Search for what?" That egg sandwich played trombone, sliding up and down the back of her esophagus.

"Miss Pembroke, you have to think." He slid a handkerchief out of his pocket and offered it to her.

She pushed his hand away. "I'm not crying." As if calling her a fibber, a tear squeezed from her eye. How did the sergeant know? Was he more observant than she'd thought? Turning toward her window, she forced back another tear, but it rebelled, trailing like fire down her heated skin. She had no control over her emotions. No control over her life. "Think about what?"

"The conversation between Cavenhalt and the killer."

No. She didn't *want* to think on that subject. And why did he say *the killer* and not *Carson*? He didn't believe her. No one did.

The sergeant rubbed his palm across the back of his neck, keeping the other hand steady on the wheel. "So you heard voices but couldn't identify what they were saying? Is that right?"

And now she was four notches beyond fatigue. Her throat burned and her muscles ached from being tense all day. Her hand gravitated toward her neck and grasped the golden chain. Oh no. "The dresser," she whispered. How could she let this happen? Exhaustion gave way to urgency.

"Pardon?"

"The dresser!" Her fingers slid from her collarbone to her flushed cheek. "Was it overturned?"

"Not sure. I didn't—"

"I need to know!" Hysterics scratched her nerves with a jagged fingernail. "I have to go back. I need to check. I just have to!" She smacked her palm on the dashboard, earning another disapproving glare from the sergeant.

"You can't go back. We can't allow anyone to see you." His

tone was annoyingly calm. "You understand that, don't you?"

"No." All she understood was he kept her from getting what she needed. What kind of brute was this man? Her heart beat out a wild song in her chest. "You can't do this. I'm not allowing—"

"They can trail you."

"Who?"

"The people who destroyed your place. They're most likely searching for you." His gaze flicked from the road to the rearview mirror as if checking to see if they were being followed. "What is it you need?"

"None of your business." She folded her arms and melted against the door. She was not about to let that one out. Not to him. Not to anybody.

"I can't help you, then."

A moment ago, her heart had thumped so hard she'd thought it was on the verge of detonation, now it felt as if it'd stopped cold. Could she be any more of a disappointment? *I'm so sorry, Grandma.*

"What was that, Miss Pembroke?"

Her fingers fluttered to her lips. Had she just said that aloud? "Never mind." She forced her eyes shut, but all she could see was her grandma's face. As if she needed guilt piled on top of everything else.

"Whoever tore up your place was definitely looking for something."

"So they're after me?" A stinging chill stole through her. Wasn't Carson in jail? Who could possibly be after her now? Her mind traveled to the man who haunted her evening numbers—Stony Eyes. Had he found out where she lived? Was the ransack related to Carson and his crime or a direct assault from the creepy stalker?

"That's why I'm to take you out of town."

"You can't hold me against my will."

"No, I can't. If you choose, I could turn this car back around and take you home." His gaze sharpened on her before darting back to the road. "Although I wouldn't recommend it. If it was

Kelly, then it's possible he has a lot of friends willing to do his dirty work."

She shuddered. Carson had a lot of connections. He'd been a gambling man—more like tycoon—and that'd exposed him to a boatload of shady characters. But would he harm her? Yes, he'd struck her when she'd questioned him about the time he'd snuck the cigarette girl into his office. But murder her? Her toes curled in her pumps.

"You need to be constantly on your guard. Not everyone is who they seem."

Something hinted in his raspy voice. What was he trying to say? Was he talking about himself?

"Why do you think the captain fetched your water? Gave you *his* dinner?"

"Because he's a swell guy."

"Because he couldn't risk you getting drugged. Or poisoned." He rubbed his brow and a knuckle hit his hat, knocking it crooked. "The badge means nothing anymore. Cash is king."

A heaviness settled over her.

"The captain asked if you had any family or friends. What did you tell him?"

"No." She shoveled all the confidence she could in that small word, but it still sounded pathetic.

"Then this is your safest bet."

"Where are you takin' me? The moon?"

His chin dipped. "Kerrville."

"Never heard of it."

If he adjusted his rearview mirror one more time, she was going to rip it off and hurl it at his square head. "That's the idea."

The onslaught of all this was hard to stomach. She'd dreamed of the day she would get to escape her surroundings but never imagined it'd be in this sorry fashion. The city limits sign came into view, then faded away.

Bye, Pittsburgh.

The tires crunched over the gravel terrain, and Mick slowed to a stop. Darkness overwhelmed the sky, trapping the moon behind ebony clouds.

Miss Pembroke stirred from slumber. A piece of him wanted her to remain asleep. Not only for the peaceful quiet he'd enjoyed the past hour, but for her sake. After the emotional exhaustion she'd experienced today, she needed rest.

"Where are we?" She yawned and extended her limbs, stretching. The poorly lit sign flickered, capturing her gaze. "Pigeon Loft Motel?" Her arms locked in midair. "No dice." She seized her handbag, posing to swing. "My safest bet, huh? A run-down, sleazy motel. Let me tell—"

He pushed his back against the door, using his hands to block her swipe. "It's not what you think. I need to make a phone call."

"Too bad, Sarge, this dame goes for hipsters, not overgrown boy scouts."

Another swing. This time his fingers caught hold of the strap. He pulled the bag from her clutch.

"Give that back!" She lunged toward him, and he grabbed her shoulders, pinning her arms to her sides.

She stiffened under his touch, sucking in a quick breath. Had he hurt her? The thought of leaving a bruise on her tender skin twisted his stomach. He loosened his grip.

She tipped her chin, placing only inches between their faces, her heavy breathing pulsing against his neck. "Let me go."

The darkness prevented him from reading her expressive eyes. "Are you going to attack me again?" If someone would happen upon them, they'd appear like a couple, cozying up, positioning for some good kissing. The situation poked him as strangely humorous.

"Are you laughing?" The disdain in her voice pinched his mouth shut. "Does the captain know of your intentions? How about your wife?"

He released her, and she skittered back to her side of the bench. "I'm not married. And don't worry. There's no fear of getting pawed."

She snorted. "I've been around dogs long enough to know what kind of meat they like."

"No, kiddo, you've been around wolves." He reached under the seat and grabbed the flashlight. When he flicked it on, the car's cabin lit enough to show the scowl cemented on her face.

"Better to be around a wolf than a liar."

Her bristly response nicked his defenses. "Liar? How so?"

"You told me your name was Mick." She folded her arms with a defiant tilt of the chin. "I heard the captain call you Ace."

"That's my nickname."

"A poker player?"

He nodded, and her eyes shifted from scrutiny to surprise, a palpable contrast, capturing his stare longer than he'd like.

Her gaze latched on his. "You're not a hustler, are you?"

"Hardly." Though he'd won his fair share of bets in high school and college. "Just happened to best the captain a time or two."

"Tell me, Sarge. Why were you there?"

"Where?"

She rolled her eyes with a huff. "At the Kelly Club. Since you obviously don't like the rowdy bunch in my circle. How come you were there?"

Silence pricked the air along with Miss Pembroke's thorny glare.

He cleared his throat. "Someone encouraged me to check it out." Not exactly a lie. Headquarters had received an anonymous tip implying the possibility of activity worse than rum-running. One that could attract the state's attention—which seemed the only way to access justice lately. Since Mick was the sergeant of investigations, plus the only officer the captain could trust, it was his assignment.

"What's this?" She pulled his jacket from the floor in front of her.

"It's mine."

"I'm not stupid." She sliced him yet another scornful look. He should keep a tally of how many scowls she could launch his way in the course of one conversation. But then, he'd been known for his severe expression, so it might prove even.

She held up the jacket. "What was it doing at my feet?"

"You looked cold and ..." *Scared*. "I thought you could use it." He shoved past her current defiant expression and replaced it with the image of her while she'd slept—the soft whimpers escaping her pouty lips and the shivers overtaking her frame.

"Here." She tossed it at him. "I'm perfectly fine."

You're welcome. He folded and laid the jacket on the bench between them.

She curled against her door and rested her head on her bent elbow.

Compassion gentled his voice. "Listen, Miss Pembroke, you've been through a lot over the past twenty-four hours. I understand why you're guarded."

She didn't move.

"I just need to call the captain and let him know we're almost there." And call his family informing them he wouldn't be at the dinner table tomorrow. He kept his lips tight, smothering the frown and restraining the rising groan. He'd exchanged his vacation to the mountains for a trip to the forest. His parents for a mystery woman with captivating eyes and a fiery temper. Following orders had landed him a headache.

Vera's eyes remained wide the rest of the way. "Did we drive north?"

"Yes."

"How far? Are we still in Pennsylvania?"

"Mm-hmm. The Allegheny National Forest."

She rubbed her eyelid, a sigh escaping. Fatigue two-stepped with anxiety across her chest, leaving a shakiness extending to her toes. "This place that we're goin' to. Are other people there?"

"No."

"So it's just me and …" She pulled her bottom lip under her teeth, tasting lipstick and salt from the potato chips earlier. Last night had been a nightmare. Was tonight going to equal it?

Alone with him.

Would he take advantage of her? She was out in the middle of nowhere. Unfamiliar with her surroundings. Nothing and no one to defend her if this man proved to be like all the others. Her throat constricted. Helplessness. Like being blindfolded and walking through a minefield. Was this man going to lead her to safer ground? Or be her destruction?

The car lurched and joggled on the rustic road. The sergeant hit the brakes for a furry critter to scurry across the road, and Vera collided with his shoulder.

"You okay?" His breath stirred her hair.

Too close.

Vera snapped straight. "I'm fine." She pressed her side against her door and held onto the armrest to avoid any future impacts.

Following another bout of the car's jostling, they drove onto a narrow lane hugged by tall pine trees. Through the dim headlights, she made out a building ahead. After driving up a slight incline, Mick put the car in neutral and pulled the brake.

The engine was off. The sergeant out. So why did she feel as if she was still in motion? The dizziness concentrated mainly in her head, but it invaded her stomach.

"Wait, Miss Pembroke." He opened her door. "The grass is pretty high."

"Yeah, and?"

"Let me set your things inside, then I'll come back and get you."

"Get me? You mean carry me?" Trying to touch her already? No. The darkness shrouded his silhouette. She couldn't discern how close he was.

He flicked on the flashlight. "I'm trying to treat you as if you were a lady."

As if? Pretty sure that was an insult. "Save it for your bride, sonny. I can manage."

With another grunt, he disappeared toward the house.

She puffed her cheeks with air and exhaled slowly. The idea of standing up caused her stomach to protest. But the quicker she got inside, the sooner she could park herself on a sofa. And there better be a sofa. She grabbed her purse and stepped out. "Ugh!" She fell back into the car.

"I told you, Miss Pembroke." His voice silenced the crickets.

She poked her chin out. "Well, you didn't say anythin' about getting drenched."

"It's just dew."

A screen door slammed shut, and she winced. Just dew? Her legs were as soaked as they would've been if she'd plunged 'em into a water bucket.

"Are you coming?" The screen opened, and this time light shone through, his broad frame illuminated in the doorframe.

Vera sucked in air and high-stepped her way to the house, the wet grass saturating her calves. Once she reached the threshold, her queasiness took over. She instinctively slapped her hand over her mouth. Mercy, no.

"Are you all right?"

Her stomach became a punching bag for nausea, knocking the egg guts out of her and onto the wood-planked floor. Ruthless. It belted her for minutes, long after she had nothing left to expel. A violent shake overtook her, and she barely felt the strong hand upholding her.

She was down for the count.

CHAPTER 8

A chirping sound floated into Vera's ears, rousing her from slumber. Not the usual cries of steam whistles or hollers from newsboys. Just the sweet song of birds welcoming the morning. It gave Vera a touch of nostalgia—Grandmother's humming, the fragrance of the lilac bush outside her bedroom window, the carefree days stitched with threads of sunshine and love.

The clanging of pots and pans punctured her reverie.

The sergeant. Subtle as an ox in a vintage wine store.

She clutched the sheets to her chest as her gaze flew to the door. Some relief came when she saw the door closed, but the anxiety returned. No lock. Not even a keyhole. Why did fellas keep giving her rooms with no locks on the doors?

She sighed and rolled over. The hem of her dress twisted around her leg. Guess there'd been no point in pinning the linens to herself a moment ago since she was fully clothed. She'd been in this garb so long that it itched like burlap. Why hadn't she put on a nightgown last night?

Last night.

Wait. She'd catapulted her dinner. Then what? And how did she get in this bed? Mick. He must have carried her. Boy, he probably hadn't appreciated her regurgitated eggs slopping up his crisp uniform. A giggle rippled out. Just a little mess in return for the big mess he'd put her through.

Sunlight poured into the room from the window beside her

bed, illuminating hundreds of floating wisps. What started as a quick glance slipped into a heavy stare. Sunlight. Unrestricted. She pushed herself to a seated position for a better view. The world beyond this window steeped with color—from the lush, emerald pines to the sapphire sky embedded with the golden sphere.

Vera could count on one hand all the days this year when Pittsburgh had been favored with patches of full sunshine. Its prison-gray skies, so much like her circumstances in that sooty city, had dulled hope for brighter times, but the vibrancy before her breathed life into the fatigued spots in her heart. She pushed the pane open and took a lungful of calmness, being cautious not to lose her balance in the process. The last thing she needed was to fall out a second-story window.

It was only when she took a step back that a sour smell assaulted her nose. Her fingers brushed the yellow-crusted hem of her skirt, and she recoiled. That egg sandwich wouldn't leave her alone. Change. Now.

She tapped her finger against her lip and inspected the door. Maybe she should scoot the dresser in front of it. That way, there'd be no risk of the sergeant playing peekaboo while she dressed. *Is Mick peeker material like Artie is?* She should say *like Artie was*. Her heart trembled as she tried to erase that dark moment from her head. His panicked voice and the sound of the shot ricocheted in the corners of her mind.

She sighed. "What a grand life I live."

Her bags sat near the door. A rush of emotions swept over her, like the breeze that came through her window. It might not be gone. She might have hope, after all. She seized the closest bag and dumped its contents onto the bed. Some dresses, three pairs of stockings, the bathrobe, and her favorite heels. Oh, and a set of flats. Mostly articles from her closet. She needed her dresser goodies. Time for bag two. Out flowed the bag's innards in a disordered heap beside her clothes. Ooh. Looking promising.

She eyed her feminine underclothing that came from the same

drawer as … her heart plummeted to the bottom of her gut as she spied it. That old handkerchief. That precious square foot of soft cotton. She held her breath as she reached for it, her chest tightening. No hope. It wasn't folded the way she had it two days ago. The lace edges were exposed. It had been unwrapped.

Her grandmother's pendant, now gone forever.

"Morning." The sergeant's voice registered no emotion. Again.

Vera smoothed a hand over her dress, its copper color matching the skillet in Mick's hand. "Yeah, it's morning." The small kitchen tweaked a sense of familiarity in her. It couldn't be considered a room, more like a hallway with a rickety stove, two metal cabinets, and a tiny icebox stuffed into it. Grandmother's place. She shook off the memory. *It's just coincidence.*

The most intriguing aspect of the kitchen, as much as it bothered her to acknowledge, was Mick. He was cooking. And looking comfortable at it.

Darts of grease shot above the sizzling bacon. He grabbed an aluminum plate, which she was certain came from the Five and Dime, and shoveled some fat strips onto it.

"Here." He gave her a hearty helping, leaving the charred scraps for himself. "Take this too."

She raised a brow at the glass he held in his right hand. "I'd rather have a cup of mud, if ya got any?"

With his other hand, he slid the skillet off the burner and then directed his eyes on her. Her breath did something funny in her lungs, as if it forgot which way it was traveling. "Miss Pembroke, please refrain from the sarcasm."

"It's coffee. Mud is jivey talk for coffee." Smokes. How off beat could this man be? "And please *refrain* from calling me *Miss Pembroke*. It's Vera."

The corner of his mouth twitched. Was he fighting a smile? Or was it a muscle spasm? "Water is all I got."

"It's awfully bland, don't ya think?" She accepted the glass with a shrug and followed him into the dining room.

Yep, this setup was smeared with masculinity. Only a man would use a dingy card table for his primary dining area. The best part was the dictionary employed under the left leg for support. Nice touch.

Steam climbed from the pile of cooked eggs in the center of the table, the odor reminding her of last night's retching episode. "I'm going to pass on those." She gestured with her hand.

"Suit yourself," he mumbled. The light streaming in from the window played on the waves of his blond hair.

Had he combed it, or was it naturally perfect? Men had it so easy. She scooped oatmeal onto her plate and perched herself in one of the chairs. Mick claimed the seat across from her. She picked up her spoon, but he remained still, head lowered, lips moving. "You talkin' to yourself?"

He didn't lift his head right away. "No."

"What were you doin'?" She better not be cooped up with a loony. That was all she needed. Escape one psycho to find another.

"Blessing the food." He smoothed a napkin on his lap and reached for his fork.

"Prayin'?"

"Yeah."

So that's why he was rigid. The man was into religion. Should she tell him now that it was a waste of time and effort or wait for a better opportunity? She'd mouthed a million prayers all to no avail. She forced a bite of oatmeal down and ignored the ache in her heart. "So ... how long are you going to hide me away in this woodland Windsor?"

He cleared his throat. "I talked to the captain this morning and—"

"This mornin'? So there's a phone here?"

"No. I went to see a friend and then went to town."

"Without me? When?"

"You were asleep." He wiped his mouth with a napkin.

And just how had he known? Had he peeked at her? From now on, she'd push that dresser in front of the door every time she was in that dusty room and not just at night. She tightened her lips around her spoon, resisting the impulse to call him on it. No. She'd wait for proof.

"Don't complain too much. You're benefiting from it."

Was he born with a stiff jaw, or was it a skill he had to master, like her with regulating her breathing for a double whole note? Even chiseled-chin Angelo relaxed when not on duty. Ah, that was it. The sergeant wasn't off duty. She'd be keen to remember that.

"Where else do you think I got all this food?"

"Oh." She scratched the bottom of her earlobe. Mick's gaze held on her movements. Why was he studying her? She dropped her hand into her lap. "What did the captain have to say? Did they catch the crumbs that destroyed my place?"

He took a drink. "No. Not yet."

Figures. "What about Carson? What's he getting, life or the chair?"

"Carson Kelly was released this morning."

Okay, so the man went from having zero humor to a sour one. "That's not funny, Sarge. I almost choked on my bacon." Just to make sure it went down right, she took a sip of her water. "I hope the trial comes soon. I'm more than ready to get my life back."

She forced her stare onto Mick. His pinched mouth and serious eyes left no room for doubt. "No." Her throat tightened as the air left her. This wasn't … it couldn't …

"I'm sorry. Kelly was released at nine this morning."

What? No! The oatmeal hardened to concrete in her stomach. A murderer on the loose. Was Carson searching for her? Was she to be victim number two? A shiver coursed through her, freezing her fingers into fists.

"No one else saw Carson's car coming in or going out at the time of the murder." His gaze pierced hers, and she forced herself to swallow. "Did you? Carson's car, did you see it?"

"No. It was raining." Didn't they go through this a gazillion times at the station? Was he testing her? Seeing if she'd give the same testimony? This took all. Carson was out and Mick wanted to play parlor games.

"We can't place Kelly on the scene at the time of the murder."

"That's a bunch of malarkey. I told you. I told you he was there!" She drilled the tabletop with her bent elbow and sunk her forehead into her open palm. "I heard him. It was him. Carson."

"Mr. Voss claimed Kelly was with him at the time of the shooting."

She ground her teeth. "Carson's lawyer?"

"Yes."

"The chump's lying." She whipped her head up, her voice trembling along with the rest of her. Compassion splashed around in his eyes, and she hardened her heart at it. If it was sympathy, it was probably for himself, having to endure her company. "Ward Voss is Carson's best friend."

"He's also a prominent figure in the city. He's got ties with bank presidents and owners of railroads and—"

"Murderers."

"Voss is respectable." Mick shrugged. "And you're—"

"And I'm what?" Her eyes watered, burning. "Go ahead and say it. A speakeasy singer's word is nothin' to a fancy-pants lawyer's."

"Yes." He stared at her as if she were going to shoot through the ceiling. "That's how they're viewing it."

Vera stiffened her features, hoping to conceal her bleeding pride. She was all too familiar with the *respectable*, and for a while, had thought she'd been immune to their condescending glares, but the squeezing in her chest proved otherwise.

"We're searching for a motive here. No motive, no case." He finished off his drink.

"There was a reason." She pushed her plate away, allowing some of the oatmeal to spill onto the table. Her mind scrambled, searching for a different road than the one she was about to travel, but none surfaced. "Artie was a blackmailer." Her voice trembled and she hated it. "I can prove it."

Mick paused, then spoke, his voice even. "How?"

"Because he was blackmailing me." And in one measly second, she destroyed all the years she'd been forced silent.

Mick shifted in his chair, openly facing her. "What about?"

"I was starving. Homeless. Artie took me in. Told Carson I was his cousin in order to get me a job at the gin joint."

There was a stretch of silence before Mick nodded. "And Kelly never found out?"

"No." Vera scratched her neck and kept her lashes lowered. "Artie threatened me that very night. Said he was going to tell Carson."

He rested his elbows on the table, leaning toward her. "I'm not sure why this is a big deal."

She settled back. "Because you don't know Carson. He demands loyalty. If he suspected I lied to him in one area, he'd wonder if I was fibbing in others."

"Were you?"

Her gaze dropped to her fingernails. "I'd also been singing off and on at the Moonlight Club. Artie found out. Pretty much told me I had to stay under his control, or he'd ruin me." She lifted her chin and got caught in his intense stare.

"Doesn't sound like a very nice guy. So you think he had something on Kelly?" Brows quirked above questioning eyes, increasing his attractiveness and decreasing Vera's ability to think.

She forced her attention on a crack in the wall behind him. "Artie was always sticking his nose in places he didn't belong." Barging in her dressing room. Pressing an ear to Carson's closed office door. "I wouldn't be surprised if he stumbled onto something worth his while." Because her pay was table scraps compared to the hearty portion Artie could chisel out of Carson. Except Carson hadn't put up with it like she had.

"Why didn't you say this earlier?"

She sighed. "I didn't want to be incriminated."

Another nod.

"So there's a possible motive." She splayed her palms on the tabletop, pressing into the cooled surface.

"I'll have my boys check into it." Mick kept his gaze trained on her, and she struggled not to shift. "But so you know, the D.A. needs hard evidence. Proof to both the blackmail claim and to Kelly being tied to it all. Is there anything else you can remember?"

"No."

"I'm going to need something more definite."

And just like that, it was dismissed. The years of dread about her secret coming to light, the moments of panic when Artie would threaten her. All of it meant nothing because she had no proof.

If only she'd caught that bus to New York.

"Look. We're doing the best we can." He stood, ducking away from the light fixture. Another reminder of his hulking physique. "Are you done?"

"Yeah." Fatigue spread through her as she held out her plate. Their fingers touched. She yanked her hand into her lap, burying it underneath her other hand.

"Do you want more to drink?"

She gave a small shake of the head.

He scooped up her empty glass. Then her silverware.

"Okay. What's your racket, Sarge?"

"Racket?" The raised brow bit wasn't convincing. She'd seen too much. They didn't make honest ones anymore.

"Yeah. Just spill it and be done with it." Then she could know where she stood. Would she be on her way to New York tonight since the D.A. considered her testimony as valuable as a wooden nickel? Maybe if she was nice to Mick, he could direct her to the nearest pawnshop. She glanced at her bracelet, her mood lightening.

"I have no idea what you are talking about."

"There's crime sprouting all over Pittsburgh. Plenty of it. You're here, cookin' my breakfast, cleanin' my dishes. What's the angle?"

"No angle."

"Gotta be."

"No, there's not."

"Then why hide me away?"

"I told you last night, we don't know who we can trust. It's safer to keep you away."

"Yeah, well, that was yesterday when my testimony was worth something." Today she was back to a nobody. "There's no reason for me to stay now."

"It was the captain's idea." He flicked a small crumb off the faded tablecloth. "He has a hunch that Carson's dealings are—

Ooh. Now things were getting good. "Are what? Out with it."

"Not sure, really. Just a hunch."

And like that, her hopes were dashed. "That was a whole lot of nothin' ya just blabbed."

The sergeant stood silent. He was keeping something from her, and she couldn't contemplate an effective way to draw it out of him. She hardly knew him, but he didn't look like one who'd dish out official information.

"Tell me, Mick. Are you on the level?"

He nodded once, never breaking eye contact with her. "There's no danger with me."

Ha! What a line! "Oh, yeah? How do I know? Prove it." If the D.A. required proof, then so did she.

"You're going to have to trust. I—"

"I. Don't. Trust." Blood rushed to her cheeks, and she slapped her palms on the table. She'd learned at an early age not to have faith in anyone. It'd kept her alive this long. "I can't trust you. The police. No one. You could be crooked like all the rest of them. For all I know, that phone call you made last night could've been to Carson's crew. And all this is a put-on to keep me here until Carson figures out how to dispose of me. There's a lot of woods out that window." She pointed. "No one would ever find me."

"I'm not crooked. And I'm sorry you aren't capable of trusting anyone."

He spoke as if he had a soul, but Vera knew better. Men only showed interest or kindness when wanting a favor in return.

His shoulders sagged slightly. "I'm not going to lie. The captain believes you're in danger. The people who destroyed your place aren't to be trifled with. He doesn't want me to take you back too soon. You're safest here."

The captain might believe her. That was encouraging. He seemed like a good one to have in her corner. "How long do I have to stay?"

"Not sure. The captain is doing this on the hush." He nodded as if Vera knew the plan from the beginning. "No one else is aware."

"Don't you think people are going to put two and two together when you aren't around?"

"No."

She sighed, wishing he filled out his answers the way he did his cotton shirt. "Why? You skip out on work on a regular basis? Not very faithful of you, Sarge."

His jaw tightened. "No. I'm supposed to be on vacation."

So that was why the man was disgruntled. He'd been swindled out of his free time.

"The captain thinks you might remember something else. Information that will help propel this case and close it up."

"I just tried and you said it wasn't good enough." Story of her life—never good enough. The words festered in her mind as her fingernails bit into her palms. "I've got nothing else. Nothing. The captain can't force anythin' with me."

Mick pulled his hand through his hair. "The captain's not like that. He's a good person. He has a heart for the lost ones."

"Is that how it is, huh?" She jumped to her feet, sending the flimsy wooden chair to the worn floor. "A rooty-toot with a badge. That's all you fellas are, and you have the brass to think you're better than me."

"Are you going to pick that up?" His gaze shifted to the turned-over chair.

"No." Vera's hand itched to slap his clean-shaven face, but another urge intensified. She stormed past him and into the kitchen. Nope, didn't see it. Into the living room. Not here either. Back to where she started, standing in front of Mick. "All right. Where is it?"

"Where's what?"

"The powder room. Where is it? In the linen closet?"

Nothing. Not even a blink.

"I'm waitin', Mick." She spat out his name like she'd been using it for years.

"So am I." The way his eyes trained on her—firm and unrelenting through a black fringe of lashes—she didn't have to imagine how severe his countenance would be when concentrated on a lawbreaker.

"Fine." She stooped down and placed the chair on its legs. "There. Happy?" She snapped her fingers in the air. "Now, spill it."

He turned and she tagged along, walking out of the dining room and into the kitchen. He creaked open the screen door. "Follow me."

She harrumphed and walked outside. "I want to use the powder room, not go on a nature walk."

They rounded the corner, and she spied an outhouse, her belly sinking. *Too familiar*. She spun on her heel, heading back inside, branding her footsteps into the soil. The screen door whacked closed with her entrance. In the main room, her gaze took in the bones of the place with fresh eyes. She plopped onto the sofa, launching a cloud of dust in the air.

How could this house be so similar to her grandmother's? No way they shared the same builder. Redding was on the other side of the state. And why couldn't the memories remain buried? Her eyes closed against the sting. She wasn't fourteen anymore. The pain, yeah, she couldn't escape it, but this place … she could.

The door banged against its wooden frame, announcing Mick's presence.

"I'm not goin' to use it. Never. Probably filled with every kind of critters. Spiders bite. So do snakes."

"Looks like you're going to be uncomfortable, then." He disappeared into the kitchen area.

"No phone. No indoor plumbing. No Vera. Get it, pal?" She'd play the role of spoiled duchess before telling him her real reasons for needing to leave this place.

The scraping of a fork to a plate was all the response he gave. What gall. The guy was cleaning food off dishes while her insides screamed.

"Quit ignorin' me." She vaulted to her feet and ambushed the kitchen.

His attention remained fixed on the wash bucket. "I'm not ignoring you. I'm choosing not to respond."

Word games again? "It's the same thing."

No emotion. No flare in the eyes. Why couldn't this man get angry with her? His cool tone broiled her temper. And why couldn't she think of a devastating reply? On the stage, she thrived off improvising, but this gig left her brain devoid of any intelligence.

He leaned over the counter, gazing out the window. "I'm going for a walk."

Perfect. Get lost.

He faced her. "You need to come too."

Ordering her around like a child. "I'm not goin' anywhere." She glared at him. "I thought I'm to be hidin' out, not frolickin' around the forest."

"Come here." He waved his hand toward the dining room table. "This is the cabin." He set his pocket watch in the middle of the table. "On either side of us is forest." He motioned to the left and right of the watch.

"You don't say."

"The woods in back belongs to the cabin. The woods to the

front belong to the government. A nature preserve that no one goes on." He ran a finger along the table and stopped when he reached the watch. "This road is only used by us and a neighbor five miles down the road."

Her interest piqued. Did he just say *neighbor*?

He shrugged. "People can't find this place. That's why we're here. We're seven miles from a back road and fifteen miles from a main road. But"—he stroked his square chin—"when we go for walks, we'll stay on our land behind the house. Just as a precaution."

Back to the walk again. "I'm not going."

He stuffed his watch in his pocket. "Okay, Miss Pem—"

"Vera."

"Fine, Vera." He emphasized her name, and some bizarre part of her liked the sound of it. The tone of his voice possessed a deep rumble like thunder in the distance—slight but powerful. In her adolescence, a thunderstorm thrilled her with its danger and unpredictability, but she'd tasted enough peril, and none of it was alluring anymore. But the brooding man who stood a yard away held an unsafe charm. Yes, his personality proved drier than day-old bread, but his confident stance and mesmeric eyes trapped her stare. Like right now.

He must've sensed her unease—or his—because he stepped back to straighten the already perfectly situated chair. "You can stay here. I'll be able to see the road from where I'll be."

"Swell." Maybe there was something to take her mind off murderers and cops. "I'll sit here listening to the noise box … and waiting for my bladder to explode."

"Sorry. No radio either."

Was he serious? How primitive could a joint be? In a shrewd manner, the police had indeed taken her to jail. But instead of a retaining cell, she had a dusty cabin with dead beetles for cellmates. She kicked the petrified insect, lying belly-up, into a gap in the floorboard.

The sergeant's expression turned sheepish, and she was relieved to see the man show a slice of emotion, however minimal. "Sorry about the filth. It's been a couple months since it's been lived in." He skimmed a finger on the windowsill, carving a trail in the grime. "There are some books over there." He wiped his hand on his handkerchief and pointed to a stack of hardbacks in a wicker basket by the sofa.

"Books are for clammy intellectuals."

"That's all I have for entertainment," Mick called over his shoulder as he hustled up the stairs two at a time.

Vera kept herself sane by pacing about the lower level. Being on the move lessened the pressure from her middle.

Mick bounded down the steps, graceful as a Saint Bernard.

Whoa. What had come over him? Her eyes could've collapsed in their sockets. The last thing she expected was for the Sarge to be donning cutoff denim trousers. His exposed arms and calves commanded her attention, the sculpted muscles flexing with his movements.

"I'll be back soon." He took the towel dangling from his hand and draped it around his neck.

What was that for? Was he going for a run? A swim? "Take it easy. No hurry." No rush at all, big boy.

His eyes locked on hers. "Except for the outdoor room, do *not* go outside."

"Since I'm not using it, that won't be a problem." With a roll of her eyes, she walked to the window, frowning at the dead flies gathered in the corner. What should she do now? Was there another option than being stuck with Sergeant Mean Eye? Maybe there was. She pressed her lips together, hiding her smile.

CHAPTER 9

Mick inhaled, taking in the woodsy-scented air.

The path to the swimming hole narrowed, and ferns brushed against his shins with each stride.

The creek whispered over stones and fallen branches, a sound he never tired of. He descended a hill and spread his towel on a yellowed patch of grass. Off went the shoes, socks, and shirt. He withdrew his pocket watch and placed it in his shoe.

His feet invaded the water, and the minnows scattered. Chilly, but it had been icier. Ankles and knees disappeared. Before Mick was waist-deep, he pulled the soap out of his pocket. Once he worked up a rich lather, the bar went on the shore and he went underwater. How that log got on its side to stretch across the creek, he'd never know, but it'd been a great lap marker. Ten or twenty? He settled on fifteen. With each lap, tension eased from his mind. Something he needed. Bad.

Mick finished up floating. With water beneath and the open sky above, his gaze looked heavenward, but his thoughts remained grounded on a certain fiery-haired woman.

Vera Pembroke.

"Oh, Lord," he whispered. Car thieves he could deal with. Unruly juveniles, take 'em any day of the week. Twenty-something females?

He let out a stream of air.

This woman had a tongue sharper than his penknife. But … it

was all an act. Everything about her screamed that she was hiding something beneath the façade. Being an investigator required a discerning eye, but it didn't take a magnifying glass to identify the lingering confusion and dread swimming in her darting glances.

He sunk in the water before planting his feet on the spongy creek floor. How deep was Vera's involvement? Would these men be combing the countryside for her? They would if they thought she knew something … and possibly if she didn't. Did she really not know of Kelly's dealings? Behind that pretty face stood a universe of secrets.

He slapped the water and it rippled away. *Secrets.* That word had become his undoing. His devastation. If the captain hadn't intervened four years ago, those black moments, the darkness, would've swallowed Mick whole. And he would've succumbed without arguing. Phyllis' death had bled him of any fight he'd had left.

He dunked his head under—a feeble attempt to rinse his thoughts free of that December day—and resurfaced. Better get back to his charge. He'd already lost one on his watch. His heart couldn't bear another.

He hung his towel on the sagging clothesline and smiled. Sure enough, the outhouse door hung open, its hinges creaking along with the mild breeze. He'd predicted it wouldn't be long before she broke down. Just like an obnoxious trainee, a taste of discipline was all she needed. He kicked his heels off the mat before entering the cabin.

Silence.

The only motion was the curtain blowing in the window.

"Vera?" He sailed up the steps and knocked on the closed door. "You in there?" He waited and then pounded again. The least she could do was respond. "Vera, I'm going to open the door." He waited a few more seconds and threw it open. Fists clenched at his sides, he surveyed the empty room.

She was gone.

He scowled at the vacant spot on the floor where he had set her bags the night before. Vera's flowery scent lingered in the silence, taunting him.

Mick sprinted out of the house, the crack of the screen door a faint tap compared to his heartbeat thrashing in his ears. He strode toward his car and settled behind the wheel. Adjusting the fuel cut-off, pulling the choke, fiddling with the spark lever all seemed to take the time he couldn't afford to waste. He turned the ignition and stomped on the starter. His Lincoln roared to life. He put the car in first gear, and with a thump of the gas pedal to the floor, he took off in search of the speakeasy singer.

He palmed the back of his neck, pressing hard against the knotting tension. Why had he told her about the neighbor? Dumb. He was about as competent as his one-eyed uncle at darts. Mick had utterly missed the mark. The captain's strategy was for Vera to remain here, guarded and safe, but in less than a twenty-four-hour span, Mick had already managed to lose her.

Didn't she realize the danger? The district attorney might be deceived, but Mick had been after crooks like Carson Kelly for years. Those kinds of men held no regard for anyone but themselves. His fingers gripped the wheel tighter, knuckles draining white. Mick knew very well of their disregard for human life. He jerked his head to shake the venom from his mind. Phyllis had made her choices, and sadly, so had he.

After a mile and a half, he downshifted and flexed his foot off the gas, letting the car cruise. The brush was tall on either side of the dirt road, but the curly mass of Vera's red locks acted as a signal flare. He slowed the Lincoln to rumble along beside her.

"Get in the car." He raised his voice above the engine's growl.

She hobbled on, her dress swishing with each stride. The only acknowledgment he received was a shake of her pretty, stubborn head.

"I told you I'd take you home. All you had to do was ask."

"Pittsburgh's not my home." She stopped.

He braked. "What about the case? You've got an obligation."

"What case?" She dropped her bags and flailed her arms in the air. "You said my story wasn't good enough."

He suppressed a groan. Why did women have to be dramatic?

"And my only obligation is to take care of me. Get it?" She cocked her head back in a challenge.

Uh-huh, he got it. "You're running away."

"Call it what ya want, Sarge. I ain't—"

"You're frightened?" *Careful, Ace.* Trained to detect signs of distress, he selected his words cautiously. "I understand, Vera."

"You understand nothing." A blotchy rash stretched across her neck. Just like the day in the interrogation room. Her voice had a quiver in it. Another symptom. "I'm not scared." She scratched the spot above her collar, reddening her skin more.

Yes, you are, kiddo.

"Quit actin' like you know me." Her stony glare didn't conceal the slight heaving of her shoulders or the trembling of her lower lip. "Because y-you don't. You have no idea the …" She pushed her palms against the sides of her head and labored for air.

Mick pulled the brake and jumped out. He placed a hand on her back, meaning to help smooth her sporadic breaths.

She leapt away as though he held fire. "Don't touch me. Ya said you wouldn't touch me."

Oh brother. He drew in a good slice of oxygen and collected himself. No reason for them both to be edgy. Control. "Vera, I was checking your breathing."

"My breathin's fine."

If *fine* meant choppy and wheezy, then yes. He had to get her calm before she hyperventilated. Engaging her in conversation would be wisest. "Vera, the thing to see here—"

"Stop! My life"—she slapped her hand on her chest—"my life was okay until you showed up!"

Soothing tones. Keep a soft voice. Her eyes rounded and alert, she resembled her nickname, Canary, ready to take flight at any sense of danger. "Your life will be okay again. It will."

"Don't ya dare make promises. Better not to vow, than to vow and not pay."

"Ecclesiastes."

She stared, lips parted and head tilted. "Huh?"

"What you just said was a verse from Ecclesiastes."

A softness swept over her hardened features. It was fleeting, like a breath of wind, making her lovelier. "Someone I knew … would always tell me that." With shaky fingers, Vera smoothed away the hair from her cosmetic-caked face. She jerked her gaze from his and sniffled.

"Here. Allow me." Mick held out his handkerchief, the same one from last night.

"I ain't cryin'." She shook her head, refusing his token. "I got a gnat in my eye."

Lie. He could point to the rock where her stray tear had landed, the darkened oval proving its existence. But just like in the car, her pride wouldn't accept his consideration. "What do you have against my poor handkerchief?" His pathetic attempt for a tease hung stale in the air, the only response from her being a rigid shoulder shrug.

Wind pulled through the trees, disturbing the shade above, allowing sunlight to hiccup across her face. Her noisy breathing quieted. Her shoulders quit heaving.

He gave her what little privacy he could offer and peered out into the web of branches. The creek burbled in the distance, constant and soothing. He snuck a glance at her and frowned. "You fell." The front of her dress was soiled, her elbow tinted with blood. He should've never left her this morning.

"I'm fine." *Brush. Brush. Brush.* Her hand worked vigorously over the fabric of her skirt. The dirt only smeared. She sighed, and her arms wilted to her sides.

"Listen, Vera." He scooped up the bags. She reached out but

wasn't quick enough. "Give it time." He tossed her belongings in the rear seat and walked back to her. "Please?"

"No."

It took all his self-control not to hoist her over his shoulder. How could he convince her of the danger? If anyone should know of the risks involved, shouldn't it be the former girlfriend of a gangster? And Carson Kelly was as crooked as they come. Mick just needed proof. Something he considered valid enough to take to the state level. Because that's the only way Kelly could be stopped.

What Mick *couldn't* consider were Vera's wide eyes that begged for stability. Or the natural pout that pulled his attention more than he was comfortable with. "No pressure. Relax up here for a couple days and then decide. All right?"

The fire in her eyes extinguished. "Maybe … a couple days." She lifted her chin, and the flames rekindled, gold specks igniting in her green irises. "But that's all."

"Fair enough."

He felt her stare as they walked back to the car. She didn't trust him. Well, he didn't exactly harbor chummiest of feelings for her either. God help them.

He held the door for her, and the side of her mouth quirked up. Slightly. Something akin to victory tugged at his heart.

However, the taming wasn't absolute. The Red Canary could take wing again.

CHAPTER 10

Vera rubbed her lips together, spreading the grit from her lipstick.

This morning marked day number two of waking up with sunshine beaming through the windowpane, warming both her skin and mood. But then the sergeant had gone and shattered her lazy musings with his persistent knocking. He now filled her bedroom entryway, all dapper in his beige suit and boater hat.

Mick released a noisy exhale. "Hurry, please."

"You're one callous cat. Do you know that? Ya don't get a dame up outta bed and then tell her she has five minutes to get ready. It's cruel." And impossible.

"I have to call the captain at eight a.m. Sharp." He held up his pocket watch as if she could read the time from across the room.

She coursed her fingers through her hair and pulled the sides up with combs. Her gaze fell to her legs. Should she roll down her stockings? It certainly would be cooler. Yesterday's sweltering heat had nearly made her faint. If she planned another getaway, she'd make sure to flee during the brisker parts of the day.

Mick cleared his throat, and she rolled her eyes. No more time to fuss. The granny garter would have to do.

"How do I look?" She popped her hip to the right and raised both arms, striking a pose like Greta Garbo's from *The Divine Woman*.

"Fine."

He didn't look. An unusual breed, this one. Most men had surveyed her like a choice cut steak, but not him. Something about it was refreshing. "Just fine?"

"Yeah, let's go." He put his arm behind her and propelled her from the room.

Once outside, Vera spread out her arms and tilted her head to the sky. "What do ya say, Mick? Can we put the top down?"

"Not today. It might rain."

"One cloud." She scrunched her brows and collapsed her arms to her sides. "It's so tiny I wouldn't call it a cloud. It's a puff. And look. It's not even over us." She shook her head. "Ya know you really should take a bath in oil."

"What?"

"You're rusted stiff. Loosen up." She rolled her shoulders a couple times. An example might help the poor soul.

"No. I'm disciplined."

"I'm surprised your joints don't squeak."

He finally graced her with a smile with … dimples. The backs of her knees quivered, and she stiffened against it. Good thing the man hardly grinned. Those deep dents framing a perfect mouth could prove distracting.

Mick reached for her door, opening it. Instead of stepping aside for her to slide in, he straightened that lousy towel where her backside would soon be parked.

The pathetic amount of attraction she'd felt was now replaced with the urge to smack him upside the head. "You sure know how to flatter the females, Sarge. And for the record, I'm not as dirty as ya think."

"What?" His brows pulled together. "The leather seat gets warm. The cloth should make it more comfortable for you."

Oh.

He shut her in and strode to his side. After settling behind the wheel, he started the car.

"So where we goin'? Atlantic City?" She shook imaginary dice and threw them.

"Of course not."

She'd only been in his presence today for fifteen minutes, and her words already set his nostrils to flaring. Getting under his skin, such a happy challenge, like mastering one of Maestro's songs. Only better.

"Thought we'd drop by the neighbor's house." He glanced over. "Since you were in such a rush to meet her yesterday."

Her? Was she Mick's girl? He seemed keen on visiting her. While he maneuvered the car down the drive, she took that moment to sneak a heavier look. Everything about the man breathing two feet away said *order*, from the perfect length of his hair beneath his hat, not too long nor too short, to the sharp incline of his chin, to his crisp beige collar. She could see why women would fawn over him. He appeared to be a man who had it all together.

"I think you're going to like her."

Vera folded her arms. Social introductions made her want to gag. "Can I at least roll the window down? I know stuffiness is your atmosphere, but it's not mine."

"Go ahead. But be careful with the glass, it's—"

"Sensitive. Yeah, yeah, I remember." Good ol' Sergeant Mean Eye. She cranked it halfway down and gazed out.

Clear skies hovered over them, a calming blue. The car's springs rattled as they drove over uneven earth and down the hill. The scent of pinesap weighted the air, the stickiness layering her lungs with each breath. One final bump took them onto the road, if she could call it that. Tire tread marks scored the ground, a seam of grass in between.

"How did Captain Harpshire ever spot this place?" She peered through timbers resembling hairy toothpicks.

He flicked a look her way. "The land's been in his family for a long time."

"Which brings up another question." She twisted to face him. "If this is his place, then how come ya know your way around? You his errand boy up here too?"

He scowled and Vera smiled brightly. She'd annoyed him twice in less than five minutes. A personal best.

"I've been coming up here for years. The captain lets me use it whenever I want."

"So that explains why ya didn't have any bags. You keep clothes here."

"Yeah."

"Glad ya lost those cop threads." Hope he made a habit of it. His taste in clothing was commendable, but even his perfectly cut suit couldn't hide the mark of his profession. His revolver seemed to glare at her, the slant of morning sun glinting off its handle.

A shiver coursed through her, and she resisted touching the scar near her temple. That bullet long ago and now the one that killed Artie. Two identical shots, a set of tormenting twins. She shoved the haunting thoughts away as they drove onto a dusty lane.

Mick stopped the car and got out. He strode around quickly, opened her door, and extended his hand.

Did he think she was helpless? That she couldn't climb out of the car without his assistance? She glared at him. "Keep your hands to yourself."

"My parents raised me to open doors for and offer my arm to a lady."

What could she say to that? Parents who cared enough for their children to teach them manners. Jealousy scratched her heart.

"Tell me what's in there for me?" She motioned her head toward the cottage. "I already know enough people. Don't feel like meetin' anyone new. With nothing new to say."

He shrugged. "I thought you'd want to get cleaned up, but if you'd rather—"

"She has running water?" This dame suddenly got interesting.

"Yeah."

"With faucets?" She massaged her sore upper arm. If she had known yesterday after her botched runaway plan that she'd be spending fifteen minutes priming an oxidized pump in order to snag a drink, she'd have gone thirsty. Yeah, Mick had offered to help, but her pride wouldn't accept it. Which was why she'd isolated herself in her bedroom for the rest of the day, humidity and silence her only companions. "Are you kidding me? Because if so, you're marked as my number one enemy."

He smiled. "The works, Vera. A bathtub, sinks, and your personal favorite, a flushing powder room."

That was the nicest thing he'd ever said. If she wasn't bent on loathing him, she'd hug him. She scooted out of her seat, not caring if her heels skidded on the floor mat.

Vera jerked her thumb as they bypassed the front porch and rounded the back of the residence. "You missed the door."

Whoa. The poor lady's house was petunia-infested. Pink petals lined the walkways, filled pots on the porch steps, and hung in baskets from the porch ceiling.

"Come on in." A squeaky voice floated from inside the cottage.

"Morning, Mrs. Chambers." He greeted a small-framed woman. The white hair and wrinkled skin answered Vera's question—not Mick's dame. "May I introduce Miss—"

"Vera." How many times did she have to tell the man? "Call me Vera." Although she didn't expect this seventy-something woman to call Vera anything but vulgar. Elderly ladies were the worst—and most vocal—when it came to handing out disapproval for Vera's overuse of the war paint. But she'd rather be called a hussy than attract curious looks with her scar.

"Vera. What a lovely name. It suits you." Her smile was kind. "Come in. Come in."

Mick held the door for Vera to pass through, and she took in the new surroundings. *Yeah, now we're talking.*

The captain's place was Daniel Boone's cabin compared to this woman's joint. Where the men had mismatched chairs and tattered cushions, she had a plush sofa with coordinating pillows. No dilapidated tables, but china cabinets and doilies galore. The cinnamon-sugar aroma sent her stomach growling. No breakfast, thanks to Sarge.

Mick pulled Mrs. Chambers in for a side hug.

Vera drew in her bottom lip, restraining her jaw from dropping. Emotion. The man could show emotion. Who'd have thought?

He approached a cat lounging in an armchair, picking it up and stroking its calico fur.

"Mick's the only one Mitzy lets do that." Mock offense sprinkled her tone, but a smile glistened in her gray-blue eyes. "Vera, I'd love for you to call me Lacey." She slipped a feeble arm in Vera's. "I try to get Mick to call me Lacey, but he won't. Flat refuses."

Mick returned the feline to the chair and faced them. "That's because your name is Frances." A broad grin split his face. And he brought his dimples along.

Okay, where did Straight-faced Sergeant go, and who was this gent with the friendly expression and the happy hugs?

"My late husband … bless his memory. He called me that. Lacey." Her voice pitched higher, her gaze upward.

Vera followed her dreamy stare. Nothing there except a plastered ceiling.

"Yes, I was his little Lacey. Won't embarrass anyone with the details of how I got it."

"Don't want to know." Mick turned on his heel and walked into the other room.

Lacey's laugh doused the air. "Poor Mick. He shies away at those kinds of topics."

"Just have to call the captain." His defensive tone made Lacey laugh more.

"Now, dearie." The older woman set a hand on Vera's shoulder. "I hear you want to get washed while you're here."

"A wash is an understatement. I think I need a chisel to chip off the crud."

"Then let's hop to it." Lacey flounced out of the room, her cottony hair bouncing.

Vera followed as the woman walked down the hall and opened the door on the left.

Ah, the toilet. Vera smiled. She'd never recalled another time when the porcelain bowl looked so beautiful. And, beside it, another refreshing sight—a claw-foot tub.

"Everything else you need is in this cabinet. Take your time."

Oh, she would. "Thanks." Vera waited until the old lady left and turned on the faucet.

She all but jumped out of her stiff clothes into the pool of steaming water. A few temps below scalding, just the way she liked it. Cleansing water saturated the pores that had been clogged with summer-induced perspiration. Her muscles relaxed as she sank deeper and leaned her head back.

"What did the captain have to say?" Lacey's voice was distant, but Vera could make out her words.

"Mostly the same as yesterday." Mick's bass-like voice could probably be heard three counties over without any strenuous effort on his part. "He confirmed that Carson Kelly was released."

Vera wanted to dip her head under the suds and stay there for the next million years or so.

"Heavens above, her hair is beautiful. Mick, I say she has a face for the silver screen. Very pretty."

The faucet dripped five times before Mick responded. "Yeah, she is."

Maybe she should tune the world out with a hum of her favorite jazz melody and not contemplate the handsome sergeant and those three words he'd just spoken.

"You're porkin' me up, Lacey." Vera stuffed another bite of pie into her craw, the tender apples a great balance of tart and sweet. She smiled. Just like tasting memories, grandmother baking all morning, then selling every pie except the small one she'd made for Vera. Perhaps not all reminiscences were bad.

"I'm not concerned about my waistline. Let me finish it." Mick reached across the table.

She raised her fork like a dagger. "Hands off, pal."

Mick raised his palms in the air and laughed. "It was just an offer."

"Ya already had two pieces." She stared at the man seated opposite her. Which Mick was the real one? The stuffy cop or Mrs. Chambers' fun-loving houseguest? The smiles and hugs he'd been giving Lacey had caused her to gawk as though he had three eyeballs. And the way he had been looking at her and talking. Real sentences.

"I need my nourishment. Just in case I need to chase some stubborn girl all over the countryside."

Vera placed her palm to her cheek. She blushed? What was wrong with her? She never blushed. Never. It was a good time to look intently into her empty coffee cup.

Mick glanced at his pocket watch. "I need to go out and check on the car."

"Boy, you are batty over that breezer." Never seen the like. If this man was this protective over a car, watch out when he found a woman. Sad girl would never be let out of the house.

"Not mine. Hewitt's." He stood, his thigh knocking into the table, spilling some of his lemonade.

Lacey swiped a napkin from the drawer and offered it to him. Mick stiffened as if the old woman had just handed him a rattlesnake. His eyes took on a wild look, his jaw hardened. *What gives?*

"It's just a little spill." Lacey took a brisk step toward a dazed Mick, snapped the napkin from his limp fingers, and sopped up the few drops of lemonade. "That's an old tablecloth. See, no harm done."

Mick glared at the wall, Lacey tight-lipped a smile that made her flushed cheeks look like busted balloons, and Vera sat confused as to why a rosebud-embroidered napkin had created such a stir.

Mitzy rubbed against Mick's legs, and he blinked, a shaft of breath escaping as if he had just surfaced from being underwater.

Vera took another sip of her coffee, watching Sarge from above the rim of her mug.

With a natural finesse, he slid his hat on his head, the brim lingering inches above his haunted eyes. "Mrs. Chambers, did those parts ever come?"

"Yes, dearie. I placed the packages on the seat. Don't forget the barn key."

Mick nodded at Lacey. He walked past and set a hand on Vera's shoulder. "Why don't you help Mrs. Chambers with the dishes?"

Vera tightened her hold on her coffee cup. Was that a question or command? Just like that, she was back to being the seven-year-old in his eyes. That man. Did he think she had no good qualities? That she had no clue in life and needed to be told what to do? She shrugged his hand off. Without a word, she joined Lacey at the sink.

"It's all right, darlin', I can handle these." Lacey's small mouth pressed into a flat line as she observed Mick stalking out the door. "Poor guy."

The only thing poor about that man was his people skills. That napkin in Lacey's hand had more personality than Mick. And at present, seemed more useful.

"He takes a while to warm up to others." She spoke of him as though he was a Golden Retriever. "He doesn't mean to be that way."

"That's all I've ever known him to be." Vera snatched the washcloth from the counter. "How about I wash and you dry? I don't know where ya like things."

"You really don't have to."

"I'm sorry, Lacey." No way was Mick going to make her look like an uncivilized tramp. "I was goin' to help before he even said anythin'."

"Well, at least take this." Lacey withdrew a white apron from the drawer and handed it to Vera. "Mick's got a lot of fine qualities, but he's aloof when it comes to understanding the female heart."

She grimaced and plunged her hands in the sudsy water. The window above the sink allowed a clear view of the barn. The truck's black body and pine-board bed blended with the woodsy setting, like a picture on one of those fancy calendars. Mick had the sides of the hood popped and stared into the truck's guts. With his sleeves pushed past his elbows, he sunk his hands and forearms into the grimy web of parts.

"He's determined to get Hewitt's truck running." Lacey leaned forward and peered out, eyes squinting. "Good to have projects. Tinkering around and kicking tires helps clear the head." She gave Vera a playful nudge. "You know how men are."

Not that one. Too tricky to figure out and too much effort. She fixed her stare on the task ahead and worked quietly until all was finished. "That's all of 'em." She pulled the stopper in the sink's drain.

"Let's have some music." Lacey closed the cabinet and smiled.

"You got records?" *Please, please, please have a noise box.* It would restore some reason to her brain.

"Yeah, but I was thinking about something else. How about a baby grand?"

"Would it be awkward to tell you *I love you*?" Heart skipping to the beat of joy, she untied her apron and laid it on the back of the kitchen chair, following Lacey so closely she stepped on the tiny woman's heels. Twice.

"Now that's a beaut." Who needed a Victrola when you could jive authentically?

"You know how to play, honey?"

"You betcha." Vera gazed at the mahogany instrument, its glossy finish blurring her reflection. The piano bench welcomed her with the perfect amount of padding.

Pressing the keys and playing a tidbit of a melody ushered in the groove. She played one song, but it wasn't enough to satisfy the musical crave. No, she needed some vocals. The keys moved flawlessly under her fingers, and her voice presented the rest.

"Lovely, Vera." Lacey clapped her hands in front of her chest. "Just lovely."

"Nothing like the sound of the ivories."

"I never heard that song before." Lacey placed a fingertip on her chin. "Did you write that yourself?"

"Yeah."

"Impressive. Keep playing, sugar." Lacey snatched a roll of yarn and scissors from the basket beside her rocker and went to crocheting.

Vera scooted the bench closer so her feet could reach the pedals easier. Oh yeah, time to drench the afternoon with a musical downpour.

Mick jerked the handbrake with more force than necessary. He was the sergeant of investigations for the city of Pittsburgh. He'd gone nose to nose with the vilest mobsters, yet he'd recoiled at the sight of a flower.

A rosebud. Like hers.

Would the torment ever end? Hadn't he suffered enough? He yanked his handkerchief from his pocket and scrubbed the grime from his hands. But dirt had lodged into the cracks of his knuckles, the corners of his fingertips. Just like the memories of Phyllis—they settled into him, always before him, and no amount of cleansing could free him from his mistakes.

Why had money been more important to her than his heart? What had made her seek out the biggest bootlegger in town? Or had the scoundrel come to her first? Either way, the information Phyllis had siphoned from Mick and sold to the rumrunners had secured her comfort. Until it'd determined her death.

His chest tightened, and he pressed a clammy palm against it. He had to get his mind off her. Off that awful day.

With a weighted exhale, he rounded the truck, standing in front of the radiator. He forced his concentration on the project before him. He'd made a promise to Mrs. Chambers to get her late husband's truck moving. And this oath he intended to keep.

He'd replaced the carburetor and the corroded spark plugs. But was it enough? Only one way to know. With his right hand, he pushed the crank in and pulled the choke lever, priming the engine and getting the fuel into the cylinders. He returned to the truck's cabin, turned the key in the ignition, and adjusted the choke to the right of the steering wheel.

Sweat gathered under his collar as he hustled to the crank. Moment of truth. This time with his left hand, he pulled the crank lever counterclockwise.

Put. Sputter, sputter. Put.

Better than nothing. "Come on, honey. Come on." He dashed to the cabin and pushed the throttle up and put the left lever down.

Vroom.

Mick pumped his fist in the air. Got it!

Hiccupping every thirty seconds, the engine didn't sing pretty, but it worked. Taking it out for a test run was next, but he needed tires that weren't flat. "Hold on, girl. I'll get you tasting the open air soon." Tomorrow on his way to town, he'd stop by Jim's Auto. Old Jim could supply him with some used tires with a decent amount of tread left.

He cut the engine and leaned back on the sun-warmed seat. The frustrating hours of poking at an old engine and flushing a rusted radiator were over. But what if he couldn't budge it out of neutral? He groaned low.

Just like Vera.

The girl dawdled in neutral, not offering any information to move this case forward. After all this effort, could the investigation stall out? Getting her to talk was challenging, but he had to discover a way.

How long had he been out here? He glanced at the cottage.

Were the women getting along? Mrs. Chambers could make friends with anyone, but this was Vera—the woman who insulted him every other breath.

He should find Vera and head back to the cabin before they overstayed their welcome. Maybe it was too late.

He jogged toward the house but stopped short of the porch. Vera. She was singing. And playing Mrs. Chambers' baby grand. He smiled. No doubt, she was in her glory. How would he convince her to go back to the cabin now?

He propped a shoulder against the wood siding, letting her alto voice surround him, the smoky flair captivating his senses, just like when he'd first heard her at the club. The variances in the music were amazing—fluctuating between subtle tones and bold pitches but holding control throughout. Dynamic. Anyone could use their voice to sing, but it seemed Vera used her heart. Passion poured from every note, saturating him with renewed intrigue for the woman who'd slanted his world in four days' time.

CHAPTER 11

"Get away from me." Vera smacked a mosquito on her neck. Bad enough, they'd returned to the Daniel Boone house. Now, pesky insects caused her to squirm like she had as a taxi dancer on payday. "Is there any reason for this happy trek in the forest? Besides a mild form of torture?"

Mick lifted a branch so she could walk under it. "Because a walk before dinner is good for you, and it's too hot in the cabin."

"News flash. It ain't any cooler out here."

Even nature agreed. The birds were either silent or squawked a complaint into the humid air. The tall grass drooped. And the breeze decided to take the afternoon off.

"Why can't we stay at Lacey's?"

"Liked her that much, huh?"

"Sure, she was swell." A bead of sweat coursed the line of her spine, and Vera wrinkled her nose. "So tell me, why does Lacey's place get all the goods and your cabin has none? Don't you and the captain believe in running water and telephones?"

"It costs too much." He lifted a shoulder. "Lacey's husband helped spearhead the project of replenishing the forest. When the government acquired the acreage some years back, they needed a few decent people who knew the land and knew what it needed. Hewitt was one of those people. So the government paid for his house to be equipped with all the goods." He tossed Vera's turn of phrase back at her along with a lopsided smirk.

"So whaddya say? Let's camp out at Lacey's cottage instead of the rickety range you got." Not mentioning, her heart bruised every time she set foot in the door. Identical to the small cabin from her childhood. The only refuge she'd known, devastatingly torn away. So wrong for a young girl to lose her grandmother and her home in a span of one day.

"We can't. You're my responsibility."

"You mean your burden."

"Didn't say that."

No, but he sure thought it.

Mick kept his glare ahead, eyes squinting from the direct sunlight, his mouth tight.

She allowed her gaze to roam over the vibrant surroundings. Before now, she could only identify two shades of green, light and dark, but brilliant hues from emerald to jade and everything in between flavored this landscape. And jade happened to be the color of the eyes now watching her.

"Vera, how close are you to Angelo Vinelli?"

Her step faltered. She didn't have to dig much to understand the direction of this conversation. Might as well peer right into the bald-faced truth—everyone thought her a floozy. She fixed her back as straight as she could. "What do you mean by that?"

"Curious how much you know about him." But his tone was obvious as the sun beaming on her and, given a long enough stare, could make her sweat just as much.

"He was a bouncer. He lived down the road from the Kelly Club."

"Vinelli's disappeared." Mick's eyes widened as though he expected her to gasp or throw a hand over her heart.

"He'll turn up." Vera swatted at her upper arm. "Why won't these bugs leave me alone? You'd think I bathed in sugar water."

He neared, his gaze sweeping from her face to her latest bite. "I have some citronella oil at the cabin." He carefully touched her arm, studying her skin. "Maybe next time you should put some on."

A tingle shot up her arm, her heart stuttering at the surprising sensation.

Forget the toned muscle and the broad shoulders. Focus on the mean eyes. She glanced over, his chiseled jaw shrouded in late-day stubble, the sun highlighting the distinct angles of his face, his eyes not mean but intense. A rugged attractiveness. Was that all her mind thought about? Handsome men? Had she not learned her lesson with Carson? No more. And she really, really, didn't want to have any interest in Sergeant Mick Dinelo—any more than she wanted to eat a salad made with poison ivy.

"Vinelli's wife filed a missing person's report."

"He has a habit of vanishin' without telling anyone. Likes the strong juice too much."

"Did you know that Vinelli is a convicted felon?"

She froze. "What do you mean by *felon*?" Maybe Angelo wasn't the most ethical with his gambling problem and shifty eyes anytime a nice set of legs strolled by, but … a felon? Did Carson know?

"A year for assault and extortion."

Her insides wilted like a flower hit by a wintry gust. Angelo convicted of extortion. What about the night Artie had been shot? Could she have mistaken the voice? Her chest squeezed. And an assault charge? Ironic he paid time in the slammer for the very thing she'd depended on him to save her from.

"Are you sure it wasn't Vinelli's voice you heard?"

Was he reading her thoughts? "Wait." She tugged his elbow, stopping him. "Angelo was the one who found Artie, right? Wouldn't it be foolish for him to return?"

He glanced up as if drawing his answer from the crystal sky. "It could have been part of his plan."

The laugh rippled out before she could stop it. "Angelo's brawn is bigger than his brains." She tapped her forehead. "No way the man could invent that kind of plan."

Understanding filled her. Mick wanted this case closed as much as she did. The quicker it was resolved, the quicker he could resume life. Maybe even salvage his vacation. What had he forfeited to stay here with her? A trip to see a sweetheart? His family? A twinge of guilt poked her iron will.

"That night at the club, when you left with Carson Kelly, who was still there?"

"Angelo and Artie."

"Vera." Mick's gaze studied her face. "Please be honest. Can you be certain it *wasn't* Angelo's voice?"

She swallowed. "It wasn't Angelo's voice. It was Carson's."

"Just wanted to make sure." He stooped, picking up a rock, running his fingers over it. "And for what it's worth, I believe you." He tossed the stone and continued on.

What was his deal? One minute he drilled her with questions, and the next he admitted he believed her? She frowned. Every other step caused her slip to stick to her legs, and her stockings gathered at her ankles. "Can we go back?"

"Not yet." He kicked a branch out of the pathway. "I think we might be going about this all wrong."

"Wow. Brilliant discovery." Those flatfoots could know how to swing a baton down the street, but when it came to sleuthing they were a couple kernels short of a Cracker Jack box. "Any chance of ya roundin' up Hercule Poirot?"

"I thought books were for clammy intellectuals." That knowing glint in his eye anchored her to the ground.

Oops. Busted.

She wasn't accustomed to people—men in particular—paying attention to anything she said. Yet, the sergeant had listened *and* remembered. "The tenant before me left a few Agatha Christie novels. So what if I read them 'cause I was bored?" And then checked some out at the local library, but no way she'd confess that. "Found out I'm a sucker for a good mystery." As long as it stayed in the land of fiction.

"Me too. Maybe we can get the little gray cells to work for us." He tapped his temple with a smile that was as much amused as it was lopsided.

"Oui, monsieur." Her French accent was hideous, but it caused him to chuckle, deep and rich. Making her want to tuck the sound into the folds of her mind.

But just as her eyes soaked in his pleasing expression, the fix of his mouth turned serious. "Going to be open with you. A week back we'd received a tip from an unknown source."

"What do you mean?"

"It was a letter suggesting questionable activity at the Kelly Club."

She rolled her eyes. "Everything there is questionable. It's a speakeasy, for goodness' sake."

"Yeah, but you know, just as I do, that shutting down a gin joint is nearly impossible in Pittsburgh. Those crooks have their paws in everything." Something in his dark tone made her breath stall. "It's going to take something bigger than a Volstead Act violation to bring the big boys down."

"Something like murder?" Then it hit her. "So that's why you were at the club that night. You were investigating."

He dipped his chin.

"When you'd said you were *checking* it out, you meant for work." She shook her head, the details sinking in. "Smooth, Mick." She'd pinned him from first sighting as one who didn't fit in with the local rowdies, but the idea of him being a policeman sure hadn't been on her mind. "Did you find anything while on the scout?"

A ghost of a smile tipped his lips. "Just a young lady in need of my services."

She scoffed as her heels crunched over a pinecone. "The young lady could take care of herself."

"Really?" One brow rose, making him look even more annoyingly handsome. "If I hadn't been there, you would've taken a hard lick."

She frowned, unable to think of a clever response. The thought of him knowing she'd depended on him, even for a brief occurrence, muddled her reasoning. At the time, regarding him as her hero hadn't bothered her, but now being aware that he was a cop and undercover, well ... she couldn't decide what to think about that.

They continued on the narrow path, and Mick waited a long moment before saying, "We've been looking at Kelly's businesses when we should've been looking at his personal life."

"I was his personal life. Me and Thundering Gallop." Something squashed under her shoe. She lifted her foot and found the remains of a caterpillar. Gross.

"Thundering Gallop?"

"His bettin' horse. He bet a lot." She shuffled her feet across a patch of grass. Mick looked at her as if she was addled. "What? I'm trying to remove a bug's carcass from the sole of my shoe."

He nodded slowly, amusement lingering in the crinkles of his eyes.

"Is that all your news from Pittsburgh?"

"Mostly. I have a couple deputies checking in on Kelly's family members and past sweethearts."

She locked her hands behind her back and nudged him with her shoulder. "Speakin' of sweethearts, do you have a dame?"

He slowed and perused her. "That's a bit personal, isn't it?"

"Yeah, that's why I asked it." She threw in a saucy smile.

"Ah." He broke off a low-hanging branch and tossed it aside. "How about another time?"

No, no, no. He wasn't off the hook this easily. And he'd better not think walking faster would cause her to give up. "Ya know all my business."

He dismissed her extremely valid point with a grimace. "I have to know in order to protect you."

"Nice out. Pull the *protecting you* mumbo jumbo. Not quittin' here, sonny." She linked her arm in his, his warm muscle solid under her fingers. The spontaneity of her action surprised her, and apparently Mick.

He tensed, glancing at her hand resting on his bicep, and then to her.

She withdrew her hand. What had gotten into her? "C'mon, dish it, Sarge. How many dolls have broken your heart? Or vice-versa?"

A tinge of something unnamed darkened the jade of his eyes, making her even more curious about his past. Had he fallen in love with the daughter of a steel factory owner, and her wealthy family forbade the match? Had he been mixed up in a tumultuous love triangle, fighting for her affection, only to lose his sweetheart to another man?

"I never wanted to be tangled in a romance. Never found the time for such things."

Never found time? That was a lot of handsome wasted on nothing.

"Can we turn around now?" Her calf muscles screamed for mercy, and a cramp lingered in her side.

"Okay. I think we've gone far enough."

She swept the hair off her forehead. "Aye, aye, drill sergeant."

"On the hike back, you can tell me why you estranged yourself from your parents."

CHAPTER 12

Her feet wouldn't budge, as if they were suctioned to the dirt. "My parents? Why?" Anxiety's tentacles clutched her throat, reaching down and squeezing her heart. No. She wouldn't let Mick arouse the emotions she'd fought so hard to keep dormant.

"Yeah. Why have you estranged yourself from them?" His gaze penetrated her, stealing the breath from her chest.

She stared into the lofty pines hedging the beaten trail. The crooked branches hovered over them, spewing a web of shadows. "You're the detective. Go find out for yourself."

"You never mention them."

"Nice deduction, flatfoot." She poked his chest with her finger, and he took a step back, his eyes wary. "Ya don't know a thing. What if they're dead? A little insensitive, Sarge."

"They're alive. Your father lives in Redding, and your mother's in Chicago."

Her heartbeat climbed to an uncontrollable rate. "You've been checkin' up on me?" A searing ache stretched behind her eyes. Of course, he'd put his nose in her business. What did she expect? Loyalty from a man wearing a badge? Colors dulled around her. Each breath exploded out her mouth in rapidity.

His gaze fixated on her chest, his mouth moving as though he was counting. "Steady, Vera. One breath every five seconds." His arm curled around her back, and he placed a hand on her stomach.

It'd been years since she had a breathing attack this

overwhelming. She slid her eyes shut.

"Keep 'em open." His command strangely soothed her, and the pressure of his touch helped her regain control.

She peered through slit lids. Her legs threatened to crumple to the dirt, but Mick's strong grip held her upright.

"Let's get you back." His thumb stroked the small of her back, each press lessening the tenseness in her muscles. "Vera. It wasn't me that dug up the information."

Her balance stabilized, and the cloudiness lifted from her vision. She braved a glance at him.

His eyes glistened with a comforting blend of concern and confidence. "Captain Harpshire retrieved the information."

"What?" She stepped out of his reach, her knees wobbly, but her balance improved by the moment. "Tell him to stop." What if he dug up the Redding incident? Her heart pounded. No. They'd promised it wouldn't go on her record.

"He's concerned about you." Mick watched her closely. "Maybe you should rest. Let's sit down in that shaded spot." He reached to guide her elbow, but she barred her arms across her chest.

"If this is your little move to get me to talk, forget it."

He shrugged. "There's nothing wrong with talking to a friend."

His words shaved the edge off her resistance. She'd never had friends. Only lovers. Only people who'd taken and never gave back.

"What about your past?"

She squinted against the sun. No doubt the scorching heat contributed to her anxiety troubles, but despite the humid air and triggered pulse, her breathing evened. Somewhat. "I didn't give you enough credit."

"What do you mean?" His forehead wrinkled, almost convincing.

"Yesterday you attempted the tough cop approach to get your goods. You came up short. Now you're masquerading as Mr. Hero. I thought ya were being kind in helping me breathe without my lungs rupturin'." She let out a sardonic laugh. "I shoulda known better by now." Men use whatever means to get what they wanted. And all Mick wanted was to get her well enough to siphon more information from her. "Leave me alone."

He stared at her as though she'd just reeled off a slew of cuss words. "I've never seen someone so delusional. Can't you see I'm trying to help you?"

"Ha! You call this help?" Forget the dizziness, because adrenaline overcompensated. She forced her legs to move swifter, leaving her interrogator behind.

"Slow down, woman," he called out. "You need your strength back."

And now he'd called her a weakling? Frustration fumed in the flush of her skin. She could've been in New York by now. Maybe even had several jobs lined up. But no, she was here, hashing out her past with a man who didn't care one straw about her.

No more.

She'd return to the cabin only to gather her measly belongings and be on her way. Maybe Lacey would help her to the town Mick kept talking about. But how could she get to Lacey's?

Feet, keep moving.

She'd crawl to the old lady's joint if that meant escaping the sergeant.

Her balance seemed off again. Was there something in her shoe? Mick's profile swept into her peripheral. She winced. Couldn't the man catch a hint? "Go away." Her elbow brushed his side, and she restrained from pummeling it into his gut.

"Stop and take a rest. Please." His fingers grazed her wrist, but she pulled her arm into her side.

"I don't need—" The heel of her shoe went sideways under her foot, and there was no way of catching herself.

Mick stretched his hands toward her but grasped only air.

Vera's shriek pierced the sweltering sky. She curled on her side and clutched her foot.

He stooped next to her, taking in her anguished expression. "Are you all right? Where's it hurt?" *Dumb question, Ace*. The girl clasped her ankle with a grip he'd seen many times over during his years in college sports. Her heaving breaths concerned him. Would she relapse into another panic attack?

"Gave out on me." Her lips quivered and eyelids pinched tight. "Can't move it."

He dropped to his knees and set a gentle hand on her leg. "Let me have a look."

"No. It hurts." She smacked his knuckles, her fingernails nicking his skin. "Don't touch me. Ya done enough."

"Come on, Vera. I need to make sure it's not broken." He resisted the dread clogging his thoughts. *Dear Lord, don't let it be fractured.* If he had to take her to get examined, the cover of their perfect forest hideout would be blown.

Vera groaned.

Okay, he couldn't wait for her permission. He removed her shoe and tossed it aside. Cupping her heel in one hand, he used the other to assess the ankle.

"Gentle with the iron fingers." Vera clenched her teeth and sucked in air.

It was already puffy, with more swelling doubtless on the way. "Take off your stocking." Her head snapped up, her icy stare colder than a hundred winters. "Listen, I'm not trying to get a cheap thrill. It'll be ten times more painful to take it off later." Not to mention he wanted to check the coloring. Probably an ugly shade of purple.

She regarded him as if searching his face for sincerity. He tightened his jaw. What kind of man did she take him for? He wasn't desperate to see a lady's leg. He held out his hand, and surprisingly, she took it. He pulled her to a sitting position.

"Turn around, Sarge. I ain't selling tickets."

Mick stood and brushed dead grass from his pants. "Call me

when you're through." A maple tree stood a few feet away. He stepped behind it and leaned against the moss-covered bark.

When would that girl realize he had no interest? None at all. The notion of him being enamored with her made his gut twist. She was impossible. She was so stubborn she made pack mules look sweet and compliant. She was—

Snap.

She was unhooking her garter belt.

What was he thinking about? Ah, no interest in the girl and her long, toned legs. He shook his head. Maybe he should've sought refuge farther out.

She groaned. Must've reached the ankle. A few seconds of stillness followed.

"All right. It's off. You can come out of hidin'."

Mick flicked a loose piece of bark to the ground. "How's it look?" He was greeted with Vera's scowl and wadded up stocking resting in her palm. He knelt beside her. Now the swelling equaled the size of a softball. "Put your hands around my neck."

She shoved her nose heavenward. "Nope, gonna wait here until it feels better."

Okay, I'll come back for you in two days, was on the tip of his tongue. But he was already fatigued from fighting with her. He grabbed her shoe. "Here. Hold this." When she reached for it, he slid an arm under her and scooped her up.

"I ain't havin' you carry me." She kicked the healthy leg. Her heel struck his hip, and he struggled to remain straight-faced. If she didn't behave, she'd knock her swollen foot.

"Vera, you can't walk. It needs elevation." And she needed sedation. He took in her pain-filled expression. The throbbing must've intensified.

She was as stiff as the logs he'd been chopping every day and making his arms just as sore. "Relax. Just relax." He wouldn't reach fifty yards this way. "Quit straining your neck. Put your head on my chest."

She complied.

His heart squeezed as he set off toward the cabin. Her curvy frame sank deeper into his arms, and she settled her head over his heart. Oh, brother. That's what he asked for, wasn't it? But he didn't ask for the wafts of lavender to tingle his senses. Or her wayward wisps of hair to tickle his neck. "How are you feeling?"

"It hurts somethin' fierce."

"Probably will for a while." He managed to answer between breaths. "Better prop it up tonight. And probably tomorrow too." He glanced at her vulnerable green eyes and pouty lips. "Sorry, Vera." His mind raced ahead. He'd have to carry her up and down the steps for meals. No, he'd bring the food to her. But then, what about the outhouse? Couldn't bring that to her.

A bead of sweat trickled down his forehead and settled in the corner of his eye. He blinked hard. This wasn't working at all as he imagined. He pressed his lips together. The solution to this case couldn't come soon enough.

"So she went to Chicago," Vera mumbled as she stared out the bedroom window. "Oh, hush up, will ya?" The sparrows seemed to mock her pain. Chirping their morning song without a care while she stewed over the offbeat screwball formerly known as her mother. The woman who'd not only abandoned her but left her alone with the monster. The pool of self-pity lured her, but if she took the plunge, misery would drain into her soul, causing all the painful memories to float to the surface.

Knock. Knock.

She scrambled toward the bed, jumping onto the mattress and kicking her left leg onto the pillow. All set. Wait, wrong ankle. It was supposed to be her right. A little switcheroo, and now she sat perfectly.

"Come in." She threw a quiver in her tone.

"I brought you some breakfast." Mick balanced a tray on one

hand. "All I had was strawberry jam."

She straightened her back against the headboard and allowed Mick to set the wooden tray on her lap. Oh yeah, a girl could get used to this kind of treatment.

He studied her ankle. "How's it feeling?"

"In pain."

"Strange. It's not swollen anymore." With a scrunched brow, he bent lower to get a closer look. "Must've bruised the bone."

"Yeah, something." She contorted her face as she centered her foot on the pillow.

"Well, I'll be back. I'm going to drive over to Mrs. Chambers' to call the captain. Do you need anything before I go?"

Yesterday morning, she *had* needed assistance, but as the day had gone on, the pain had lessened to almost none at all. Even the bruising had turned a faint yellow. Could she help it if she was a quick healer? The decision to keep on the injured list had been made when she'd realized she wouldn't have to pump a million buckets of water. Million meaning five or six, but still her forearms felt like snapping in half every time she'd worked that rusty pump.

Vera even had her fix of attention as Mick doted on her, keeping her company by playing games of gin rummy and then explaining his favorite pastime—poker. He'd told her stories of how he connived his younger cousin to spy on other players' hands and that they'd use a code of tapping to communicate the cards. Mick taught her how he'd tap out *Ace*, and it wasn't unlike Morse code. Plus, he hadn't approached the subject of her horrid youth. Maybe he'd keep it that way.

But now, her little deception forced her to sacrifice a trip to Lacey's. Sour deal. "Go on. I'll be fine."

"I almost forgot." He handed her a napkin he'd stowed away in his pocket. "The jam is runny." His dimpled smile made her insides flutter. "I won't be long."

Then he was gone.

Vera filled her cheeks with air and exhaled. Hearing the car's engine lowered her mood. She spent long moments staring out the window, watching the willowy clouds stretch across the sky. Maybe she could write a new song about a radiant girl who was plagued with unending boredom.

But then, an idea formed. One she hadn't thought of—or rather had an opportunity for—until this pivotal moment. A twinge of guilt poked at her heart, but she pushed it away. If he could know her business, then why couldn't she know his? Only fair. She stuffed the piece of toast in her mouth and slapped her feet on the floor.

Destination? Mick's bedroom.

Only a pinch in her healing ankle argued with her quick steps, and she entered the square room that breathed of musk and order. "At ease, Sergeant."

The bed was made with the sheets tucked tightly under the mattress and a blanket folded at the bottom. Not one wrinkle. His shoes were lined up against the wall, and every other one had a rolled-up pair of clean socks slipped inside the sole. Wow.

She brushed her hand over the top of his dresser. Where was the clutter? No loose change or rumpled receipts. Nothing. Not even a candy wrapper.

But on the top of the nightstand lay a book. She picked up the black leather binding and ran her fingers across the gold metallic script—*Holy Bible*. When was the last time she had seen a Bible? An envelope protruded from inside the cover. Easing the flap from its tucked position, she peeked inside.

A newspaper clipping?

She slid the paper out and placed the envelope on the bed next to the Bible.

Woman, 22, Fatally Shot on Fifth Avenue

Vera stared at the bold black words, biting the insides of her cheeks.

Why would Mick keep only the headline? Who was this woman? She turned over the paper and was met with jumbled words from another story. No other markings. No other clues as to who this person was in relation to the sergeant.

She glanced at the Bible. Maybe he had more mementos stuffed inside the pages. Vera held the book in the light of the window and flipped through it. There weren't any more hints to Mick's awkward keepsake, but something else caught her eye—passages she'd heard her grandmother say. For some strange reason, poring over the familiar words made Vera feel close to her again.

"I'm back."

What? No!

She must've been reading longer than she'd thought. Pulse racing, Vera shut the Bible, dropped it on the nightstand, and bolted.

The creak of the steps gave her five seconds to hop into bed.

"How you feeling?" He filled the doorway, his presence numbing her senses. "Are you okay? Your face is red." The ten feet that separated them disappeared as Mick strode to her bedside. His large palm covered her forehead, his touch steady but gentle. Physical contact with the man made her stomach do strange things. "You running a fever?"

Oh, please, don't take my pulse. She'd be found out for sure. "Oh ... um." His enormous hand shielded most of her eyes, leaving only slits of vision. "I'm heated." She pointed to the window. "I closed the window last night, thinkin' it was going to rain."

"I'll open it." He dropped his hand and lifted the pane, then stuck the metal screen in. "I'll be outside if you need me." With his brows pinched, he stared at her beneath long, thick lashes, making her fidgety. "You sure you don't have a fever? Your face is very—"

"Yeah, yeah, I'm sure. Just got warm." *Because you were faster than a crazed race horse.*

"I'll check on you later." A scowl fixed on his face.

Was he mad at her? Did he know she was faking? He couldn't possibly suspect her of having been in his room. Had he learned something about the case at Lacey's? "Mick, what's wrong?"

"I don't want to talk about it." His fist tightened at his side.

"I'll bring you a sandwich when I come back in." He walked out, his footfalls thundering down the stairs.

What about the captain? The case? Carson? She threw the pillow on the floor. Ugh. She should've never devised this fakery scheme. She was pinned to her bed, being held captive by her own ploy.

Mick knew something. She needed answers.

CHAPTER 13

The weeds invading the firepit bore the brunt of his wrath. Mick stabbed the soil with the blunt shovel and twisted, loosening the cantankerous roots. His shirt clung to his damp skin, choking his movements. With Vera being isolated in her room, he yanked off the bothersome shirt and threw it.

Smack. He struck the earth again. The captain's words sifted through him. What had he gotten himself into? He tossed the dirt behind him.

A woman shrieked. He turned to find Vera, brushing soil off her blouse. He ground his teeth. "What are you doing out here?"

"A fine apology." She picked a clump of grime from the crevice of her collar, then lifted her gaze, stopping when it hit his bare chest. Her mouth opened, then snapped shut.

Speechless? Ah, the redheaded jabber jaw had no words. He pressed his fist against his lips, hiding a smile. A moment of silence. Was this what it felt like? He should go without a shirt more often. "What about your ankle?"

The evenness of her stance revealed her secret. What an actress! She'd played him for the fool that he was. But why deceive him? Why fake an injury? He tightened his grip on the shovel's weathered handle, the splintery wood jabbing at his calluses. Was she deceiving him on the case?

"You chatted with the captain, and I want to know about it."

"No." Definitely not now. His trust in her was as fragile as the pile of leftover ash from lasts night's fire. Any wind would carry it away.

"I wanna hear about the case."

A growl rumbled in his chest. "You're stubborn."

"Yeah. And I'm going to hound you until ya tell me." With arms crossed, she tapped her elbows, fast at first, then slowing. "What do ya say to a competition?" A spark shone in her eyes.

In a million days, he'd never be able to predict what would come out of her mouth. A half smirk adorned her face, baiting him. "What kind of competition?" A confusing mixture of curiosity and amusement surged through him. She couldn't know his boyhood reputation for never turning down a challenge, but the playful glint in her eyes lured him more than any double-dog dare ever thrown at him.

"Do you still have the canned bean container?"

"I think so." He palmed the back of his neck. Where was this leading?

"Targets." She stooped and picked up a rock from the dirt he'd just dug up. "Put the can on that fence post. First to knock it down, wins." A smile played on her lips, but it was the light dancing in her eyes that sparked every one of his nerves to life.

"Vera, I don't think you want to hear it—"

"Scared?" She arched a perfect brow.

He laughed. "Not at all." Lightness replaced the anger that had stirred in his chest. Yes, she'd tricked him with the ankle, but to be fair, he wasn't innocent in the courtroom of honesty either. Saying he'd never courted a woman? That would set the polygraph to dancing.

"Uh-huh." She lightly tossed the rock in her palm. "You're afraid to be beaten by a puny woman."

Puny wouldn't be his choice of words. Attractive. Leggy. And several more adjectives that his mother would box his ears for. "I'd hate to see a woman lose."

"Okay, Micky boy, choose your weapon." She pointed at a

small heap of stones on the ground. "So if I win, you tell me what happened with the captain. Deal?"

"What do I get when I win?" At his question, the smile slid from her face, and regret pulsed through him. She'd misinterpreted his meaning. He would never take advantage of her. Never. Wouldn't dream of using this sorry contest as a way to push his advances. But she didn't know that. "Listen. Let's forget about this. I'll tell you."

"Good." She lobbed the stone. "I was hopin' you'd say that. I flunked phys-ed."

Another pretense? "Looks like I'm the chump today."

"Don't take it too hard, Micky." She showcased an expression of mock sympathy.

Her intrigue baffled his senses. One minute she'd be crushed by life's pressure, and the next she tossed the world in her palm like that little stone. She lowered onto the log stump stool he'd set by the firepit and stared at him until he took a seat on the grass.

"It's about Kelly." What did she see in that man? Sure, he had money, but a guy like that didn't settle down. "Vera, I know it's tough. Finding out the man you love was—"

"Who said I loved him?" Her forehead creased with small waves like the ripples from the stream. "I never did."

Okay, now what? "I guess I misunderstood."

"I was keen on him, but nothing serious." She ran her fingers back and forth over the side of the stool, dried flakes of bark floating to the grass. "We never had the whole love thing. Besides, he never wrote me a song."

"A song?"

"Sure." The corners of her mouth hitched up. "I'll know it's love when I hear the perfect song. Words are better when set to music."

Heaven help him. This woman lived on another planet, one that spun on an axis of fantasy. She had no grasp of reality. Selecting your soul mate based on a song? He grabbed his shirt off the grass and pulled it over his head, the extra moment of silence necessary so he didn't say something rude. But really, was there any logic in this woman?

"Why are ya lookin' at me like that?" Two auburn eyebrows pinched to a V. "I'm no loony. You ain't a musician, so you can't relate."

So now her unreasonableness was his fault?

"I can sing about love being lost or survivin' a lover's jilt. 'Cause I feel songs like those. Feel it." Her hand fisted over her heart, rumpling her blouse. "So far, I haven't found one that moved me. They're all filled with the sappy unending-love stuff."

"You don't think it's possible?"

"I ain't sure." She stared at her crossed ankles, her left foot swinging to a silent rhythm. "If a gent comes along and shows me a love song I can feel, then I'll consider it."

Love wasn't based on feelings. Feelings came and went. Real love was a choice. Mick's gut churned. Look at him, contemplating the perfect relationship advice when he hadn't followed through with any of it himself. Would Phyllis have changed her ways if he'd exposed her betrayal to her face? He'd never know.

Vera leaned forward on the stool, setting both her bent elbows on her knees, cradling her chin in her palms. "Now about the captain. What's the story?"

He took a deep breath. "Vera, it's like this. Kelly's attorney—"

"His partner in crime."

"He's been digging up information about you."

"Me?" A shadow flickered across her face, and her hand pressed against her chest. "I'm not on trial."

"He's trying to do his best to discredit you." The soft wind pushed red wisps of hair onto her cheek, and Mick restrained from smoothing them away, folding his hands in his lap.

"How?"

"By making you look like a vengeful ex-girlfriend."

"W-what?" Her features froze, lips taut and eyes round. "I-I don't … I mean … what do I have to be vengeful of?"

"He claims that Kelly tried to end it with you, and you turned spiteful." Mick shifted. Vera's expressions went from hurt to anger and back to hurt again. If she didn't love him, then why the pinched mouth and darting gazes beneath a shroud of lashes? "That you conjured up this story so Kelly would go to prison."

"I didn't. That *was* what happened." She pushed a finger to her lip and breathed hard. "A little excessive, don't ya think? If he did end it with me, as he said, then why would I … I mean, blamin' someone for murder because of gettin' the brush? That doesn't even make sense."

Mick placed his hand on her arm. She stiffened at his touch. At least she didn't swat him away. "This is about the gift shop. Did you rob it?"

"What?" She pulled her arm into her chest, wrapping her other hand around it.

"The captain told me about Redding." Her eyes widened at the last word, but he continued. "You got caught stealing. Maybe we should talk about that before anything else."

Her cheeks reddened further with each of her stifled breaths. "I …. that is …. no one was supposed to know about that."

"What do you mean?"

"She didn't press charges. They said it wouldn't go on my record. Those chumps, how'd they find out? How did …" Her tone fizzled out like yesterday's fire.

"Don't know. His men are good at what they do."

"It's not fair." Her lower lip pouted, stirring something in his core he wished would remain solidified.

"They don't play fair." He shoved propriety aside and pushed the curl behind her ear. It was soft, like touching strings of silk. "Their job is to make Carson Kelly look like a model citizen and Vera Pembroke like a thieving gold-digger." He couldn't sugarcoat it. She'd find out sooner or later. But a punch in the gut would have been more comfortable than viewing the hurt in her eyes.

Without a word, she crept off the stool and walked away.

He went after her. "Let's talk. We can figure this out together."

"Listen, buddy." She faced him and shoved a finger so close to his face, he could kiss it. "I have to visit the outdoor powder room. Is that okay with you, or do I need approval first?"

And that was how she managed hurt, huh? By consuming it in anger. Fine. Mick raised his hands and took a step back. For now.

The motor sound was as faint as a fly's buzzing, but it launched Mick to his feet from the couch. He dashed to the window, heart racing with each step.

The late afternoon sun bounced off a black Chrysler invading their territory, driving down the private lane.

"Vera, keep inside!" He yelled up the stairs and bounded out the back door. He withdrew his gun, the overpowering sun slicing his vision in half. He crept along the side of the house, making sure he left not even a shadow.

The motor's hum grew louder, and Mick pulled in a breath. Who was driving? Carson? One of his henchmen? He crouched low, the sound grinding in his ear like a jackhammer. He couldn't fail this. She needed him. Whether she'd admit it or not. Her life hinged upon his ability to protect her. Every muscle tensed.

Would Vera obey him? Keep indoors?

A sickening sensation soured his gut. If she strode out the front door, she could be shot on the spot.

Silence deafened the air.

A car door slammed shut. Mick flattened to his stomach and crawled to the narrow area behind the holly bush. With his pulse pounding in his ears, he inched to the right, gun extended, eyes narrowed.

"Hello? Anybody home?" a feeble voice called.

What on earth? It sounded like an old man, but Mick wasn't a rookie cop. Never drop your guard. Never jump to conclusions until guesses were proven facts.

He stretched his neck to get a quick glimpse. His eyes slid closed as he lowered his gun. A guy older than the captain, supporting himself with a cane, hobbled closer to the house.

Mick put away the weapon and stood, keeping a hand on the holster just in case. "Can I help you?"

The man almost fell backward. Probably not expecting a full-grown man to pop up from behind a bush.

A slow smile spread on the gentleman's face. "I'm Pastor Peterson. I was wondering if this is Frances Chambers' residence."

Ah, Mrs. Chambers' pastor. She'd told him the board had voted on a replacement. The last minister had left for a bigger town with a higher salary.

Despite his grass-stained, dirt-ridden trousers, Mick walked over. "Nice to meet you." He stuck out his hand.

The older man had a surprisingly strong grip.

"You passed it." Mick pointed the direction from which the man had come. "Just turn around and keep your eyes peeled for a lane on your right. It will practically bring you to her doorstep."

The pastor nodded. "Thank you, young man." He gave a weathered smile and returned to his car.

Mick rolled his shoulders.

Vera was safe.

His heart rate had returned to normal by the time he entered the house. He expected to be ambushed by an inquisitive Vera, but all was quiet. Too quiet. He rushed up the stairs and down the hall to her room. With the door ajar only two inches, he could see in.

Hands pillowed under her head, Vera had closed her eyes in a peaceful slumber, completely oblivious to the situation that had just rattled his composure. He shouldn't stare. Shouldn't be captivated by the strands of hair that had fallen across her porcelain cheek. Or the soft pink of her lips, colored the same as cotton candy. Would they taste just as sweet?

He scolded himself for the thought. Besides, when she awoke, she'd more than likely still be fuming.

She'd worn pride as thickly as her makeup, covering her flaws, concealing her shortcomings. Didn't she know to be flawed was to be beautiful? That no matter how layered, how far beneath the surface was scarred, mercy ran deeper. To be healed by His wounds and to be freed by His surrender, now that was a beauty no cosmetic could duplicate.

He winced at his own revelation. If her flaws were covered by grace, weren't his? The prickly fingers of guilt squeezed his heart. His situation was different. More severe. Her spiritual hands may be a bit soiled, but his were smeared with blood.

CHAPTER 14

"Kotex."

Mick fumbled the scrub brush in his hand. "What?"

Surely, he'd heard of them, because, my goodness, she needed them. The cramps that woke Vera this morning hadn't subsided. Now that it was early afternoon, she needed to act fast before the store closed. "Kotex. Ya know, feminine napkins."

The straight line of his shoulders stiffened. "What about them?"

Did she need to spell it out? Yes, she was interrupting his private time with his prized car, but the man could scrub his whitewall tires later. "I need some. I had a couple, but I'm all out now." Fabulous thing that the sanitary belt got packed into the bag, or she'd be needing one of them too. "And would ya hurry up with it? This kind of thing doesn't wait for a dame's approval." She talked to his broad back.

"No, I can't."

"Too busy?" Nothing like a little sarcasm before lunch. She shifted her weight from heel to heel. Wasn't he going to look at her?

Maybe he was angry with her. Sweet victory was in sight. She was getting closer to the target. His Christian faith was like a dartboard. If she'd keep launching, she'd hit a bulls-eye. "You know those tires are whitewalls?"

"I know." He scrubbed harder.

"That's a dirt road we've been cruisin' on, genius. The tires are gonna soil the moment the treads hit it."

"I know that too." Testy, testy. And still not looking. With both his knees planted in the low grass, he cleaned away as though she didn't exist. He might consider looking if she picked up that bucket and gave him a bubble bath.

"Why clean it, then?"

"Because."

"You tryin' to stay away from me? You said two words at breakfast." *Morning, Vera*. "You practically drank your toast. Then out the door to do yardwork for hours. And now you're scrubbing your precious tires that'll get dirty again when the wind blows." She shoved her nose in the air and popped her hip to the right. "That's all right, Micky boy, stay away, 'cause I am havin' the time of my life sitting on that musty couch. So far, four birds passed the window, and I killed an ant. Mm-hmm. Things that make the locals jealous."

"Anything else?"

She never knew a man's voice could cause her blood to boil. "Yeah. The Kotex."

He shook his head so slightly. Was that a no?

She swatted a bug away from her face. "Okay, haul me to the store and I'll get 'em."

Not only did she have to deal with cramps that made her feel as though her insides were juggling hacksaws, now Mick can't-leave-my-Lincoln Dinelo wouldn't get her what she needed.

He turned slightly. His jawline set harder than the steel of his breezer. "Can't take you either."

"Listen, Mick, either have it out with me about whatever it is you're stewin' over or get along with ya before the store closes." She took a few steps to the left to view more of his face. His fixed scowl tempted her to take the scrub brush and scour it off. "If you're embarrassed, sonny, these setups have a discreet box. It's right there on the counter. Just slip the nickel in, grab the napkins, and cruise on out. That's it." She snapped her fingers. "Set up for cowards like you."

Mick catapulted to his feet and chucked the scrub brush into the bucket, suds erupting over the sides. With palms spread on the Lincoln, he leaned on his car, keeping his back to her.

"Doesn't that hurt?" No way his skin wasn't blistering something fierce. The June sun and the metal car frame couldn't make a happy resting place for human flesh.

"It feels good."

"Yeah, sure it does."

"Give me … just a minute, please." His *please* sounded forced.

"Did I finally get a rise out of ya, Mick?" Took long enough. She huffed loudly. How long was he going to stand there, motionless?

"Too risky."

She deflated like the tires on Hewitt's rusted truck. He was supposed to holler, flail, and make a scene. She had her Christian hypocrite speech all primed to deliver. But no. Instead, Mick's two words were uttered in complete calmness and in more of a soothing tone than he'd had all day. And yesterday, to think of it.

She sighed. "What's so risky? It's just a drugstore."

"I can't make that purchase." Mick turned to face her. Finally. Soapy water or sweat discolored his shirt. But the sun brightened the pigments of his eyes. "That store has two clerks, and they both know me. They know I'm not married." He held up a ring-less hand.

Just what was she going to do? Sit in the creek for four days? "Mick, I need—"

"I can't allow any questions to be raised. It's dangerous." He palmed the back of his neck as if talking to her was a fatiguing activity. "And as for you going, that's not an option whatsoever. You have to remain hidden, and I don't feel comfortable leaving you. In fact, from now on, every time I go to Mrs. Chambers, you're going with me. You can't—"

"Can't this! Can't that! Can't this! Can't that! Your record's broken, Sarge!"

"Calm down. Don't yell."

"I can pitch the pipes if I well please to!" She stormed up the porch steps and into the house, the percussion of her heels against the wooden floor echoing off the wall.

Her bags would be packed in less than an hour.

Mick squinted and held up the sliver of paper against the blinding afternoon sun pouring through his car's windshield. "Are you sure you got this right?" A multitude of scenarios invaded his thoughts. None of them good.

"Now, Mick, don't let these wrinkles fool you, I have plenty of good years left in these two ears of mine." Mrs. Chambers rolled the window down, allowing in the faint scent of her treasured petunias, and hung her arm over the side of the car.

"Vera's mad already." He shook his head to clear the image of Vera thrashing her arms through the air like a bi-plane propeller. Maybe he should seek a bomb shelter now because when she read the news sitting in the hollow of his hand, she was sure to explode.

Mrs. Chambers gave a sympathetic smile. "You still haven't told me what the favor is that I am performing for you."

The car roared to life. "Vera's going through …" Amazing, how he could challenge the gang lords but couldn't spit out the word *menstruation*. He reversed the car onto the road. "It's personal. It's a …" He cleared his throat. "A womanly issue." The captain never warned him to expect this when he was appointed as her guardian. Menstrual cycles went beyond any training he'd received. "I thought if I gave you the cash, that you'd—"

"Buy the feminine napkins for you?"

Heat crept up his neck. "Yes."

"Sure, dearie."

Relief surged through him. Mrs. Chambers had the excuse of having female visitors ever so often, including her daughter and two granddaughters. He pulled the wheel to the right, avoiding a divot the size of a hubcap. "Thanks, Mrs. Chambers."

"You could put a little smile on, sugar. It makes your face look better."

"It's complicated." He let off the gas and glanced over. "Vera's been snooping in my room."

"What?" Her expression clouded. "That's a bold accusation. You sure?"

No doubt. He'd known as soon as he'd stepped into his quarters yesterday that Vera had snuck inside. "Personal items I keep in my Bible were scattered on my bed." The envelope. The newspaper heading. He squeezed the steering wheel. Vera had discovered memories he regarded as classified. And painful. He only kept the envelope for those moments he required a reminder of his own folly.

"Hmm. Suppose you could've done it?" Her gaze flitted his way as the wind poured into the car. "You might have left it on the bed. You have been under abnormal stress."

"No. I didn't. The point is, she's snooping." Mick's pet peeve—someone trespassing in his personal space. In the Army, there'd been discipline enforced for that kind of behavior. "She's harder to control than Hewitt's truck with a bent chassis."

"Is it your job to control her?" The words might have posed a question, but she was driving home a point. With a sledgehammer. "Vera's not sheet metal and bolts like that Ford, she's flesh and blood."

Blood. Vera was out for *his* blood. Mrs. Chambers didn't understand. If she did, she would take sides with him. "The girl is difficult. I think she takes joy in it … you know, being difficult. If I say *yes*, she says *no*. When I say *left*, she says *right*. The other day, when I asked her … What? Why are you laughing?"

Her hearty chortles weren't comforting. "Mick, I've never known you to get so worked up."

"I've had a bad day." And it wasn't over. He needed this break from Vera, but he didn't want to be gone long. Her alone at the cabin, though well-hidden, didn't sit well with him.

"Where's your sense of adventure? You've withstood all the lawlessness the prohibition has brought about but can't endure a headstrong female? I know you don't want to hear it, sugar, but this granny is going to speak, anyway. You need to trust God."

"She's too emotional. She needs more discipline."

"There. Right there is your problem." Her light tone turned serious. "You treat her like a child."

"I do not. And please don't look at me like that." If her jaw dropped any farther, it would be in her lap.

"What about the other day, darlin', when you told her to help me with the dishes?"

"Nothing wrong in that. Listen, I'm not above helping. I would've, but I'm so close to getting that truck running."

"And that's more important?"

"That's not what I meant." Mick thudded the steering wheel with his thumbs. "She needs direction."

"No, she doesn't need to be told what to do. She resented it." Mrs. Chambers smoothed out the skirt of her floral dress. "She apologized to me. Said she would've helped without being told. You, young man, embarrassed her."

"Vera apologized to you?"

"Surely did. Looks as though you need to gain her trust."

Maybe Vera had taken a liking to Mrs. Chambers, but this account … this wasn't the redhead he knew. How come? *Because I'm an idiot. That's why.* "What can I do?"

"She needs to trust you. The work is gaining her trust, darlin'. That will establish a relationship."

Mick gazed steadily on the road. "Vera's doesn't trust. If she even suspects she's being pushed, she—"

"Not pushed. We never push … we draw. Rules without relationship always lead to rebellion."

Rebellion. The word summed up the situation. Mick commanded an outfit on his terms—shipshape, while Vera declared mutiny.

"This might go smooth, but then"—he shook his head—"I can't predict how she's going to respond." Women. "This is going to be complicated." More than he'd thought at the beginning.

"Usually, anything worth anything is."

Frances Chambers, the cotton-haired Aristotle. "Thank you, Mrs. Chambers."

"That young lady hasn't handed over all her trust to me yet, but I think I've made some progress. Treat her kind. She acts tough, but her heart is as tender as one of those apples I used in that crisp you devoured. She's just as sensitive and easily bruised."

Mick breathed out slowly, releasing the tension in his shoulders. "I needed to hear that." He braked at the stop sign. Kerrville's one and only. The drugstore was situated at the end of Main Street. With only seven shops total, Mick could never tire of its charming view. Quiet. Uneventful. So different from the streets of Pittsburgh.

"Did you consider, Mick, that she had your Bible? If she took some things out of it, then it's possible her eyes were reading it. Looks like the good Lord is doin' a mighty fine job of drawing her already."

Mick could beat his head on the dash. "Why didn't I think of that?"

"Cause your head's been shouting, and your heart's been whispering. It takes some persistence to hush the thoughts, but when you do, the right power can direct. The heart never makes a mistake. God's in there, sugar."

Maybe Vera *had* read it. If God was working on her heart, then he wouldn't interfere. But getting her to trust him? How could he ever find a way?

"Something pleasant could develop here."

Here it comes.

"She could be just what you need."

And like that, the conversation took a nosedive. "Mrs. Chambers." Always someone. Always marriage. It never failed.

She heeded his warning with a chipper smile. "You aren't

getting younger. You need a good woman behind you."

"I swore off matrimony for—"

"Yadda-yadda." She opened her hand and closed it, making it look like a mouth yapping away. "You say that every time."

And he'd continue to do so.

"Mick, being a policeman doesn't mean you can't have a family."

"I've never said that's the reason."

"No, but it is. You think your job is too dangerous and don't want to leave behind a wife and children. I watched my brother struggle with it when he became a policeman. God can take care of you. Never let fear call the shots, Mick."

He forced his mouth tight, controlling frustration with several hard breaths. How did they get on this subject, anyway? If she knew why—the real reason behind no relationships—then maybe she'd leave him be. He'd made an oath on the snow-ridden ground on Fifth Avenue. An oath sealed in death.

CHAPTER 15

"Vera?"

Mick's deep voice drifted beyond the closed door into her bedroom. She sighed. What should she do? She wasn't in the mood for talking, but if she didn't respond, he'd bust open the door. Better to keep the message simple enough for a man to understand. "Go away."

"Vera?"

Okay, maybe it wasn't simple enough. Something slid under the door. A slim, baby-blue box now rested on the coarse hardwood floor. Followed by another box and another.

"I didn't know how many of those you needed. Can I come in?"

Let him in? Don't let him in? If another argument rose, then that was it. She'd be on her way. Her bags were packed, but something in her couldn't leave just yet. "You know there's no lock. What's keeping ya?"

"You."

The look on his face when she opened the door would be the deciding factor. Her head hoped she'd be met with angry eyes, but her heart … well … who thought with their heart, anyway? She twisted the circle knob and pulled. *Here goes.*

"Thank you, Ver."

She expected enraged Doberman-like eyes, not sad Bassett Hound. Regret and humility looked good on Sergeant Mean Eye.

"I believe you, Vera. I want you to know that. And …" He dug in his pocket. The corners of his mouth turned up as he jangled his keys. "I lowered the top."

"The breezer's freed up?"

"Yeah." His dimpled smile made her breath hitch. "Want to take this square for a ride?"

"You better believe it, buster." She snatched the keys. "And as for the square part, admission is the first step to recovery." She patted his shoulder.

His laughter filled the room. The glimmer in his eyes was everything swoon-worthy. *Take it easy, heart.* Romance for her was about as possible as landing on the moon. Besides, she didn't want his adoration, right?

"Mrs. Chambers gave us a mission. She's out of teaberry."

"I have no idea what that means, but as long as I get to drive the breezer, then I'm golden." She gave a saucy wink. "Let's get a move on." Oh, but first . . . "Just give me a few minutes to get things taken care of."

Mick handed her one of the Kotex boxes, pinching it by its corner, touching as little of it as possible.

"Don't worry. It's not catching."

"Now this here—"

"Is the choke. Mrs. Grable taught me all this." Vera huffed for the umpteenth time. "You know it's going to be dark before we get this mechanized baby rollin'." They'd gotten a late start, but Vera had to admit it was worth it, considering Lacey had sent a basket of her delicious fried chicken home with Mick for supper. But now, the early evening sky teased her.

"We have some daylight left." Mick adjusted the mirror and then glanced at her. "How's that? I think that suits your height."

"Dandy. Can we go?"

"Yes, but first tell me who taught you how to drive." He inched to his side of the bench.

"Mrs. Grable, my landlady." Pinching her lips, she went through all the motions, checking them off in her head. The pad of her shoe pressed down the starter pedal. Ah, the motor's smooth purr. "We had an agreement. I would help her run errands, and she'd let me use the car if I needed it. Like to get groceries and such. Carson wasn't keen on the idea."

Mick raised a brow. "Why not?"

"He wanted me completely dependent upon him. He'd been like that ever since he claimed me as his girl."

"Claimed you?" The sun shone on his face just right, casting a bronze light on his skin and drawing out hidden layers of green in his eyes. "If he respected you, valued you, then he would've asked you to be his girl. Not demanded it."

Her gaze slid to her lap. Mick confirmed what she'd always felt. It had been unfair for Carson to stake her as though she was a piece of property and not a human being. Carson had bullied her, and she'd let him because she'd needed the job. The ache in her heart was a cruel reminder of her stupidity. "Can we go?"

"Yeah."

The trip started with her clutching the steering wheel and leaning so close to the dashboard she could press her nose on it. But a few minutes on the dirt road cured her rigidness.

She relaxed her grip and straightened. "So do you miss not being at work? I'm sure loads of rumrunners are running roughshod over your officers."

A muscle pulsed in his jaw. "It's getting to be a lost cause."

She couldn't help but agree. Speakeasy owners shelled out more dough to policemen than the city government's payroll. It was either money or a free pass to unlimited liquor that enticed the boys in blue. Sometimes both. "Do you think the prohibition was a good idea?"

"I get paid to enforce the law, not challenge it."

Something lingered under the surface of his clipped words. Was he not in favor of the amendment? Did he secretly enjoy drinking, and now his integrity wouldn't allow him to sip the juice? Had that left a sour taste in his mouth, or was there another reason?

Curiosity took hold of her mind with the tenacity of a badger. "If the big men never had signed the Volstead, would you be in the Kelly Club on Saturday nights?"

"No."

"Somewhere else, then. Maybe the Star, sipping champagne?" Of course, he wouldn't want to loiter around a factory-laden avenue where the soot hung thicker than the stench of vomit from the clumps of drunks.

"No champagne. No Pittsburgh Scotch. Even if the sorry law was repealed, I wouldn't drink."

Another thing in common? "Ya wouldn't?"

"No. My job gives me upfront views of an alcoholic's lifestyle. Hauling 'em in and locking 'em up until they're sober. It's not my ideal pastime."

Boy, had she had an upfront view too. "I don't like alcohol either." She glanced at him in time to catch his brow raise. "I've seen too much of it in my family. I can't stand the stuff."

"But you worked in a gin joint?"

"What can I say? I'm a walking irony." Or plain pathetic. A man like him wouldn't understand her father's plight. How alcohol had turned him into a monster, causing Vera to flee to Pittsburgh—broken and hungry, forcing her to succumb to Artie's manipulation. Then Carson's.

"You can pull over coming up." He pointed to a shaded area on the left. "The teaberry patch isn't far from here."

"You got it." She eased off the gas and steered onto the open space. There. Nice and smooth. "How's that?"

"You drove well. Mrs. Grable was a good teacher."

"Nah." She gave a cheeky grin. "I was a good student." She put the gear in neutral and pulled the brake.

Mick twisted in his seat to face her, and Vera caught sight of the gun ever strapped to his hip. "If you ever want to talk about your past, you can confide in Mrs. Chambers. Her grandfather was an alcoholic."

"Sure." Like the day after never.

Mick smiled as if he'd heard her thoughts. "Might help you to talk."

Sorry, but Vera Pembroke didn't talk. She ran. Although she hadn't figured how to outrun memories. Wasn't time supposed to be a healer? Somebody lied on that one. "Don't feel sorry for me. I turned out okay." Okay? *You have nothing to show for the past ten years.* Sure, her voice got her the canary job, but what had that landed her? An all-expense-paid vacation to the sticks with a cop for an escort.

"Just trying to help."

"I got all the help I need. See this?" She unclasped her bracelet and suspended it in the air like a pendulum, the diamond's prisms sparkling in the sun. "I have plans for this baby. Straight to the pawnshop. This sucker is my ticket to anywhere I want to go." *New York, here I come.*

"Pretty. Where'd you get it?"

"From the big lug. Ya know, the one getting away with murder."

"Kelly?"

"You know of another person getting away with murder? Of course it was from him."

His eyes narrowed on the bracelet. "Can I see it?"

She held it out for him, and his warm hand carefully picked it from her palm.

Mick examined the piece of jewelry and returned it. "Is that necklace from him too?" His gaze went to her neck, and so did Vera's hand.

"No." She lowered her lashes and focused on the buttons of her day dress. "It's my grandma's. She gave it to me."

"Is she still living?"

Oh, if she was. Life would have been so different. "No, she

passed when I was fourteen. She was a Christian." Why she felt the need to tell Mick that, she hadn't a clue. "It's a shocker looking at the way I turned out, huh?"

"I wish I could have met her."

Her defenses scattered like sheet music in a breeze, confusing her as to which emotional tune she should pick. Angry? Surprised? Sappy? No, not sappy. He probably wasn't sincere, anyway.

"You should get a pendant to hang on it."

"I did have somethin', but it's … lost." She forced a smile. "At least, I think it's gone. I won't know for sure until I see my apartment again." If she even got the opportunity. Probably wouldn't. "But, hey, that's how the song sings sometimes."

His eyes filled with tenderness. "I would like to show that bracelet to the captain."

She sat straight, her back catching resistance from the warm leather seat. "We're goin' back to Pittsburgh? When?"

"Me. Not you."

Those short responses. She wanted to grab his shoulders and shake him. "What's that supposed to mean?"

He reached in his pocket and gave her a folded paper.

"Urgent." Vera read aloud. "Mandatory meeting Wednesday with the D.A. 11:30." She read it again. Each word pushed her heart farther into her gut. Wednesday. Three days from now. "What's this about?"

"Not certain. The captain called Mrs. Chambers this morning with that message."

Vera scowled as she handed it back to him. "So where am I getting shuffled off to? Is it the deputy's turn or the sheriff's?" She suppressed a groan. What was it that bothered her, being thrown into the power of another policeman, or Mick leaving without her?

The sun bounced off his windblown hair, highlighting golden tones. "I had hoped you wouldn't mind staying with Mrs. Chambers."

"Um … no. Not a bit. We jive well together."

"Good. I'm taking you Tuesday night, and—"

"I thought the meeting was Wednesday?"

"It is. But I got to be there at nine. Leaving here by five. So you—"

"Ya said enough." No way she was rising before good ol' mister sun. "More time at Lacey's means baby grand unlimited." Beautiful. And to lounge at a place that didn't reek like mothballs and smelly boots was a priceless perk.

"It's settled, then." Mick gave a satisfied nod. "Ready to get Mrs. Chambers some teaberry? It's just a little walk up that hill."

"*Little*?" She eyed him suspiciously. "Will you shake on it?"

He grinned, not his put-up-with-Vera smirk, but a genuine, dimple-dashing smile. What had happened between earlier and now? My-oh-my, the marked difference in this man did funny things to her insides. She would've sent him out for Kotex sooner if she'd known she'd get these results.

Mick played along and stuck out his hand to which Vera happily shook.

Her thumb grazed his index finger, and her jaw dropped. "You've been holdin' out on me, Micky."

CHAPTER 16

Mick shifted on the car bench as Vera practically yanked his hand onto her lap. Palm upward, his knuckles rested on her thigh, and man alive, he should be slapped silly for the thoughts pummeling his head.

Her thumb grazed his rough fingertips. "You're a strummer."

"How'd you come up with that?"

"See? Right there? Those are calluses." She stared at his hand, still within hers. "The way they're placed on the ends of your fingers is a dead giveaway. Why didn't you say you played the guitar?"

He offered a nonchalant shrug, gently withdrawing his hand from her grasp. "You never asked."

"Where'd ya hide it?" She folded her arms. "I glommed every inch of that cabin, and it couldn't be in your room because ..." She blanched. "I mean ... I've never seen it lyin' around." She clamped her mouth, and her eyes widened as if she was bracing herself for a good scolding.

His lips twitched, fighting a smile.

She became more fidgety than the pesky crickets that camped outside his bedroom window, and it wasn't until his smile spread into a full-blown grin that understanding registered in her emerald eyes.

"You know I went in your room." Her cheeks reddened. "Don't you?"

"I was wondering if you'd own up to it."

"You ain't angry?"

"No." He winked.

"I thought if you found out, I'd be peeling potatoes or scrubbing the outhouse as penance." Her shaky laughter made his ribs pinch.

This wasn't the picture he wanted her to have of him—a disciplined idiot who offered no mercy. How stupid for him to think letting her drive his car would be enough to gain her trust. He needed to give more, work harder, to change that image. "Look what's tucked on the floor behind you."

She shifted onto her knees and peered into the backseat. Her squeal could've rattled the branches above them. "Your guitar. And it's a Gibson!" Her gaze swept the hard, black case with its gold-toned hinges, then she faced him. "It's been behind me the entire time?"

"Yes ma'am."

She gave an incredulous shake of her head. "I need to be more aware of my surroundings."

He smiled. "How about you try it out?"

"Okay, now ya got me concerned." She leaned toward him and pressed a palm to his forehead. "You feeling okay?"

"Never been better."

Her hand dropped from his face, and her pink-tinged lips spread into a heart-pounding grin. "Then, in that case, I'd love to play your fancy guitar." She scurried out of the car and eyed the lush vicinity. "There's a decent-sized rock over there with plenty of room for us both."

He didn't even fight the laughter rumbling in his chest. What she'd considered *decent-sized* was hardly enough space unless she sat on his lap. The image caused heat to climb his neck. Maybe this wasn't the best idea. But the eagerness in her step and the lightness in her voice made him want to give her anything she desired.

"Sounds good." He stepped out, the tall grass skimming his trousers, and he unlatched and opened the case. With careful handling, he withdrew the Gibson, the guitar's red spruce body absorbing the fading daylight.

Vera, already settled on the moss-carpeted rock, patted the area beside her.

He smiled. "I'm good right here." When he handed her the instrument, she gave a low whistle.

She spent the following half hour playing several songs comprised of basic chords. Mick introduced her to some complex fingerings to give her a broader scope when creating new music. He positioned her hands on the rosewood fretboard, and the look of triumph in her eyes when she mastered the chord was enough to undo him.

He slid a thick finger under his collar. "Are you ready to head back to the cabin?"

Her strumming paused. "Don't we need to get Lacey those berries?"

Ah, yes. The teaberry. "We should probably fetch some before the sun goes down." Mick never trekked through the forest after twilight. Those nocturnal hours were reserved for black bears and other creatures.

With a wistful sigh, Vera handed back the guitar. "Thank you, Mick." The marked appreciation in her expression peeled away her coarse edges, baring a layer of Vera Pembroke he'd never seen.

Perhaps he could yet gain her trust, as long as he didn't lose his sanity in the process.

Vera cupped her knees and bent over, catching her breath. "So when you said a *little* walk, I didn't know you meant all uphill."

Mick stopped mid-stride. "It's just up yonder."

Maybe she should have him shake on that one as well. They continued on the narrow foot path supposedly taking them to this famous teaberry patch.

"How much of this stuff does Lacey need?" Shouldn't they have brought baskets or something? Vera had never laid eyes on a teaberry. Was it as big as a strawberry? Would her fingers get stained by the juice?

"We'll fill up the pouch I brought." He patted his pocket.

Her brows rose. They must be smaller than blueberries to fit in a little bag. Her foot skidded on loose dirt, and Mick caught her hand, keeping her from tumbling down the hill in a tangle of limbs and humiliation. She gave a grateful nod, and they resumed at a slower pace. It wasn't until they crested the hill that she realized he hadn't withdrawn his fingers from hers.

What was with him? This wasn't like Sergeant Mean Eye. Earlier in the car, he'd winked at her. Winked! That gesture alone had tickled her gut as though she'd swallowed a bucket of feathers. Then he'd handed over his expensive guitar, not only giving tips on her playing but teaching her new chords. Now he held her hand?

Maybe the steep climb had been to blame for his continued touch, but they were currently on level land.

As if reading her thoughts, he released her and pointed to a pine-framed patch of earth dappled by the lowering sun. Vera followed him and her gaze turned inquisitive. She scanned the area, turning in a slow circle. "I don't see any berry bushes."

He dimpled. "That's because they grow on the ground."

"Oh." Her voice registered her surprise, and she stooped to snatch a better glimpse. "Okay, where are the berries?" Because all she saw were oblong leaves, canopying dainty, white, bell-shaped flowers.

Mick crouched beside her, sending a pleasant whiff of soap and musk her way. "They don't appear until the fall." He plucked a leaf and handed it to her. "We've actually come here for this. Try it."

"As in *eat* it?" Her nose wrinkled at the waxy texture. The deep-green leaf with red edges was no bigger than her thumbnail, but she wasn't sure she could stomach it.

Mick snapped off another and broke it in half. "At least smell it." He brought it close to her nose, and she sniffed the sweet fragrance.

She could see how a touch of that would make Lacey's tea more flavorful. Maybe it wouldn't hurt to sample one. Before she lost her nerve, she shoved the leaf into her mouth and bit into it, tasting almost a wintergreen zest.

"Atta girl." Mick grinned and sat back on his haunches. "What do you think?"

"Hmm. I've had something like this before. Do they make chewing gum this flavor?"

"Yeah. Clark's brand." He nodded and withdrew a navy pouch from his shirt pocket. "Mrs. Chambers likes that too. The captain always brings her some when he visits."

Was she missing something? "Pops knows Lacey?"

Mick looked at her sideways. "I thought you knew. He's her younger brother."

She laughed. "That makes sense. They have the same eyes." And say *darlin'* every other sentence.

They filled the next several minutes stuffing the pouch with the teaberry leaves, a comfortable silence stretching between them. Mick stood and helped Vera to her feet. A flash of bright color over his shoulder pulled her attention.

The sunset.

She stepped past him, moving to a wider clearing. The hilltop gave her an impressive view of the radiant skyline. "Oh, wow."

Mick joined her in admiring nature's show. The scene looked as if it longed to be set to music, trills of pinks and golds blending—rather, harmonizing—across the expanse, giving her slice of the world a grand finale. The strong-willed sun was belting out one last fiery melody. Soon it'd bow behind the jagged row of pines, and the moon would strut onto the inky stage.

She sighed. "It's sad they call this gorgeous place the Allegheny Forest."

Mick gave her a curious look.

"It sounds starched. Flavorless." She could think of rat holes with better names. "Too much like—"

"A map."

Was he teasing her again?

"Okay, Vera, name this place." He spread out his arms. "Can you do better?"

Ooh, nothing like a good challenge. "I could. Give me a minute. Gotta let the creativity soak in." She allowed her gaze to rest on the trees huddled on her left. A slight breeze brought the branches to life, gently touching one another. "Whispering Pines." It was like watching poetry. "Listen." She cut a glance at Mick. "When the wind blows, the trees make a *shh* sound, like they're tellin' secrets."

"Whispering Pines." He rubbed the sharp turn of his jaw. "I like it."

Vera's heart swelled at his approval. His magnetic smile drew her gaze to him, almost overpowering her defenses. She hadn't missed the softness in his touch when he'd helped her to her feet a moment ago, harnessing his strength as if she were a treasure to be handled delicately. A couple days ago, it would've insulted her, but the kindness in his expression unraveled something inside her. Enough to make her brain jostle. So much she could almost hear it rattling. Wait, that sound came from outside her.

"Vera." Mick's tone held a serious edge. "Don't move. There's a snake behind you."

CHAPTER 17

The rattler blended into a pile of leaf litter, its beige body coiled and fanged head lifted, poising to strike.

About four feet separated the snake from Vera. Mick had a clear aim of the serpent, but—Lord, help him—he had to shoot between her legs to kill it.

"Stay still." Mick locked his gaze on Vera's panic-stricken eyes and inched his fingers toward his gun.

"Can I run for it?" Vera's voice was as shaky as Mick's confidence.

He had only one shot. If he missed, the spooked snake would surely launch at her. "No. You're in striking distance. You won't be quick enough."

With slow movements, he unholstered his gun. He'd never claimed to be a sharpshooter but today, he had to be. Vera's haunted gaze fused to his gun, and her eyes pinched shut.

"Don't move. I'm shooting between your legs."

Fear ravaged her face, blanching her complexion, twisting her mouth. Perhaps it was a good thing her back faced the venomous reptile. Its black, forked tongue flicked the air, and slit pupils sized up Mick, challenging him to a duel of deadly proportions.

Holding still, except for a bead of sweat coursing his temple, Mick drew a steadying breath. Like a finger's snap, he withdrew the gun and fired.

The snake's head flopped to the ground, and Mick exhaled his relief.

With a shriek, Vera sprang toward him, half tripping, half charging like a linebacker. She smacked flush into his chest. Her fingernails bit into his shoulders as she clung to him.

He holstered his gun with one hand and ran his other over the back of her head, hoping to soothe. Mick wasn't the best at calming frantic females. Her frame visibly shook. Offering gentle words, he pressed his palm to her tense back, anchoring her against him.

He eyed the snake. Still dead.

Man, he disliked—no, hated—killing wildlife. Especially when men like Hewitt Chambers had worked for years to rebuild this forest's depleted habitat to what it was now. But he'd had no choice.

Vera tipped her head back, glancing up at him with eyes dewed with unshed tears. "That was close." Her gaze traveled from his to the gun at his hip. "I never thought I'd be thankful for a pistol."

And Mick was thankful he'd been able to lodge the bullet between the rattler's eyes. Otherwise, this would've all ended differently. "Came in handy" was all he could say. Truth was, it'd take him the whole evening to get his heart rate normal.

She tossed a look over her shoulder. Her gaze landed on the bloodied snake, and her rigid frame responded with a shiver.

"Thank you, Mick." She turned to face him, the deep-green of her eyes more vivid than the bed of ferns surrounding her. With a delicate smile, she eased away from him, his body now void of the warmth hers provided.

Oh brother.

Trust shone in her expression, but Mick couldn't let out a victory whoop because something else stirred in his heart. Something he would never acknowledge. "Let's get back to the cabin."

"No!"

Vera shot up in her bed, clutching her sheet to her chest. Was that a man's yell or a crazed night owl?

"Stop!" Mick's voice penetrated her ears.

She sucked in air.

An intruder!

Panic strangled her chest, forcing her breath to snag in her lungs. Darkness shrouded the room. The shadows mocked her blurry eyes.

Was Carson here? Or his thugs? Was Mick hurt? Alarm coursed her veins as she fumbled out of bed. Her foot caught in a fold in the sheet, sending her to the floor with a thud. If the intruder hadn't known where she was, he did now.

Trapped.

If she jumped out the window, she'd break a leg and still get caught. At least braving the hall would give her a fighting chance. She grabbed the plank of wood Mick had used to brace the window open.

A pain-filled groan made her toes curl against the cool floor. Mick needed her. If he could take on a rattler for her sake, she sure could try to wallop any intruder. With the board raised like a baseball bat, she crept to her bedroom door that was cracked only an inch and nudged it open with her foot.

A stillness settled in the hallway, but her heart pounded such a thunderous beat it could produce its own echo.

Mick's door was ajar. She strengthened her grip on her weapon.

"Phyllis!" A rustling noise mixed with his anguished voice. "No!"

She stilled. *Phyllis? Who's she?*

With all the courage she could scrape together, she peeked in. The moon's silvery haze poured in the window. Mick wrestled in his bed with an imaginary assailant. She rested the plank on her shoulder, the splintery stubs poking her skin.

No intruder. It was only Mick having a nightmare. He writhed in a bedframe not much larger than him. She welcomed air back into her lungs. Should she let him be or wake him?

She placed the board on the floor, careful not to let it clunk.

He groaned and turned toward her, his frame stiff, his face contorted. She bent low and put her hand on his bare shoulder. His eyes popped open, and he lurched back.

"Mick, it's okay. Just me." She touched him again, smoothing back his hair from his forehead, as her grandmother used to when nightmares came. "You were yelling."

"Vera." His voice was a sleepy, yet haunted, drawl.

She sat next to his recumbent form, her fingers traveling to the nape of his neck. "I'm here." With light movements, she massaged his balmy skin, the tension in his muscles lessening.

"Haven't had … one of those for a while." His loud breaths tugged at her heart. "Sorry."

He shifted and held out his hand. She pulled her touch away from his neck and placed her fingers in his.

"I didn't mean to wake you." Moisture collected in the corners of his eyes.

Sweat or tears? She reached for the handkerchief stowed in her robe pocket, but her fingers hit only the satin of her nightgown. Her pulse quickened. In her frenzy, she hadn't grabbed her robe. Great, she was half naked and in a man's bed. Maybe he couldn't see. She turned her shoulder and yanked at the thin material, trying to cover more of her chest.

She glanced over. He faced the window, and his body lay motionless. Phew. He'd fallen back asleep.

Now to get off his bed without disturbing him. She inched her way until only her palms put pressure on the mattress. Slowly, she pulled her hands away.

"Goodnight, Mick," she whispered and left the room.

But she lay awake a long time, wondering who Phyllis was.

CHAPTER 18

"I want her protection withdrawn." Robert Shultz folded his arms and scowled at the captain.

Mick swallowed the refute billowing in his chest. The D.A.'s word sizzled in his ears, blazing his insides, but he had to remain calm. For Vera's sake. He couldn't let her down. Especially not now. She'd proven herself a friend by not badgering or ridiculing him for his nightmare the other day.

His neck grew stiff. In his dream, Phyllis, covered in her own blood, had been calling—more like accusing—him. And just like all the other times in those dark visions, he hadn't been able to save her. As much as he hated the torment, it served as a reminder—he couldn't get close to Vera. He couldn't open his heart to her. But that didn't mean Mick wouldn't do everything in his power to protect her.

"You can't withdraw our service now." The captain sat straight in his chair, his posture like granite. Even his jowls seemed rigid. "It's only been a week and a half."

"Too long." Shultz's beady eyes turned to Mick. "Sergeant, can you provide me with something substantial, a reason to extend her guardianship?"

The D.A. occupied the exact chair Vera had sat in the afternoon he'd brought her to headquarters. So much had transpired since that day.

"I'm waiting, Dinelo." Shultz dipped his chin, making his

receding hairline more obvious.

"Sir." Mick regarded him with a smirk of his own. "I know Miss Pembroke is in danger. Remember her apartment was broken into?"

Captain Harpshire nodded in agreement.

"That's old news. Besides, her apartment isn't in the most respectable area of the city. Could have nothing to do with the case. Anything else? Have there been any more attempts on her life?" He tapped his pen repeatedly on a stack of loose papers on the table.

"No." Mick forced the word out. "There haven't been any other assaults or attempts."

"None?" He quirked a brow, a note of victory smearing his eyes. "Any threats?"

"No."

"Well." Shultz dropped the pen in his pocket with an exaggerated nod. "Guess we can conclude the young woman is no longer in danger."

Mick cleared his throat. "Sir, I think—"

"And the manner in which you've hidden her raises my suspicion. You've told no one." Shultz's glare displayed an arrogance that tightened Mick's stomach more than a hundred push-ups. "I'm trusting she's not at some high-end hotel, loitering away the city's funds."

"She's at my summer cabin in the Alleghenies," the captain said.

Shultz's expression twisted into a mixture of surprise and disgust, as though he'd swallowed a fly. "Captain Harpshire, we should use our manpower to find the criminal behind Cavenhalt's death. We need to build a strong case, not entertain a nightclub singer."

Mick gritted his teeth. A left hook to this man's jaw would be an improvement.

The captain set his coffee mug on the table, a frown settling between his brows. "The police protection was my decision."

The D.A. practically growled. "And now it's mine."

Mick folded his hands, squeezing his fingers against his knuckles. It was ingrained in him to respect his superiors, but people like Shultz made it difficult. Who was to say the criminals hadn't been looking for Vera? That the hideout hadn't been the very thing keeping them from finding her? To bring her back into Pittsburgh unguarded—like a lamb to the slaughterhouse—could be what they were waiting for. The thought sickened him.

Shultz glared at the captain. "The city of Pittsburgh needs a prosecution, and we don't have a suspect since Kelly's alibi surfaced."

"One more week." Mick's fist thudded the tabletop with more intensity than planned.

Shultz blanched. Captain Harpshire smiled.

"She knows something. I'm convinced to the point I'd risk this." He withdrew his badge and tossed it on the table like a bargaining chip. "Give me another week, and I'll have your evidence."

Shultz cocked his head, his eyes more thunderous than the storm Mick'd gotten caught up in on the way here. A long silence hovered between them.

"One week, Dinelo." Shultz held a bony finger in the air. "One week and you better have something." He stood and shoved out his right hand.

Mick answered with a firm grip. God help him.

Mick groaned at the disarray before him. The thought of scouring Vera's apartment had tapped his heart ever since Vera had hinted about a precious token left behind, but after the meeting, the idea had nudged him like an elbow to the ribs. Maybe there might be something linking to the case. His words from the meeting wrapped around his chest, squeezing. His badge was on the line. More importantly, Vera's safety.

He shrugged off his jacket and loosened his tie. No doubt, he'd expected a mess, but this resembled the remains of an explosion. Clothes and papers littered the floor. Lamps smashed. Everything torn off the walls. He ran a hand over the back of the sofa. The same sofa he'd sat on the day he'd brought her to headquarters. The once plush cushions now hacked open, stuffing spilling out.

Who had done this? And what had they been looking for?

Hunched over the last pile of rubble, he came up empty and stood, stretching his sore muscles. He twisted, cracking his back. Glancing at his watch, a sigh escaped. An hour of searching had landed him nothing but a slice on his index finger from remnants of a vanity mirror.

He stood, pressing a palm to the stiff spot on his neck, sweeping the shambolic room with a doubtful gaze. Nothing could be salvaged here. All junk. Worthless and broken. The realization hit deep and strong. Was that how Vera felt about her life? Ruined and fragmented?

If only he could help her, show her that a marred history didn't have to stain her future. An exasperated huff swelled in his chest, and he kicked a mangled hatbox out the way. He couldn't escape the past himself, let alone guide Vera to.

And this little scavenger hunt wasted valuable time. Couldn't find Vera's token. Couldn't locate anything to help the case. He rolled his shoulders, a vain attempt to shrug frustration away. Fatigue pressed in, and a five-hour drive awaited. He took his key from his pocket, his pen coming out with it, dropping to the floor, rolling beside the radiator.

He stooped. His favorite fountain pen cozied up next to something he never thought would be in Vera's possession. He scooped them both up, shoved them in his pocket, and strode out.

Being in direct line with the afternoon sun, the exterior doorknob burned his palm as he pulled the door shut. A shuffling to the right drew his attention. He glanced over. A fist propelled toward him. He jerked back, missing the full impact but receiving a knuckle to his cheek.

The attacker, a scrawny man with shaggy hair, cussed, then sprinted the opposite direction and down the stairs. Mick charged after him, leaping off the last five steps. The man moved swifter, expanding the gap between them. The assailant turned the corner of the building, and Mick slowed, withdrawing his gun. He couldn't afford the mistake of rushing into a bend and getting jumped. Gun raised, he rounded the turn.

Gone.

Heavy breaths fought their way out of his chest. Trigger finger holding steady, he scanned the dumpsters. He dashed farther down the graveled way, dust flying up behind him, but only came across a rusty bicycle.

Mick dragged a hand down his sweaty face, heart pounding. Who had that been? And what had he been doing outside Vera's apartment?

Vera walked over to the window and pulled back the sheer white curtain. The empty drive stared back at her.

"Watching for him won't bring him back sooner, darlin'." Lacey stood in the living room doorway, wiping her hands on the front of her apron.

"Who said I was watchin' for anything?" She dropped her arm to her side, the curtain falling back in place. "Thought I heard something. That's all." A small lie, but no harm done.

"He won't be long. When I talked to him this morning, he said he had a few errands to run before his drive here."

What errands could he have? Was he enjoying his freedom away from her? Vera thought she'd enjoy the break from his company, but even with all the musical options, she found herself bored, listless. Last night, she'd had trouble falling asleep despite Lacey's guest room mattress being softer than anything she'd ever slept on. What did all this mean? She couldn't be … could she?

"Anything on your mind, dearie?"

Just Mick. "What date is it?"

Lacey puckered her lips and raised her eyebrows as if it would help her think. "It's the sixth."

Vera's hand went to her mouth. "You foolin'?"

"No, sugar, I'm not." Lacey walked to the hutch and pointed to the calendar. Two little fat angels held the word *JUNE*, and above Lacey's fingernail was the number *6*. "Is there something important you have to do?"

Nine days she'd been hidden away. And it was the sixth already? She pressed her lips together. It was just a day. "Nope. Nothin's important, anymore."

Lacey tilted her head. "I'm wondering who's going to clear the air first? You or Mick."

"Clear the air?" Maybe Lacey was frustrated with their arguing. They had been getting along better, a lot better.

"Come on, sugar. Don't think I haven't seen it." Lacey waved a hand at Vera. "Mick's calf-eyed looks. Goodness, he's love-struck."

"For me?"

"No, for Mitzy." Light-hearted sarcasm coated her tone. "Of course, for you."

Vera's breath hitched in her throat, a heady wave coursing through her. But then … Lacey was a matchmaker. Even the first day they met, the woman tried to pair her and Mick. And as for the calf-eyed looks, Lacey had imagined it.

Outside the window, a flash of yellow arrested her attention.

Mick's car.

Vera gulped so hard she might have swallowed a tonsil.

"I think I heard Mick." Lacey gracefully stood and stepped to the window. "That's him, all right. I wonder if he's hungry."

Vera's stomach and heart were at odds with each other, one queasy while the other turned cartwheels.

CHAPTER 19

Mick killed the motor and relaxed against the seat. The soreness in his neck extended to his fingertips. The five-and-a-half hours of strain, finally over.

No one had followed him. He'd skirted towns, venturing backroad routes, dodging any form of traffic.

Leaning forward, he pinched the bridge of his nose, restraining the throb in his temples. The dull ache had lingered since he'd informed headquarters of the attacker at Vera's apartment. The captain had received the news seriously, but the D.A. had dismissed the incident on account of it being in a high-crime district.

With a heavy exhale, he stepped out into the summer air.

Nothing looked out of place. He checked the barn, jiggling the knob. Locked. The leaf he had wedged between the barn door and the shovel's handle was still there. Satisfied there hadn't been any foul play, he made his way to Mrs. Chambers' car.

Her Buick was parked in the same spot as it had been the day he'd left. He crouched down and, guilt nibbling his heart, saw the stick he'd set behind the front left tire. He should trust Vera more, but he'd been unable to shake the fear of her convincing Mrs. Chambers to take her into town. Or worse, her sneaking off by herself.

He stood and took in the area. No movement anywhere except the clothes on the line, almost horizontal with the steady breeze.

Mrs. Chambers waved and pushed open the screen door.

"It's good to see you." He side-hugged the woman, her fragrance of vanilla and bleach making him smile.

"How did everything go?"

He shrugged. "I think I got us into a mess." A big one.

Mrs. Chambers' brows rose. "Speaking of messes"—she waved her embroidered handkerchief—"you have dirt on your cheek."

Mick shook his head. "It's a bruise." He determined to leave it at that, but Mrs. Chambers inclined her head as though she was ready to hear some juicy gossip. "I was leaving Vera's apartment and ran into some trouble."

Her eyes widened, and he held up a finger. "But I'm fine." Even if the bozo got away. "Everything is all right." He forced a tight smile and shuffled his feet on the tweed doormat. "Do you have anything to drink?" Mitzy greeted him, rubbing against his leg.

"Lemonade all right?"

"Yes, thank you." Was it hotter in here than outside? Having discarded his suit jacket in his car, he rolled his sleeves up to his elbows. "Where is she?"

"In the powder room. Took off like a pelican when she saw you coming up the drive." Lacey sidestepped to him and stood on her tiptoes, pulling on his shoulder. "We all know why."

"Yeah. She's hiding."

"Oh, stop that. Give yourself a little more respect." Mrs. Chambers swatted his arm with her handkerchief. She hummed the wedding march as she stooped to pat Mitzy's side. "Da-dum da-da."

"Mrs. Chambers, I'm exhausted." He hated to be blunt. But the matchmaking had to stop.

Her easy smile flattened. "I just don't want you to miss out on anything. Yeah, you have a fear of getting killed in the line of duty, but that doesn't mean—"

"I've sworn off matrimony." His voice sounded gruff, but it was all he could do not to explode. His nerves had taken a severe beating today, and the worst was yet to come. He still had to tell

Vera about the meeting. "Please don't push that topic with me."

"Mick, I only—"

Vera appeared in the doorway.

His gaze met hers. What had she heard? A surge of regret rushed through him. He should've kept quiet. Mrs. Chambers never listened to his objections, anyway.

A warm smile danced on Vera's lips, and his chest burned from the welcome.

Something had happened between them since that evening with the rattlesnake. They'd bonded. And now, her appearance made him realize even more what a woman she was. Mercy, did she have to look so fetching? The sundress hung over her modestly, but there was no hiding her curvy frame. He'd never seen her hair fixed such a way, all piled on top of her head with ringlets framing her face. Had she done that for him? The urge to pull her into his arms surprised him. Hadn't he just resolved not to let her crowd his heart? He steeled his mind against her pull.

"Hey, there, Sarge." Vera glided closer and regarded him with eyes greener than the fields behind Mrs. Chamber's cabin.

"How are you? Feeling okay?" He broke the long stretch of eye contact with her, studying her face for any sign of stress. "I have a lot of news from Pittsburgh. I want to wait until you're …" Why couldn't he think of the word? Maybe he should sit for a time before delving into the business that'd been the subject of his prayers. "Let's go into the kitchen."

He held out his arm, giving Vera the right of way. She smiled but concern framed her eyes. This wasn't going to be easy.

It was maddening. Nothing short of torture watching Mick slowly sip on the tall glass. At the pace he was going, she wouldn't know about the meeting until next month. She shifted in her chair a couple times, traced the design of a flower on the tablecloth with her fingers, and patted Mitzi when the furry thing rubbed against her leg. Lacey was outside watering her petunias, leaving Vera to stare at Mick drinking his lemonade like a parched camel.

Stretching her arms out on the table, she tapped softly, repeating the rhythm.

His mouth inched up and his eyes met hers. "You've been practicing."

Ah, Mr. Dimple, I've missed you. And missed his voice, the strength of his deep resonance. She plain missed him. She had to resist slapping her forehead. *Wake up, Vera-girl, you heard him.* He'd sworn off matrimony. Not like she was in contention for the accompanying role, but knowing he was closed off made her heart wilt. "I wasn't sure if you'd notice." Or notice her.

Mick wiped the ring his cold glass left on the tablecloth with his napkin. "You tapped out my code—ACE." He pulled his chair closer to the table. "You mastered it. I'm impressed." His perfect lips slanted in a crooked smile that didn't quite reach his eyes. "Any chance of you being my poker partner?"

"Hardly. But tell me, are you impressed enough to share about the meeting?" She leaned forward, keeping her stare locked on his. "And why do you have that shiner on your cheek?"

The smile dropped from his handsome face, and Vera's stomach tangled like Lacey's darning yarn. Maybe she didn't want to know.

"A man was outside your apartment. I barely missed his punch."

Her breath caught. "My apartment? Who?"

"He got away." His expression struggled between frustration and disappointment. "And as for the meeting, District Attorney Shultz wants you off police protection."

"What? Why?" The sudden news drove her heart racing. On her own. "How soon?" She couldn't stay in Pittsburgh. Where could she go? New York had been her goal for years, but now being forced to go—when Carson was still on the loose—unsettled her.

"We've got seven more days." He jerked the knot of his tie loose, the frown on his face pushing more and more caution into her heart. "I told them that you—"

"What?" The word came out a reedy whisper.

"That you might know something."

She sucked in air and held it. Why would he do that?

"It was the only way to extend your safety." He rested his elbows on the table and looked at her. "Is there something, Ver?"

"No." If only she could snap her fingers and have the answer. But she couldn't. She'd told them everything she knew, and it wasn't good enough.

"Here." Mick reached in his pocket and pulled out his handkerchief. "Take this before I forget." He withdrew her bracelet, the one Carson had given her, from the cotton cloth.

"And?" She coached herself to be strong, whatever the news. Stolen. Fake.

"It's a Tiffany. Worth a little over a grand," he said. "Here. Let me help you with it."

Vera held out her wrist, and he latched that puppy. A grand? That could help her start off right. She could go anywhere. Even abroad if she wanted to. Something pricked her heart. That was what she wanted, wasn't it? Mick would go back to Pittsburgh and resume his life. Without her. "I thought for sure he put the heat on that bracelet."

"It's great for your sake, but it didn't help the case any. You and I have a lot of work to do. We have to come up with a motive by June thirteenth. One thing is going for us. Because of what I said this morning, everyone thinks you have the evidence to nab him." The glint returned to his eye. "Good strategy."

Would the news travel to Carson? Angelo? Whoever it was that desired her death? An icy chill coursed through her, freezing her thoughts and stopping her heart for a breath. "You're usin' me as bait? A little fish to catch the big one." He was supposed to be on her side. And this was why she couldn't trust. "How could you? No way I am goin' to be found belly-up in the Ohio River." She pushed off the table to scoot her chair back, but he stuck his foot out, stopping the chair, keeping her seated.

"Nobody's using you as bait."

"Oh yeah? What do you call it? Besides that, you lied." Her jab didn't work—his face revealed no offense. In fact, it had a smile on it.

"I didn't lie. I believe you know something. I just don't think you realize it yet."

She glared at the floor. He lifted her chin with his thumb, and their gazes connected, the intensity in his eyes overpowering her objections to pulling away.

"Ver, I have a gut feeling."

Now she was stuck. Gut feelings were powerful. And usually true.

CHAPTER 20

Mick scooped up the flat board and wafted the fire, launching hundreds of fiery darts into the black sky, the soft crackles and pops a comfort in his ears. He'd never tire of that sound.

After they'd returned from Mrs. Chambers' place, he'd suggested building an outdoor fire and enjoying the pleasant evening.

A familiar noise hooted in the dark.

Vera startled.

"It's only an owl." He focused his gaze on the glowing oranges and intense reds of the blaze.

"You can stop smilin' anytime." She snapped a piece of bark off the log stool she sat on and threw it at him.

"You missed." His laugh shot out like his grandpa's rifle.

She folded her arms. "I missed ya on purpose. Consider that a warnin'."

"Sure. I'll make a note of that." He'd also make a note of how the fire's light intensified her beauty. The soft glow danced across her gentle features as the light wind played with the ends of her hair, teasing him to test its softness. *Eyes on the fire, Ace.*

"Is he far?"

"Who?"

"The owl. It sounded like he was right behind me." Vera glanced over her shoulder, her eyes holding an innocence that made his heart squeeze.

"Actually, he's in front of you." He pointed to the line of

trees about forty yards from them. The darkness made the pines look like giant fingers scratching the sky. "He's perched in there somewhere."

"Well, I wish he'd pipe down. He gives me the creeps."

"Everything gives you the creeps." Mick shook his head as he stooped closer to the fire. The log on the left needed more centered. The silver scales on the burning wood illuminated brighter as he poked it in place. Better. "The bat you saw earlier. The raccoon I shooed from the garbage. Even butterflies. All of them made you wince."

"Can I help it if critters give me the jumps? And the only shakes I enjoy is when I'm dancing the Shimmy, thank you very much." Silence hovered like the smoke above the fire, until Vera's laughter broke through it.

"Care to share?"

"I better not. It's about you."

He pointed the tip of the poker stick at her. "Now you *have* to share."

"All right. All right. I was thinking about you attemptin' the Shimmy." She covered her mouth and another laugh escaped. "Sorry, couldn't help that one."

"I take it by your laughing you weren't imagining me as F. Scott Fitzgerald."

"More like a tin soldier. All stiff and half a beat off."

"Honest. A little brutal, but honest. And probably not too far from the truth. I don't dance that one. Or the Charleston." Was she laughing or shivering? He set down the poker and climbed to his feet. "Stand up. I'm going to move your chair closer to the fire."

"It's a log. A chair has armrests." But she stood.

He scooted the log stool about two feet closer to the blaze. "Here." He stripped off his jacket. "This might help too." He wrapped the jacket around her slim shoulders after she sat down. Her perfume had lingered on the fabric for several days after he'd covered her with it the night they'd left Pittsburgh. Not that he'd minded.

"So, Micky, what dances can ya do?"

"The slow ones."

"And are you *careful* with your hands, sir?" Vera flashed her palms and wiggled her fingers. "I've yet to meet a gent who is. But then, being forced to be with sweaty-palmed men for a coin a dance can really give a person a slanted opinion on the subject."

Mick's chest squeezed. "You were a taxi dancer?"

"Off and on at the Kelly Club. I was first hired to sell cigarettes, but I also had to serve as the dime-a-dance girl. That's why I was so happy to become the canary."

The image of drunken idiots with their grimy paws all over Vera ignited something in him. No wonder she had a tough time trusting men. Between Kelly, Cavenhalt, and the sordid patrons at the Kelly Club, the poor woman couldn't help but carry a loathing prejudice against his gender. "Did you always want to be a singer? Was that your dream?"

"I gave up on dreams long ago. Survival trumps fairy tales." She sighed. "I hated to be pinched. Grabbed. Being the canary, I went out and sang. That's all. Nobody touched me." She glared at the fire. "Angelo was my bodyguard. He'd throw out any creep with forceful hands. Usually, I found them in the crowd before anything happened. Except for that one time."

A nerve throbbed in his temple. "What happened?"

"I finished my number, walked offstage, and …"

The flickering fire could be blamed for the shadows on her face, giving her a haunted look, but Mick knew better.

She shivered like the moment she'd spotted the dead rattler. Were the memories just as poisonous to her? "A man pulled me by the arm outside."

He tensed. "Did he hurt you?"

"No. Carson found us and slugged the man, sending him running."

"Did they find him? Was an assault charge filed?"

"No, they didn't find him. And Carson didn't take the trouble to search." She blew out her cheeks with a noisy exhale. "How did we get on this topic again?"

"Dancing."

She gave a ghost of a smile. "Oh, right. Men and their hungry hands."

"Not all are like that." Mick stepped toward her, thinking if he was at the Kelly Club right now, he'd pin all the men up on the wall by their collars.

"What? You goin' to move my log closer?" She stood and took a step back.

"No, I am asking you to dance with me."

She looked at him sideways, but the fire's light revealed traces of pleasure in her eyes. "What did Lacey put in your lemonade?"

He didn't move. She needed to know what it was like to be treated with respect. While he couldn't surrender any portions of his heart, he could offer her this dance.

"You serious?"

"Yes."

"There ain't music."

"Best around." He motioned toward the fire. "The rhythmic crackles could rival any melody. And we have a spotlight." He tipped his head back. "I ordered a full moon, just for you."

She set his jacket on the log, and he outstretched his hand, fully aware that she could reject his offer with one word or even a shake of the head. Keeping his eyes trained on her, he hoped with all his soul she could feel the security in his gaze. He'd never harm her, and Lord help the man who tried while he was near.

The sides of her mouth slowly tipped up, and his patience was rewarded with a smile that throttled the air right out of him. She stepped into his arms, and the swell of victory rose in his chest.

He placed his palm on the curve of her back, and with his other hand he held hers. Her frame fit snugly into his. And they danced, swaying under the chunky stars set in a black velvet sky. Vera rested her head on his chest, and a comfortable silence lingered between them. "Am I putting you to sleep?"

"No. I was thinkin'." Her hair was fragranced like every man's dream—lavender hinted with campfire smoke.

"What about?"

"How different you are to the man who showed up at my door."

Mick laughed. "I'm not any different. I have to harden myself. It's important in my line of work. You know me better. That's all." He felt her nod, and most likely she felt his pounding heart. "Besides, I could say the same thing about you. You're a different girl than that mouthy redhead who stuck her tongue out at me." He glanced down, reveling in the way she nuzzled her face into his shirt. "You know I saw that, don't you?"

Vera's gentle laughter floated into his ears, and his eyes slid shut. "I did do that. Sorry."

"Your world was crashing." And the urge to be the one to help her put it back together raged within him.

She relaxed against him. "I'm glad you were at the Kelly Club that night." The admiration in her voice speared him, like a hundred bullet casings in the heart.

Did she know how much she affected him? Made him long for things forever out of his reach?

He pressed a kiss to the top her head, lingering, letting the action speak what his voice never could.

His hot breath blazed her neck, while the pungent odor of whiskey burned her nose.

"Get off me!" Vera wrenched, but he sat on her legs, pinning her to the bed. The steel barrel of the pistol stabbed her gut, making her choke on her own saliva. "Stop!" Tears squeezed from her clenched eyes as his fingers bit into her throat.

"Give it to me." His snarly voice grated her ears.

"No! It's all I have left of her!" She shifted and thrust her knee into his groin.

He moaned and rolled off her thighs, his dirty hand still clutching the pistol. His finger grazed the trigger.

Thunder cracked, rattling the window. Her eyes popped open.

Vera's fingers were tangled in her necklace, her legs twisted in the sheet. Her nightgown clung to her chest, dampened with sweat. It was only a dream. She was safe in the Boone cabin. She breathed out, releasing the tension in her muscles. It'd been eight years, and she still couldn't get away from him? Eight years to the day.

Thunder roared again. She glared at the charcoal clouds strangling daybreak, a scornful laugh pushing from her gut. Dark and somber. Indicative of the kind of day it'd always been. Rain pelted the window in a fitful rhythm. She'd let the skies cry instead of her.

The effort of dressing and not burrowing under her covers all day added an extra strain. Could she possibly take on the task of pretending today meant nothing? As though the nightmare had never occurred? If Mick detected one shred of her unease, he might try to uncover the whole incident. And she couldn't have that.

Maybe she could dwell on happier times—one so recent as last evening. She could've melted into a puddle, and it hadn't been from the fire's heat. She relived it, the planes of his face in the moonlight, the beat of his heart against her ear, and the pressure of his lips on the crown of her head. That one dance had done more for her heart than a hundred other dances had.

She dressed and went downstairs. Ten steps in various directions revealed Mick wasn't anywhere nearby. But something else close drew her stare. Donuts. Her stomach growled. She neared paradise on a plate and found that wasn't the only item on that dilapidated card table. No, there was a wooden box and a note.

"Because every girl should have a present on her birthday." Vera read the message aloud and slowly descended into the chair. What? How'd he know? She glanced around to catch any trace of him, but there was only the sound of rain and her thoughts. She read the note again and smiled at the letterhead—*Allegheny County Police Department.*

Goodness, how long had it been since she'd gotten a birthday present? She fingered the gold chain around her neck, the last gift she'd received. Well, *half* of it, anyway. She'd always remember the delight which had coursed through her when her grandmother had bestowed it. Her fourteen-year-old heart had been filled with excitement to look all grown up with a real gold necklace. Such innocence. Vera's heart panged. Oh, for life to be simple again. Pure.

She focused on the box. It was small, almost like … a ring box. Her heart spiraled into her stomach like the rain rolled down the roof. She remembered his words from yesterday to Lacey and dismissed any suspicions of that kind. Mick wasn't interested.

Running her fingers across the carved paisleys, she studied the box's elegance. Slowly, she lifted the lid.

She sucked in enough air for her lungs to explode. Resting on a folded handkerchief was … the other half. *The other half!* She cradled the golden cross pendant in her hand, gazing at the token she'd thought was gone forever. Where had he found this? Memories swirled—her grandmother's faint scent of peppermint oil, the soft rasp of her voice, and the peace that permeated her cabin. A hot tear trickled as she pressed the pendant against her cheek.

"It was under your radiator." Mick stood in the doorway between the kitchen and dining room, hands anchored in his pockets, his shirt dotted with the rain.

Vera ran and threw her arms around his neck. "Thank you!" She planted a kiss on his clean-shaven cheek. "Thank you so much!"

"You're welcome," he said in a strangled voice.

"Sorry, Micky." She laughed and released her hold. "You made me so happy!" Another tear, but who cared? "I used to keep it in my drawer folded in my grandmother's handkerchief."

"Not bad for an overgrown Boy Scout."

"You goin' to hold that against me?" She waved a hand at him. "That was ages ago." Well, about eleven days, but it'd seemed like forever. "You're on my A-list now, sonny."

Mick grinned, and she'd swear that he rocked slightly on his heels. "If I'm on you're A-list now, I'd hate to know where I was before." He motioned toward the box she held. "That's from me. I bought it to put the cross in."

"It's perfect." Her heart filled with an emotion she hadn't experienced in years—hope. She shamelessly shed another tear. "I was sure, so sure, the cross was lost forever. And here it is."

"Happy Birthday, Ver."

"Thank you," she said on a sigh, turning toward him. "What do I say to the man who gave my grandmother back to me?"

He shook his head. "I only gave back the good memories."

She allowed her gaze to pour over the cross. "Well, it's the closest I can ever get to her."

"Doesn't have to be," he said. "You can look her straight in the face again. She's alive. Heaven is a real place."

Rain pattered the roof, Vera's emotions welling. How she longed to see her. Hear her. Touch her.

"Want to know what to say to the Man who gave your grandmother back to you? Tell Him that you believe on Him."

All elation drowned in the sincerity of Mick's eyes. "I ain't good enough for that kind of place. I could never be."

"Your grandmother wasn't good enough either."

Vera opened her mouth.

Mick lifted his hands. "I say this respectfully. No one's good enough. God's Word says that all men have sinned and fallen short of the glory of God." He stepped closer, the air between them thinning. "And makeup may cover that scar on your face, but it can't heal the ones on your heart." He reached out, barely touching her cheek.

Vera reeled back, the realization stabbing her heart. Her tears must have exposed her ugliness. She turned her head, shielding the scar from his view.

"I saw it the day we met."

And he'd never mentioned it until now? At once, it was difficult to face him. The hideous, discolored skin was never to be seen by anyone.

"Ver, it's okay." He slid his hand under her hair and traced his finger along the curve of the scar. Again and then again.

Her thoughts stumbled into each other. Didn't he know what he was doing to her? And why did the aching tenderness of his eyes make her want to collapse against him? To be held, not only in a passionate manner, but in a way she craved, yet had never experienced.

"You don't have to be ashamed. Whatever it's from, you're safe with me."

The usually firm lines around his mouth now soft, his open stance relaxed, his voice soothing. Could she breathe in his calmness and hold onto it forever? "It's my last remembrance of the monster." And the one that'd never left her.

"The monster?"

"My father." She drew in a shaky breath. "You're not the only one with nightmares."

Sympathy filled his eyes, pulling her gaze to his.

"When my grandmother passed, I was forced to live with my parents. My father drank, sipped the stuff like water. My mother was gone a lot. Who knows where or with who?" Shame and bitterness emerged from the shadows of her soul, pointing their twisted fingers to her distressing past.

Mick tugged her hand into his.

"Most of my days were spent staying at a friend's house or hiding in my room. That way my father couldn't get to me when he was drunk." It was all so fresh—her quiet sobs, her stomach panging from hunger, and no one caring if she lived or died. Had anything changed from her childhood? She studied Mick's pensive expression. He cared, didn't he? "I went from having my grandmother's love to nothin'. Mick, I told ya it was a bad ballad." She squeezed the cross in her hand, the edges pressing into her palm. An awareness of the Man who'd hung on the real cross swept into her soul. He knew pain. He knew abandonment. "Then, one day, my mother never returned home. She was gone for good, leavin' me with the violent old man."

Mick cupped her face with his hands, the gesture stealing her breath. "Did he beat you?"

She could only manage a nod.

His Adam's apple bobbed, and she slid her eyes shut, pulling strength from his touch. "I'm sorry, Ver."

"I usually could escape him by locking myself in my bedroom. But the last night I ever saw him, I forgot to bolt the door."

Mick removed his hands from her face, but held his gaze on her. "What happened?"

"He was always needin' money with that crummy addiction. I woke up to him clawin' at my neck, choking me. He held a gun. I'd never seen him that desperate." Her breath shortened as her chest tightened. "He wanted my necklace. To sell it like he had most of the things in the house." She swallowed. "I hit his middle with my knee. He shifted off me, and I was able to get away. Somewhat."

Mick stiffened.

"I was scared, crying."

"Aw, sweetheart." He ran his fingers along her hair, then pulled her to him.

She cuddled into his chest, the vulnerability both freeing and frightening. "He came after me, waving the gun, cussing, and stumbling all over the room. He tripped, and the gun went off. He shot the window I was next to." She touched her scar. "The glass cut my face. I can still hear his voice as I ran out. *You aren't worth anything to anyone.*"

He stepped back and squared her shoulders to face him. His jaw set. His muscles taut. "That's a lie, Ver. Not true."

Her heart yearned to believe him.

"So I ran away. Tried to steal money from the local gift shop to buy a bus ticket." There. She finally answered his question about her short life of crime. "The lady caught me and told me to work a full day. She gave me the coin I needed to skedaddle." She shrugged. "You know the rest of the story." Vera Pembroke's life summed up in three minutes. Shame lowered her gaze, and she scuffed her toe along the line in the floorboard.

"Can you look at me?" His eyes were dangerous to the brick walls around her heart, chunks crumbling to dust with each penetrating look. "What you went through wasn't right, but it doesn't disqualify you from God's love."

Didn't he get it? Why was he being so cruel? "Mick, my own parents couldn't love me. I was a nuisance to them. No matter how hard I tried." Vera didn't know what burned more, the salt tears over her flushed face, or her father's words branded on her heart. Not worth anything. Mick stood so sure, so confident. Someone like him couldn't understand. "It's a lost cause. Because then I went to Pittsburgh, and you know what happened there." Her breath hiccupped in her chest, and her legs wobbled, threatening to buckle. "Can't ya see the pattern? It's impossible. He can't love me." She balled her fists. "Can't."

"Too late. He loved you before time."

"How?" Vera dropped to her knees and muffled her sobs in her hands. "How?"

She felt Mick's warm presence beside her. "He always has."

"No. How … did you know?" Her hands fell limp against her sides as she sat back on her haunches. "I never told a soul."

"Ver, I don't under—"

"My grandmother told me that. Every night before bed, she'd kiss my forehead. *He loved you before time.*" The last words she'd spoken to Vera before she'd died. And now Mick had said it? "How on earth did you know?" Hearing those words was like water to her dehydrated soul.

"He's reaching out to you." Mick seized her hands, his gaze passionate. "Embrace him, Ver."

She couldn't keep living like this, heart gaping open and wounded. Fear and anger voiced in the depths of her mind, shouting condemnation, but the whispers of her heart drew her longing. "Jesus, I need you."

CHAPTER 21

Mick let out a low whistle, catching sight of Vera on the top of the stairs. He couldn't have been more surprised when Vera had asked him after her buffet of donuts to take her for a shooting lesson. But now, by the hesitant look in her eyes, she appeared as if she had second thoughts. Or perhaps she was just miffed with her necessary attire.

"I look like a gent." Vera's lower lip protruded as two fists settled on a slim waist. "This is awful."

"My clothes never looked better." And the way she filled them out made his heart pound against his ribs. He liked her this way, her frame swimming in his flannel shirt. She rolled up the cuffs so her hands could escape. And the necklace hung perfectly over her exposed collarbone, making him want to trace his nose along the slim gold line. He swallowed and asked God to help him control wayward thoughts. "My question is, how do the pants fit?"

Vera lifted the hem of the shirt. A rope was pulled through the belt loops, tied tightly, the material bunching in the front. "Found it in one of the dresser drawers." She gave the end of the rope a tug.

Mick laughed, and Vera scowled.

"I'm glad someone's gettin' pleasure out of this." Red ringlets swooped up in a navy ribbon, allowing visibility of her full face, causing his stare to linger a bit too long.

"I think we learned from that day gathering teaberry that you can't climb hills in a dress." The terrain on the hillside was littered with sticks, thorny bushes, and patches of bur weed. Stockings wouldn't make it ten feet before being sliced into silky shreds. And even though the rain had stopped, the ground was sure to be wet and slippery.

Vera picked a loose string off the shirt and then looked to Mick, her eyelashes resembling tiny fans. "Maybe I can just watch you shoot today."

Stay strong, Dinelo. Her eyes held a persuasiveness powerful enough to make a grown man's knees buckle. "It never hurts to learn how to shoot. And with your situation, it's a necessity. You can do it." He patted the holster on his hip and winked. "You'll see."

The backs of Vera's legs flamed. "How much longer?" And how come her body wasn't nimble after all these forest treks? She reduced her pace as Mick quickened his.

"We're almost there. About fifty more yards."

He called that *almost there*? Sheesh. "I'm takin' a break." For like two days. She bent low, rubbing her calf muscle.

Mick stopped and set the bags of dirt on the high grass. Was that what they were going to shoot into? Shoot. The silly notion had her heart skittering faster than the squirrels racing up the pines.

She should've never asked. At the moment, it'd felt right. Her objections about guns had lessened after Mick had protected her from the rattler. But why did she have to go all Annie Oakley? As soon as the request had left her big mouth, she'd regretted it. But Mick had turned all Buffalo Bill and devised this little shooting adventure. Vera hated to disappoint him. He'd been so sweet about her birthday. She fingered the cross resting on her collarbone, and all the memories of the morning swept in. She smiled. Being right with God felt good. Being right with Mick did too.

He wiped the sweat from his brow with his forearm. "You

thirsty?" He slid the canteen strap off his shoulder, unscrewed the cap, and poured water into the lid. "Drink as much as you want." From the lid that was the size of a teacup?

Vera received it with a smile. She drank two gulps, the icy temperature of the spring water enough to make her teeth chatter, and handed it back.

"More?"

"No, you go 'head."

"I brought it for you." He put the lid on. "Let me know when you want another cup." He swung the strap over his shoulder and picked up the bags. "The landing is right past that maple."

Vera stuck close to him during the rest of the hike, in case some rattlesnake or any other creepy thing would want to cozy up to her. They reached the summit, and Mick set down the two gunnysacks in an open space.

He slid the gun out of the brown leather holster, and she fought against a cringe. *Don't be a scaredy-cat.*

He motioned to her. "Come stand by me."

Vera did so, her heart accelerating with every step.

"This is a Smith and Wesson thirty-eight caliber."

She took in its wooden handle and silver frame.

"Always keep it pointed away from you." He directed the gun toward the gunnysacks. With his left hand, he stroked the steel. "This is a standard barrel. See this raised groove? This is the sight. It's how you aim." Then he showed her the hammer, the trigger, and the cylinder.

For his sake, she tried to act interested.

"Now this gun can shoot decent up to thirty yards, but we aren't going that far." He led her about twenty feet from the gunnysacks. He held out his right hand with the gun pointed straight ahead of him. With his thumb, he pulled back the hammer.

Click.

Vera shivered. The horror of those nights rushed through her, her father's gravelly voice, Artie's shrilling yell, the fear setting its claws into her and not letting go. The glass window shattering. The scar. The feeling in her gut during her number. Running from the club in the storm. Fragments of those memories sliced her soul, knifing the air in her chest.

"Ready?" Mick glanced at her, determination tightening his features.

No! But her voice wouldn't work, and fear pressed hard, smothering her from the inside out.

He fired all six rounds.

Vera screamed and buried her face in her hands. Strong arms wrapped around her. His muscles pressed into her back like the day he'd saved her from the snake. She exhaled.

"Shh. You're safe, Ver." He whispered in her ear, rubbing between her shoulder blades in rhythmic strokes. "No fear, sweetheart." The warmth of his breath coated her cheek, and he held her close.

"Do you really think I can do this?" She drew back to read his eyes.

Mick traced the curve of her face with his finger. "Yes."

Vera slid her eyes shut, breathing out a prayer. Courage rose within, an empowering she could never have produced on her own. Mick must have detected it in her eyes, for he regarded her with a full smile. "Now it's your turn."

Mick reloaded the cylinder and looked up at Vera. "You can do this." He nodded, hoping she could feel his faith in her. He held out the gun.

She took in a breath and gently lifted the revolver from his hand.

"This is your trigger finger. That's right. Now extend toward the target." He ran his fingers down her arm, ignoring the sensations coursing through him, and gently pushed on her elbow until she locked it in place. "Keeping your joints and muscles tight will help your aim." He wrapped his fingers around her forearm. "I'm going to help support your arm until it stops trembling."

Vera glanced up at him, and compassion filled his heart.

"Bring up your other arm. Yes, just like that. Fold your left hand over your right. Perfect. You doing all right, Ver?"

She nodded.

"Now, with your right thumb, pull back the hammer until it locks." It clicked and Vera stiffened. "You're doing great."

Her silence bothered him.

"Let's try this." He moved closer, standing behind her. "Please don't take me wrong. I don't know how else to help."

She nodded again.

He enveloped her frame, arms over arms and hands over hands. Her body relaxed against his. "Okay, I am going to help support you, and when you're ready, fire."

Vera's shoulders rose with a deep breath.

"One, two." Her voice was a breathy whisper. "Three." She pulled the trigger.

Her shoulders spiked, but the rest of her remained rigid.

"Atta girl." His lips touched her earlobe, and his own flamed. "Shoot again when you're ready."

She counted and fired. And then again, four more times, emptying the cylinder.

He smiled. "I'm going to change your name from the Red Canary to the Red Baron." Her soft laughter made his heart soar. "You can relax your arms now. The gun has no more bullets."

Vera dropped her arms freely, her left hand still clutching the .38.

Mick turned her to face him. "You did it." Her lips quivered, and the yearning to press his own against hers was as present as the sun in the sky.

Their eyes met, and a small smile graced her face. She glanced over at the gunnysack filled with holes. "Not too bad, huh?"

"You can't count that. I was holding you." Yes, he had held her. It had been a struggle to let her go. "When I took your hands, I adjusted your aim." Her eyes narrowed, and he laughed. "But you pulled the trigger. That's all I wanted."

"Is that so?" She arched one brow. "Let me try again, then. Without your gorilla arms blocking my vision."

She was back. The challenge in her eyes, the sassiness in her tone, who'd have thought that would be a relief to him? "If you think so." He smiled and withdrew the pouch of bullets from his front pocket. She gave him the gun to reload. With pleasure, Mick filled the cylinder and snapped it in place. He handed her back the pistol.

She looked relaxed. Her body wasn't shaking, and her eyes were focused, not scared. She stretched out her arms, the gun pointing directly at the gunnysack. She glanced over at Mick and smiled before firing six bullets.

"That was a lot easier this round." She stepped beside him and crouched down, brushing her hand over sack's surface and frowning when she saw she'd missed a shot. "Hmm. I'll get 'em all this time."

"Whoa there." Mick grinned at her newfound confidence. "We're all done for today."

"Ya out already?"

"No, I have a few left." He pulled out the pouch and reloaded. "But what kind of cop would I be if I ran out of bullets? Besides, we don't want to be up here too long. I know of a certain birthday girl who needs to visit Mrs. Chambers." Then he'd planned on sitting down with her and discussing the entire case from the beginning. It felt as if a clock sat on his head, counting down until Shultz's deadline. They had to figure this out.

"Lacey." She clasped her hands together. "I almost forgot." Gazing south, she scrunched her nose. "We have to ankle it back down that hill?"

"Yes, but it won't nearly be as hard."

Vera's mouth quirked up. "How about ya give me a piggyback ride?"

Tempting.

"You were gonna carry me into the house the first night we arrived. Can't I cash in now?"

He laughed. "The hill's steep. I might fall, and then you'd have to carry *me*." He returned his gun to the holster. "Might want to fix your rope." He pointed to the loosened knot hanging below the hem of her shirt.

Vera's nose wrinkled, and she gave the ends of the rope a good yank. "I'm so ready to look like a dame again. These threads are eating away at my femininity. Now I understand how Artie's sister feels."

Mick put his hand on her shoulder.

Vera regarded him with a sideways glance. "What? You have the funniest look right now."

"Artie … doesn't have a sister."

"Huh? Yeah, he does." Her eyebrows lowered, bunching the skin between her eyes. "Artie brought her 'round the club."

Notepad. He patted his pocket. *Where is it?* He must have left it on his dresser when he went to change out of his rain-soaked shirt this morning. "What was her name? Can you remember?"

"I think it was Marlene. No, that doesn't sound right." She fingered her cross as she thought, something Mick had noticed she'd done several times since this morning. A sense of satisfaction billowed in his heart. He would have searched all over again and twice as long to see that pleasure ripple in her eyes. "Millie!" Vera snapped her fingers. "Millie Walters. I know that's it. Poor girl always wore clothes two times her size. Cute dame, though. Tough to imagine her as Artie's sister."

"That name wasn't on any reports. The records only said he had two brothers." He motioned with his head. Time to start back. "Is she in Pittsburgh?"

"No, that pottery city on the river. The one in Ohio."

"East Liverpool."

Her mouth curved up in that familiar way he was becoming

attached to. "Yeah, that's it. I think she's a photographer or something."

"Ver, I think we got a lead."

Vera walked alongside him down the hill, every so often her hand brushing his. And Mick said going down the hill was easier? He'd had to catch her arm twice to keep her from tumbling down the hillside like the rocks she'd been kicking up.

"Look, the roof of the cabin," Mick announced. "Almost there."

"I don't see it." Brush and trees. That was all. She held out her hands, letting the ferns tickle her fingertips.

"Right there." Mick stopped and shoved his pointer finger in the air. "See that tree? And before you give me that look, I mean the tree that has leaves growing off the bark."

Vera spotted it and laughed. "It looks like it needs a shave." Mick could use one, too, though she liked his five-o'clock shadow. Gave him a roguish look.

"Now direct those pretty green eyes to the right of it, and you can see the slate of the roof."

"Still not spyin' it." He was definitely making it up. And did he mention pretty eyes? Probably to boost her morale. The only thing that needed a boost was her aching body. "You should've given me that piggyback ride." Then her legs wouldn't feel like warm marmalade. "Do you think—"

Mick's hand covered her mouth, pushing her air back down. He pulled her in close, his lips brushing the spot behind her ear. "Be quiet, Ver. They're here."

CHAPTER 22

Vera swallowed a gasp as Mick helped her to the ground, his head turning as if it were on a swivel.

"Keep down."

"Mick, what are you going to do—"

"You've got to be quiet." He squatted to her level, eyes intense. "Stay here."

She stared at Mick soft-footing away, her breath turning shallow.

His hand went to his holster, and her heart beat wildly.

She saw nothing out of the ordinary, and that raised more alarm. What exactly had Mick seen? Had he spied the thugs, or only heard something? She pulled her knees to her chest and remained motionless, her thoughts scattered like the heap of dry pine needles she sat on.

The silence chilled her. There was no breeze to make the pines whisper. No songs from any winged creature. It was as if the forest held its breath along with her.

Moments stretched until she didn't know how long she'd sat alone.

Had they gotten Mick? Or had he gotten them? The questions hollowed her gut, sending a shiver to her toes. She had to find Mick. Maybe it'd be better if they were together.

Pushing herself, she stood, looking in every direction. She padded in the direction of where he'd gone. After about thirty feet of walking, she found him crouched down, peering through the branches of a pine.

A stick snapped beneath her foot, and Mick spun around.

"I told you to stay there." He must've taken in her anguished face, because his hard eyes softened. "It's dangerous." The cords of his neck bulged as he stared down the hill. "They're armed."

Vera blinked, hoping her dry eyes could interpret what Mick saw. She shifted and spied a silhouette. The blinding sun restricted any clearer inspection, but even from a distance she could discern the man was large. No, enormous. Almost like—

"We need to get out of here." Mick wrapped his hand around her fingers. "I counted at least two. One is in the house."

A fiery spasm rushed down her. The hunt was on, and she was the prey. The form extended his arm toward Mick's car. "What's he—"

Gunfire pierced the sky. Vera clutched Mick's chest, his heart thundering against her palm.

"My tires." A shadow flickered across his face. "Come on." He tugged her elbow, his olive skin ten shades beyond scarlet.

She struggled to keep pace with him.

The sound of glass shattering sliced in her ears. Those thugs destroyed more than the tires. She glanced over her shoulder, and the sight squeezed the air from her lungs. *Angelo!*

She gasped and scrambled back. Her foot rolled on a loose rock, and she fell, sending the chunk of stone into the tree's trunk with a loud smack.

Angelo's head whipped her direction. The sun bounced off his gun, raised and pointed.

"Stay down!" Mick tackled her, and her chin struck a mossy rock embedded in the ground. He stretched himself completely over her. Two shots followed.

Vera, winded from the weight of Mick's body, clenched her eyes closed and whispered a prayer.

"Out of the house!" Angelo bellowed. "They're in the woods."

"He's got to reload, Vera. Hurry." She felt hands on her waist.

Mick hoisted her up to standing.

Her balance was off, the taste of earth and blood bitter in her mouth.

"Follow me." His voice was low and gruff.

She staggered the first few steps but fell in stride. Shouts and curses came from behind, stabbing her ears.

Where were they running? Her legs, already on the verge of cramping, throbbed each time her foot smacked the ground.

"Watch out for mud." Mick jumped over a sludgy spot. "Can't leave tracks."

The ground squished under each step. Hair fell in her eyes. Trying to shake it away only made more curls fall loose. All she needed was to collide into a tree or trip over a rock. She pushed her hand over her forehead to catch all the wisps, smoothing them back in a quick motion.

"It gets steep here." Mick reached for her. "Hold onto me."

Her eyes took in the slope, a thirty-foot descent leading to a narrow canyon. Mick hooked his right arm around her, and she slung her hands around his neck. They trudged down, Mick carrying most of her weight.

"When we reach bottom,"—he adjusted his hold on her and pulled in a strained breath—"sprint up the valley, but be sure to run alongside the cliff wall."

"Up?" Her legs protested with a pulsating ache that spread to her toes.

"The path down meets the road. They'd expect us to do that." His foot skidded on a rock, but he maintained control. "Up the trail is thick brush to limit visibility. We have a better chance of surviving." He released her when the ground leveled. "Okay, Vera, we got two minutes, maybe less, before they can see us." He motioned to the tall overhang, now acting as their earthen buffer. "Make it count." One side of his mouth hitched up. "Race you to the top?"

With that, she dashed off, trying to convince herself it was just a game, but her mind knew better.

After what felt like miles, they paused for a breather at the top of a ridge.

"My feet are goin' to fall off." Vera glanced at Mick, who laced his hands behind his head, extending his torso and getting much-needed air.

Those goons would need to have the noses of bloodhounds to find them. Her hero had navigated them through hills, fields, and one slippery creek, which she had been blessedly carried across. Mick, the Tarzan of the Allegheny Forest. And Vera, the girl who wished she'd consumed something more substantial than donuts for breakfast.

"Thank you for coverin' me from Angelo's shots. You would've taken a bullet for me." For her. Was that instinct? Love? Her already tender muscles shivered with the thought.

"I told you, I'd do whatever it takes to keep you safe." He turned to her, gaze so piercing it made her wonder if she should toss that shield down now or keep struggling to hold it over her heart. "You're worth it."

Okay, now the shield had a gaping hole. *Just chuck it to the ground, Vera, and be done with it.*

"Come on." He held out his hand and assisted her over the trunk of a fallen tree. "I hate to bring this up, but that was Angelo with the revolver. Not Kelly."

"So what are you sayin'?" The same thing that had been spinning in her own mind for the past half hour. Could she have mistaken Angelo's voice for Carson's that night at the club?

"Can you think of a reason why Angelo would kill Cavenhalt?"

"Probably the same as everyone else. He hated him." But that still didn't mean he'd killed him, right?

With brows drawn together, he glanced over. "Was Cavenhalt that bad of a guy?"

Vera swatted a bug. "Artie was a first-rate creep. He bossed you around with a lazy smirk on his face. He'd cuss ya out, even if it was his fault. And you better keep a close eye on your check because he'd chisel and keep it for himself."

"Then why did Kelly keep him on staff?"

"Question of the century." Vera shook her head. "On top of everything, he'd say some of the strangest things."

"Like what?" He ducked under a low branch and then turned his attention to her.

"The night he died, he barged into my dressin' room wanting to know about Carson and me, then out of the blue, he said 'Good thing Betsy got hungry.'"

Mick stopped. "Who's Betsy? Could that be something for the case?"

"The only Betsy I know is the cleaning lady at my old apartment building. I don't think Artie was talking about her."

"Why?"

"She probably never met Artie. And besides that, Betsy left Pittsburgh a while back to live with her family across the state."

"I'll still mention it to the captain."

She shrugged. "Won't do you any good." This was getting ridiculous. "Listen, I'm a singer. I rely on my ear. It's a heightened sense for me." Yes, the rain had been loud against the roof. Yes, there had been a sizable distance between her and the closed office door. But she could distinguish Carson's voice out of a million. Couldn't she? When Angelo had sprayed bullets at her, he'd shot doubt into her judgment. "I need a break." From walking and thinking.

"Good news for you." Mick motioned forward with his head, and her spirit lifted.

"It's the back of Lacey's garage!" She squealed and quickened her pace. Oh, to see her white-haired friend.

Mick brushed past her, leading the way, gaze sweeping the area, obviously back into danger mode. "We need to leave in ten minutes."

Vera's stomach sank.

CHAPTER 23

"What on earth?" Lacey's forehead rippled like the creek, surprise filling her dull blue eyes.

The strong smell of onions and beef smacked Vera in the face, swirling her stomach.

"Are you okay, Mrs. Chambers? Any strange visitors?" Mick bolted the door and then slipped past her and Lacey, his movements guarded as he searched the house. He pulled down the shades and closed curtains.

"No one." Her feeble voice held a twinge of alarm as she watched Mick grab Hewitt's rifle out of the closet. "What's going on?"

"Let Vera explain. I'm calling the captain." He glanced over his shoulder at Vera. "Sit down and rest if you can. Like I said, ten minutes. Sooner if we can."

"Wait, wait, did you walk here? Where's Mick's car?" Lacey's voice was so high it cracked. "What about ten minutes?"

"We're okay, Lace." A chair. A stool. Anything. Vera's legs trembled with exhaustion. "They came and brought their big boy guns." Vera grimaced. Angelo. She now had a full ten minutes to call him every foul name in her vocabulary. Back-stabber was a good one. What a laugh that the fella who used to protect her was the one who'd taken a shot at her. No, two shots.

"Who came? Is that what Mick's calling the captain about?" Lacey's gaze flitted to the kitchen as she wrung her hands on her apron. "Are you sure you're not hurt? Your face is bleeding. Was there shooting?"

Probably should steer clear of Lacey's couch. Maybe she could sit on the wooden chair at the kitchen table. A muscle in her leg twitched. If she could get there. "Yeah, they shot at us, but we're fine."

"Thank you, Jesus." Lacey's eyes watered. "So it was Mr. Kelly?"

"No." Even now, Vera's mind couldn't wrap around it. "It was Angelo. A bouncer from the club."

"So he was the one. Mr. Kelly might be innocent after all."

Vera winced. What if she was wrong? What if Carson didn't have anything to do with Artie's death? She'd accused him of murder. A million thoughts whirled as a cyclone through her exhausted brain, leaving debris of confusion. "I'm not sure anymore. But Mick's car—"

"Vera, sugar, would you mind telling me while we clean you up? I can't stand to see blood on your face."

"I smacked a rock when Mick shoved me to the ground." The reminder provoked a burning sensation on her chin.

Lacy gasped. "Oh, poor dear."

Vera sighed at the sight of the porcelain claw-foot tub. This was one of those fall-asleep-in-the-bathtub kinds of days, but there wasn't time. She'd have to settle for a face- and handwashing.

Lacey turned the faucet on full hot and pulled a washcloth from the closet, then handed it to Vera. "Now, what about all this? Was there more than just the bouncer? Are you wearing Mick's clothes?"

Vera sucked on her bottom lip to keep from frowning. Seeing Lacey was supposed to be a comfort, but the questions Lacey hurled raised her blood pressure. "Mick's car is destroyed. They shot out the tires. Killed the frame."

"His baby!" Lacey put her hand over her mouth. "Is Mick all right? I hardly saw him."

"I don't know." Vera tested the temperature of the water with her fingers. The warmth stung her skin but felt good. "I've never been more exhausted in all my life." She spoke above the water's trickle, while scrubbing hard to get the dirt from underneath her fingernails. "I'm not sure where we're goin'." Or *how* they were going. Mick's car was out of the equation. She flicked the water off her hands into the sink.

Vera glanced at the mirror, the light glinting off her necklace. She ran her thumb over the cross and faced Lacey. "Look. Mick gave this to me for my birthday." Even creepy Angelo and running for her life over mini-mountains couldn't spoil the day. She smiled as a sliver of tranquility glided into her soul and landed on a curl of contentment. "I can wear it now. I said yes to Him."

The hand towel slid out of Lacey's hand, dropping on Vera's foot. "Mick asked you to marry him?"

"What? No, no." Had she given that impression? "Jesus. I said yes to His love for me."

The woman's astonished expression bolstered into excitement. "Oh, Vera!" The older woman pulled her into a tight embrace, surprising Vera with the amount of strength in those slender arms. "My heart is turning somersaults." Lacey pulled away with tear-sheened eyes. "Welcome to the family, love."

Warmth kindled Vera's heart. *Family.* It was nice to belong again.

"I want to hear all about it, darling." Lacey picked up the hand towel and dabbed the corners of her eyes. "Start with the beginning."

"It'll have to wait for another time." Mick's voice floated in from the hallway. "We have to leave. Pack up, Mrs. Chambers—you're coming with us."

Lacey's eyes widened and mouth parted simultaneously. "No, honey. I'm not leaving my home." She took a step back into the hall so she could see Mick.

No way Vera was missing this. She squeezed behind Lacey to get a good view.

Mick's countenance was serious, and Vera noticed a scrape by his right eye. "Mrs. Chambers, if they could find your brother's place, they can find this one. I'm not having you in danger."

"God protects me." She lightly hit his shoulder with her hand towel. "Besides, Vera is your responsibility, not me."

"You are the captain's sister." Mick draped an arm around her small shoulder. Ah, going for the affectionate approach. Wise move. "Which makes you my responsibility."

"No."

"Yes." Mick removed his arm only to fold it with the other across his chest. "I'm already uncomfortable with the amount of time we're wasting here. I have great respect for you, Mrs. Chambers, but if I have to carry you out, I will."

Vera believed him. Sergeant Mean Eye showed no mercy.

"All right, Mick." Lacey waved the towel in surrender. "Have it your way."

"Thank you."

"Though I am not going with you. Three's a crowd, if you ask me."

Mick breathed hard. "Mrs. Chambers, I've had a rough day. I'm not—"

"I know, darlin', my heart hurts about your Lincoln. But I am talking about Doris. I'll stay with her. She's been asking me for a visit."

His brows pulled and then relaxed. "Doris from church?"

"Yes. She's moved over a couple towns over. Can't make it to church as often. So last time she invited me to stay with her and—"

"Fine. Stay with Doris, but get moving. Please." The *please* was definitely forced, and Mick's eyes held no apology for interrupting the older woman. "Finish cleaning up, Ver."

Vera couldn't allow the uncertainties to linger in her mind any longer. She waved Mick to come closer. His features were controlled, but she could hear his heavy breathing even from several feet away. He nodded and approached her.

Lacey scooted to her bedroom, mumbling something about

having to take Mitzi.

"Mick, we don't have a way to get anywhere if Lacey's goin' to her friend's house." You'd think the cop would have thought of that first. Yowser. "Your car is—"

"We're takin' Hewitt's truck."

Oh no. The jalopy.

"We'll have to stop a lot." He popped a shoulder against the wall, fatigue lining his eyes. "Got to make sure it doesn't get overheated. I'll fill some jugs with water for the radiator. Fill up some extra gasoline—"

"Do you think it can make it?"

"You doubt my mechanical abilities?" Mick raised an eyebrow with a tilt of a smile, his voice low, gruff, and way too dreamy.

"I'm learnin' not to doubt you." Her mind lingered on his actions back on that muddy hill. He'd have died saving her. Every cell in her body seemed to tingle. *Don't cry. Do not cry.*

"So ... you trust me?" A slice of the strain he'd been carrying scraped away from his voice.

"Yeah." She stepped closer to him, as if by an invisible pull. Could his eyes get any greener? Or clearer? "I trust you."

Mick leaned in close to her ear, smelling like sweat, dirt, and a hint of musk. "Good." The way he whispered that word. Mercy. "Because we're going to have to do something uncomfortable for us both."

CHAPTER 24

Mick pressed the gas, allowing minimal space between the truck and Mrs. Chambers' car. His gaze flickered between the road and the surrounding areas. How had Angelo Vinelli discovered them? If they weren't safe hidden in the middle of nowhere, then no shelter would be out of harm's way. Tension's iron fist squeezed Mick's heart. What if he couldn't protect Vera? Hadn't he promised her she'd be safe with him? He ground his teeth.

One consolation was Hewitt's hunting rifle resting snugly beside him. He dared them to try anything now. He could pick off those bozos one by one with shells to spare.

Lord, help me. Only the power of God could calm his rage. It blazed strong when he thought of Vera's scraped face and ruined birthday. Then there was his car. He sighed. It was just a possession. A thing. Vera was still breathing. He was still breathing. Life held value, not things.

"It stinks down here."

"Lay low for a little while longer." He patted her back and raised his voice over the rattling floorboards.

Vera was being a good sport, curled up on the floor between the truck's bench and dash.

"The main road is about five miles away. So far, so good." He pumped the brake, not wanting to smack into Mrs. Chambers' bumper. Hopefully, he'd made the right decision in letting her lead the way. If she followed Mick and those henchmen crept up on her, it would be easy for them to take a shot at her. But then, what if they set up a blockade? Mick adjusted the side mirror, the steering wheel shaking with only one grip on it. "You're doing great, Ver."

"Easy for you to say. You disguise yourself in Hewitt's goofy straw hat while I'm stuck down here smelling stinky air."

"It'll be over soon."

She harrumphed.

He thudded his thumbs against the steering wheel, eyes alert for anything out of place. For all he knew, those men could be waiting by the main road, ready to fire at whatever came their way. Vinelli seemed trigger-happy. He downshifted over a rough spot in the road.

"Can ya cool it on the bumps? I think my stomach rolled into my toes."

"Sorry. Not much I can do. Almost there, though." Two miles to go. The golden sun blazed through the windshield, challenging his vision. He glanced over his shoulder. Good, no one following.

The town's main road crept into sight. His breaths deepened. "You can get up if you want." Mick motioned with his head. "Might want to wave to Mrs. Chambers. We're parting ways here."

"Would if I could, but I'm stuffed in here." Her voice was muffled. "Like a human jack-in-the-box."

"I'll pull over when I get a chance." Mick held his hand out the window and waved to Mrs. Chambers. The lady wiggled her fingers in return, and he said a quick prayer for her safety.

He pulled down a side road, spotted with only a few houses and a dingy barn. "Okay, Ver, one more bump. Brace yourself."

The tires tumbled over dirt clumps and grass patches, and she groaned. He stopped the truck and jumped out his door to open Vera's. He was met … with her backside. His fingertips skimmed his jawline as he admired the view, wondering how she had squeezed in there to begin with. "You're going to have to turn around somehow."

"Genius," Vera huffed. "And just how's that gonna happen?"

She wiggled, getting nowhere. "Maybe … if I … no, that hurts."

"Push yourself up with your hands and then turn."

"Are you laughing?"

"Yes." Any man would.

She twisted halfway, head angled down in an unnatural way, chin tucked into her chest.

"You almost have it. Now." *Man alive*. He reached in and tugged down the hem of her skirt.

Vera popped her head up, smacking it off the bottom of the dash. "Ow!" She worked her hand free to rub her crown. "Hey, what's the idea?"

"Your skirt was hiked." His skin warmed, the sight of her full leg playing like a nickelodeon in his head. He missed the trousers from earlier. The dress and stockings she'd left hanging on Mrs. Chambers' line yesterday was now Vera's only set of clothes. But at least they were fresh and clean, unlike Mick's. He hadn't borrowed anything from Hewitt's closet because while the man had been tall, he'd been more on the lanky side.

"Here." Vera wagged her hand in the air. "Grab and pull."

Mick crawled in the door and wrapped his hands around her, hauling her out like a sack of potatoes. Her feet touched the ground, but Mick hung on to her a second more.

"Sheesh. I hope I don't have to do that again." Vera evened her stance and smoothed out her clothes. "Are we clear of those goons?"

"Hopefully." And hopefully he could expel from his head the picture of her upper thigh and the way the seam of her stockings roamed up the curve of her toned, long leg. First the nightgown and now this.

I'm trying, Lord.

It was going to be a long drive. Which reminded him. "Got to check the radiator." He walked around the front, thankful for the turn in his thoughts. His job was to protect this woman, not gawk at her as though she was a calendar girl. He unscrewed the radiator cap and read the thermometer, checking the temperature of the water vapor. He nodded at the results. Perfect. Hewitt's truck was holding up beautifully. "Looking good so far. Going to stop at the closest filling station and fill the gas containers."

"No prob." She climbed into her seat. "If it's all the same to you, I'll be snoozin' the whole way." Then she looked at him, head tilted and face thoughtful. "I just realized, I have no idea where we're heading. Back to Pittsburgh?"

"No, East Liverpool." He shut her door and leaned in the open window. "And you can't sleep the whole way. You have to come with me inside the filling station."

"No can do." She folded her arms and tipped her nose heavenward. "My makeup is in my bag … which is at the Boone cabin. You dressed me up like a man, and now I look like one."

Hardly.

"Look at me, Mick. Just look."

With pleasure.

She pulled up a chunk of hair, exposing her scar. "If this wasn't hideous enough, I have a bloodied-up chin." Her gaze shifted to the warped mirrors of the Model A. "Which is now turning purple." She pressed a finger on it and winced.

"Lift your head a little." When she did, he ran his thumb over the wound. "Does this hurt?" He applied minimal pressure, watching her reaction.

"Just burns."

"How about here?" He pushed on the flesh under her jaw, her skin warm and supple.

"No." She pulled her head back, staring into his eyes. "What's with the examination?"

"I wanted to be sure nothing was fractured." He tipped his straw hat, and Vera released a soft laugh. He knew he looked somewhat ridiculous in Hewitt's hat, but he'd wear a sombrero if it made Vera smile that way. "I'm sorry about your bag, Ver. We'll get you makeup at the first store we get to."

"Will you shake on it?" Vera slid her hand out the window, her slender fingers straight and stiff.

As their hands connected, so did their eyes, and her stare held more to it than just a silly deal. Was she falling for him? The thought made him break eye contact and release her hand. "I'll keep my promise. Though we probably won't be able to get it until tomorrow. Haven't yet seen a filling station with a cosmetic shelf."

Her lower lip protruded.

"Until then, how about this? I'll let you know if you have food in your teeth or something hanging from your nose. Deal?"

"No deal." She swatted his arm. "For goodness' sake."

Mick laughed, pulling himself away from her window and straightening tall. He was relaxed, and it bothered him. He had to stay at high alert. "Let's go." A lightning bug flew past, reminding him of the wasting daylight. The closest filling station was a good twenty miles away. He jogged around the car and settled in the driver's seat next to her. "But so you know, from now on, everywhere I go, you go. I'm not letting you out of my sight."

"This should make for some interesting powder room trips." Her lip curled up in a way he found adorable.

"I'll wait for you by the door for those excursions." Why did she fascinate him so much? Her laugh. Her touch. The way she brushed her hair away from her forehead.

Let it go, Ace.

She trusted him. Words from her own pretty mouth had clutched his heart so fierce, it was a struggle not to clutch her. Doggone. Why was he so attached to this woman? It couldn't be love. He'd only known her two weeks. Two weeks. When he'd fallen in love with Phyllis, he'd known her for years. He turned on the truck, and the noise of the engine wasn't loud enough to his overpower his thoughts.

No. He had a plan. A plan he intended to stick to. She'd given him her trust. He couldn't be foolish with it.

CHAPTER 25

"I am going to introduce you as my wife."

Vera jerked her head, instantly regretting the quick motion. She pushed her palm on the burning cramp pulsing in her neck. Rotten truck. Getting comfortable in this jalopy was just as challenging as holding her bladder over the bumpy roads. With the door making a lousy headrest, she'd fallen asleep on Mick's shoulder. "Your wife?" Her heart rate quickened. "Why?" She looked out her window at the black sky, yawning. "Where are we? East Liverpool?"

"Uh-huh. You said you trusted me, right?"

"Yeah."

"I told you I'm not letting you out of my sight. We're at the motel, and we're sharing a room."

"What?" Was that what he'd meant earlier when he'd said they'd have to do something uncomfortable? He could have expounded a bit more. That would've given her time to process. But in the darkness, with her half-asleep brain, the translation got muddled. "All right, let me make sense of this. You're concerned about my safety. Okay, understood. We're sharin' a motel room. Sounds strange comin' outta my mouth, but I get that too. The wife thing. Not gettin'?" She couldn't see the details of Mick's face, just his outline.

"We can't use our real names. Captain's orders." His large hand covered hers. "I got cash. And when I sign in, I'm going to use fake names. And I think it sounds better and respectable to have you as my wife."

Twenty-two years old and playing house. "Can I pick my own name?"

He chuckled low. "If you want to."

"Would ya let me pick yours too?" Oh, now this was getting fun.

"Sure." He pulled his hand away just as she was getting used to it. "It's late. I should go ring the bell. What did you have in mind?"

"Okay, then, how about you be Raymond?"

"Raymond? That sounds fine."

"I'll be Tessa. I always loved that name." She smiled, resisting the urge to nuzzle into his shoulder. "You can pick our last name, Ray. But don't use Smith. Dead giveaway."

"Let's see. How about we be Mr. and Mrs. Girard?" He slipped his arm around her and gave her shoulder a friendly squeeze. "My high school football coach's last name, my dear Tessa."

She tilted her head back on his arm and looked into his face. "Sounds swell." And if he didn't move soon, she'd melt into his arm. It was terrifyingly comfortable, and the way his thumb stroked her sleeve gave her an appetite for more of his touch.

He gave her a reprieve by withdrawing his contact and rummaging his pockets. "Here, slip this on." He dropped something small and circular into her palm.

"A ring? Where'd you get this?"

"Mrs. Chambers. I asked to borrow it, but she said you can have it. It's not real."

"Oh."

"I thought that would make things more believable."

"Sure." She shoved the metal on her left ring finger. "A fake ring for a fake marriage." It only made sense. She leaned back, and her neck met something lumpy. Mick's arm again. This could get dangerous. Especially this time, when his torso was closer, touching her side ever so slightly. "Mick?"

"Yeah." His masculine drawl engaged every one of her senses. The dark clouds joined in the intrigue, pulling away from the moon, allowing a milky glow to pour into his window which highlighted the angles of his face. She wasn't sure if it was his presence, the emotion of the day, or the ambiance of the summer night that caused her hand to stretch over, but she didn't have the strength to restrain it. Just one touch. Her fingertips swept over his face, starting at his temple and slowly wandering to his jaw, the curve of his perfect lip just above her index finger.

He dipped his head closer to hers, not breaking the touch. "Ver." Said on a sigh, but it thundered with hunger. Everything she felt. His arm collapsed around her, pulling her closer to him.

She slid her eyes shut and waited for his lips to claim hers. A few hot breaths and she was still waiting.

Mick kissed her forehead, the pressure of his lips lingering for only a second. "We should probably go in." He withdrew his arm, his touch, his interest.

Vera released the air her lungs held hostage.

"They're probably waiting for us." Mick picked up that dumb straw hat he'd shed hours ago and plopped it on his head.

Mick Dinelo, the man of steel emotions, possessing the superpower of phenomenal resistance.

They wandered the uneven walk until he found seventeen. "Here we are." He jingled the key the motel manager had given him.

"Yuck." Vera swatted her hand in a frenzy. "There are bugs everywhere."

He pointed to the dim light above the door. "When the light's on, the bugs come."

"Now you're sounding like Grimby." She slid behind him, using him as a bug-shield. "Wonder how he's doing."

"Who's that?" He put the key in the lock. It stuck, so he jostled the door knob when he turned it.

"Ah, just an old hobo I'd see around town. Poor guy. He'd say the same things over and over again. What you said reminded me of something he'd say all the time. 'When the light's on, the boats come.'"

"What does that mean?" He pushed the door and motioned for her to enter first.

"Don't know. Could be anything."

Stale cigarette smoke assailed them on the threshold.

"Whew. It smells like Sunday morning at the club." Vera pinched her nose and wagged her hand.

He turned on the lamp.

"There's only one bed, buster." She made a grand gesture with her arm toward the room's centerpiece—a queen bed. "What are we going to do, Micky? Arm wrestle for it?" Grinning, she made a muscle pose. "Loser gets the bathtub." She threw a thumb in the direction of the bathroom.

Ah, Vera. How far she had come. He relived the night he almost had his teeth knocked out by her handbag after pulling into the Pigeon Loft Motel. Her words, even now, jolted his thoughts. *I've been around dogs long enough to know what kind of meat they like.* Her statement screamed the truth. Those men weren't men, only animals. "There's no bathtub. Just a shower."

"Stakes are higher, then."

"No arm wrestling. That's yours." He motioned with his head to the steel-framed bed. "Floor's mine."

She looked down and grimaced. "Ew. You can't sleep there. It's disgusting."

"I've slept in worse conditions." Littered cement pads on a stakeout, dusty wood floors when helping his parents move, and out in the open air during one of his stays at the cabin. "Besides, Ray wouldn't treat Tessa any other way."

Her mouth spread into a warm and inviting smile, as if her lips were entreating his.

What if that ring was real? What if instead of being Mrs. Girard, she was Mrs. Dinelo? Only last week, he'd pictured her growing horns and breathing fire, and now she was wearing white and saying *I do*. Imagination was a fickle comrade. "I might borrow a pillow. If you have an extra."

"You can have them both. Don't use pillows." She reached over and plucked them from the head of the bed. "Ready? I'm gonna launch 'em."

Mick held out his arms. "Hit me." One white blob flew through the air. Then another.

"Guess this is what ya get for a dollar-fifty a night." Vera stuffed her hands on her hips and surveyed the room, clucking her tongue with every turn of her head. "Compared to this, Mick, your cabin is the Waldorf Astoria."

"Been there once."

Vera whipped around and looked at him as if he'd just told her he vacationed on Mars. "You've been to New York?"

"Mm-hhm. My cousin lives there. I visited him once. It's a fancy place."

"I'd like to go there." Her starry-eyed expression pulled him in. "Anyways, I'm beat. Who'd have thought turning twenty-two would be so difficult?"

"You held your own today." Not to mention his heart at times.

She pulled the ribbon from her hair, and crimson locks cascaded just above her shoulders.

Come on, Ver, show a man some mercy. His eyes put up a fight, but he wrestled his gaze away from the beautiful woman and onto the pale face of his watch. "You have fifteen more minutes of birthday bliss. Spend it wisely."

"Because every girl deserves a present on her birthday." She repeated his note in a tone of voice that put a chokehold on his heart. "Ya know, that was one of the nicest things anyone has ..." She stopped.

Was it because she was happy? Unhappy? "Done for you?" The look on her face made him want to gather all her dreams in life and present them to her on a golden platter. Truth was, she was going to have to return to reality. Find a new residence. Go back to work. Would she go back to singing at a speakeasy? He inwardly winced. Her heart was changed, but that existence was how she survived. All she knew. He put a fist in the pillow, loosening the clumps of imitation goose feathers and releasing frustration. They didn't need to address the future. Not yet. Let her enjoy her last minutes. "Happy birthday, Ver."

"Thank you, Mick."

"Now, you need to rest. Got a big day tomorrow."

"Artie's sister?" She folded down the covers, her face skeptical as if she could encounter a critter at any time. "I don't need this thing." She pointed to the bulky quilt. "It's too hot. Ya want it? Might make the floor softer."

"Sure. I'll take it." He pulled it from the bed's bottom. "And yes, Artie's sister. Got to call the captain in the morning for her information and address. G'night, Ver."

"'Night." She tugged the sheet under her chin. He could see the dark fabric of her day dress through the thin cotton sheet. Tomorrow he would buy her a change of clothes with her makeup. Shoot, he'd buy her anything she wanted. If he only had a few days more with her, then he was going to spoil her.

"I'll get the lamp."

He dragged the blanket over to the spot in front of the door where he'd tossed the pillows. His gun was beside him, within arm's reach. He pulled his New Testament from his pocket.

Vera had been still for the past five minutes or so. He checked the door to make sure it was bolted. He walked to the window by the desk. It was shut and locked. Everything looked secure. He reached under the lampshade to click off the light but not before stealing a glance at Vera.

Wisps of hair fell across her face. Her lips, which took every ounce of his strength to keep away from, were now relaxed and parted. Lips that, tonight, almost pulled him into a kiss. As much as he wanted to taste, to explore, he wanted to do what was right. And to kiss her would've been wrong. For more reasons than his tired brain could count.

He stole another glance at her. Man, she was beautiful. Now she had a beautiful heart to match. With that, he shut off the lamp and found his spot on the floor. All other emotions aside, his heart overflowed with awe and gratitude. Gratitude for the saving grace that still flowed from nail-scarred hands.

CHAPTER 26

"You weren't foolin' about following me." Vera pulled the diner's powder room door closed as she exited and looked at Mick, leaning against the wall, anchoring his hands in his pockets.

"I told you I'm not leaving you alone. Anywhere." He stood straight and scratched a jawline darkened with stubble. This morning, she'd missed her toothbrush, but she'd bet all the nickel tips ever thrown at her that Mick had missed his razor.

They walked into the dining room, and Vera resisted the urge to slap one hand over her scar and the other over her chin. She instead focused on the inviting atmosphere. Natural daylight streamed into the bright-colored space, contrasting the dark, shabby motel they'd just left ten minutes ago. The aroma of coffee and bacon wafted to her nose. Long-legged men were stuffed into booths, their fedoras bobbing over opened newspapers. The corner housed a table of women, leaning over steamy mugs, competing to see who could talk the longest without taking a breath.

"I wonder if their coffee is fresh." They'd only entered this diner to use the payphone, but her stomach begged for any sort of nourishment.

"Let's grab a quick bite." Despite Mick's welcome words, his eyes had a faraway look, and his mannerisms were rigid. He wasn't nervous, was he?

Vera pulled her chair out and sat, the chill of the metal carrying through her dress. "What did the captain say?"

Her attempts to angle close by Mick's side during the phone conversation had revealed her eavesdropping skills could stand improvement.

He picked up the menu from the stand in the center of the table. "Her name is Camille Walters. She's not Artie's sister. Not by records, anyway." He shrugged but didn't pull his eyes away from the grease-stained paper.

"Art-man introduced her that way to me. I'm sure of it." And she was sure those donuts in the glass case by the register didn't stand a chance. "So what about her?"

Mick motioned for the waitress. She gave the *be with ya in a second* wave. "They had trouble locating her. I have an address." He patted his pocket. "But it's a gamble."

The fifty-something female approached them. "Welcome to Chuck's Cafe. My name's Alice." She rambled this information off in a lethargic manner. "What'll it be for you two?" Pulling a notepad and pen from a pouch in her apron, she turned her amber eyes to Vera.

Vera returned her menu. "Coffee and a donut."

Alice scribbled it down and didn't look up.

Vera glanced down at her ring, still nestled below her knuckle. Were they still pretending the marriage stuff? How could she forget to ask? She had been too occupied this a.m. with trying to look socially acceptable. No brush, combs, or hairpins meant a lot of finger fussing and splashing of water to tame wayward curls.

"I'll take scrambled eggs and a side of bacon."

"To drink?"

"Juice, if you got it." He stuffed the menu back in the wire stand and looked up at her. "That should be all. Thank you."

Alice spared a quick nod, then hustled off as quickly as she'd come.

Mick relaxed against his seat, his gaze casually sweeping the area before settling on her. "Did Artie mention anything about where Camille lived? In a house? Apartment, anything?"

"No, I don't think so. Artie and I weren't the best of friends."

"I'm not sure what we're going to find. We might not discover anything at all." His eyes flooded with uncertainty.

Where was her confident sergeant?

"As I said, it's a gamble. A long shot."

She rested a hand on his, like the many times he'd done for her over the past week. "Then we'll take the gamble together." Okay, maybe a little forward, but the dimpled smile came in full view.

"I don't want it any other way, Ver."

Holy smokes. He had to stop looking at her like that. His gaze seemed to stretch beyond the surface. She wasn't sure how to respond to such a gesture, but the warmth extending to her toes seemed to say it wasn't so bad.

"Here you go." The waitress returned with the grub, which could've broken the moment between them if Mick hadn't aimed his smirk at Vera for a direct hit to her heart.

The waitress set Mick's food on the table and then Vera's.

Yum. Her stomach sang an ode to coffee and fried pastries.

"Here are some cream and sugar." Alice looked to Vera's hand still on Mick's, and her expression softened, the taut lines in her face relaxing. "Nice to see young people in love. Refreshes this old heart of mine." She eyed Vera's ring. "So how long have you been married?" This question was directed to Mick.

Vera pulled her hand away and worked on fixing her coffee with two sugars and a whole lot of cream.

"How long? Seems like only yesterday." Mick smiled, his eyes downright rascally.

Vera's talent for improvising was rubbing off on the man.

Alice wagged her pen at Vera. "I think you found yourself a keeper."

He grinned. "No, I did." Oh dear, there was that mischievous eye again. "Did you ever see anyone so gorgeous, Alice?"

Vera pulled her lips tight and prayed coffee wouldn't come out her nose. She hid behind her mug and refused to look at the adorable grin lighting his face.

"Now I know he's a keeper." Alice put the ticket face-down on the table and looked at Vera, smiling widely. "Hang onto him, honey." She shuffled off, the scent of roses and talc powder going with her.

Mick wielded his fork like a dagger and stabbed his eggs. It was just like him to throw a remark out there and then go back to business as usual.

"You satisfied with yourself?" She spread her napkin over her lap.

He gave her the *who me* look.

Vera narrowed her eyes. *Yes, you.*

"Just enjoying the silence." He dabbed the corners of his mouth with his napkin. "I discovered something worthwhile."

Whew. And so had she. Staring at Mick while drinking a blissful cup of coffee was a beautiful pastime indeed. "Yeah, what is it?"

"I discovered if I want a moment of silence from you, then all I have to do is call you beautiful."

"So you didn't mean it. Lying to Alice like that. Tsk. Tsk."

"No, I meant it, gorgeous."

Man, oh, man. The guy was flirting—and brutally good at it. So how could she control a heart melting faster than the lump of sugar in her coffee? His eyes, his smile, the way he kept finding avenues to be close, all of it working together to make Sergeant Swoon-face more endearing to her.

"See? Tongue-tied. Point made."

And then he said that.

His eyes sported a note of victory. Maybe her foot could knock it off key.

"Playing footsy with me?"

"I was crossin' my ankles. Could I help it if your shin got in the way?"

"Crossing your ankles while bruising mine." He took a sip of his juice and winked at her from over the glass.

Heart, you have my permission to head for the hills. Somehow, over the past couple weeks, Mick Dinelo had gained entrance into her heart, unlocking portals to her soul that she never knew existed. The waitress' words resurfaced. *Hang onto him, honey.* Mick was everything whimper-worthy, all in a delicious, six-foot-two package. If she saw it, and Alice, a total stranger, saw it, then how come some doll hadn't dug her claws into him ages ago? There was a mystery behind the man across the table from her. And she was determined to find out.

CHAPTER 27

Crem's Hardware. Mick stared as if a house would magically appear in its place. Yet this was the address the captain had given. He glowered at his scrawl.

32 W. Park Ave.

The paper matched the numbers on the window front. But … a hardware store? A garbage-strewn alley and a barbershop bookended the place. Frustration clouded his mind. Why couldn't he get a break? Just once.

"There's somethin'." Vera pointed down the alley. Beyond the stack of broken wooden boxes was a door.

"Just a side entrance to the hardware store."

She cut him a look.

He quickly amended his response. "But let's check it out."

Vera stepped ahead, and Mick refrained from pulling her back to keep her alongside him. Ever since Angelo took those shots at her, Mick's desire to protect her bordered on obsession. He slid his hand over the leather holster. He couldn't fail. For her sake as well as his own.

"Uh-huh. Just what I thought." She paused and tilted her head back, a flat hand over her brow, shielding her eyes from the sun. "Twelve o'clock, Micky."

Mick's gaze went straight up, and with it came the corners of his mouth.

"Those are frilly curtains in the window." An *I was right*

demeanor plastered her face. "I've never seen a hardware store garbed in lace."

Vera led the way, stepping over broken bottles and rumpled newspapers. Mick kept two steps behind. Not smothering, but close.

"An apartment over the store." The mail tag on the door read *Camille Walters Photography.* Hope gathered in his chest. "You found it."

"There's no bell." Vera frowned at the weathered door. Peeling paint exposed slits of the dark wood underneath.

"Then let's give 'er a good pounding." Mick flashed her a smile and rapped hard on the rotted entrance. He stepped back and sought her gaze. "Ready?"

"Yeah, but I don't know if she'll remember me."

"I have no doubt she will." Mick's eyes glistened in the sunlight like glossy green stones. "You're unforgettable."

Vera rewarded his words with a smile. Noticing something amiss, she reached over and turned down the flipped-up collar of Mick's jacket. The backs of her thumbs brushed his neck and stubbled jaw. Her hands trailed down, smoothing the wrinkles on his broad shoulders.

His lips twitched. "Thank you."

The deadbolt unlatched, pulling Vera's attention from Mick and his charm.

Millie's expression shifted from confusion to a smile. "Miss Pembroke. How are you?" The gentle breeze didn't disturb her blonde hair, pinned neatly in an up-do, but did ripple the faded fabric of her dress.

"Hello, Millie. Please call me Vera. This is—"

"Mick Dinelo." He stuck his hand to greet her, but his greeting was stiff.

What was he doing? He didn't say *Sergeant* or flash his badge.

Did he not want Millie to know he was a policeman? Confusion pinched her as she watched their exchange. Maybe she should take it like a dance and let the man lead.

"Nice to meet you." Millie folded her hands in front of her, a nervousness marking her expression.

Vera could relate. Mick's hulking presence did that to a woman.

"Just about out the door to run some errands." Millie gave a weak smile. The dark circles under her blue eyes aged her, but she couldn't be more than mid-thirties. "I can't afford to turn down business, though. That's why you're here, right? For pictures?" She opened the door wider to allow them to squeeze through. A small laugh riddled the air. "That Artie, he's such a great brother. He promised to send clients my way, but ya really didn't have to come all the way from Pittsburgh. Hope he didn't praise my work too high."

She doesn't know. Vera shot Mick a wary look.

"It'll be all right. I'll handle it." His low whisper seemed troubled. He put his hand on her back as she walked up the stairs. The dull wood creaked under her shoes. Vera took one look at the dilapidated railing, which seemed it would snap into splinters with any weight on it, and clung to Mick's arm.

"Who is it, Mama?" A little girl popped up from behind a wingback chair, her blonde hair like her mother's but in braids tied with ribbons.

Millie planted two fists on her hips. "Abigail Walters, you better not be standing on the furniture."

The small form dipped out of sight.

"That's my daughter. Mischievous as ever." Millie adopted a wearied look, but amusement lit her eyes. "Abby, come here, baby."

Abigail skipped to her mother, her shoes smacking against the wood planks. Vera's gaze skimmed the bare floors. No area rugs. Even with an apartment the size of a piccolo case, the poor woman didn't have the means to fill it.

Seconds later, blue eyes peeked around Millie's flowing dress covered in rosebuds, and Vera smiled.

A hand took hers. Mick's. His posture was rigid, and the twinkle in his eyes deadened. No doubt this task ahead wasn't going to be a barrel of laughs, but Mick was a policeman. Shouldn't he be used to this? Then again, how could one become immune to news of death?

"Would you care to sit down?" The cheery grin on Millie's face showed she had no idea of their struggles.

Mick led Vera to a small sofa that was adjacent to the wingback chair. Vera sat, noticing several patch jobs done to the cushion.

"What kind of event are we celebrating? Engagement?" She glanced at Vera's hand. "Oh. Are you married already? I can never tell by the ring anymore." Her conversational tone increased Vera's uneasiness.

How long was Mick going to let his go on?

"Don't count me forward, Miss Pembroke, but you are a photographer's dream. Your features are so defined." Her buoyant smile fell when her gaze hit Vera's scabbed chin. "What happened?"

"I fell." Vera wondered if her tone was strained. She ran her fingers along the corded trim of the armrest. At least her hair covered her scar.

"I see." Millie's mouth tipped up into another warm smile. "Nothing a little powder won't fix." She scampered about the small living area, picking up things from the floor. Abigail's sweater. A wooden puzzle piece. A dish towel. "Sorry 'bout the mess. Wasn't expecting company." She set the items on the table behind the couch.

Mick shifted beside her. Vera could tell by his expression that a plan was forming behind those green eyes. To her heart's relief, he was not Sergeant Mean Eye, but a sympathetic soul.

"Miss Walters, we're not here to have our portrait taken." He withdrew his badge from his trouser pocket and held it out for her to see.

Millie's jaw slackened and her eyes rounded.

"I'm a sergeant with the city of Pittsburgh." He paused. "I regret I have information that you need to hear. It's—"

"Hold on, Mick." Vera stood, her legs trembling. "Millie, can I take Abigail into another room?" If she could get there. The anticipation of the impending conversation shook her heart harder than Hewitt's truck over gravel.

"Yes. Yes, certainly." Her voice tensed, and her chipper attitude fizzled out like a wet firecracker. "Abigail, take Miss Pembroke to the bedroom."

"Why, Mama?"

Millie didn't respond.

Couldn't they have done this differently? Vera bent to the girl's level and smiled. "Abigail, do you have any toys we could play with?"

"I have a dolly, but she's napping."

"Aw, well, it's almost lunch time, so don't you think you should wake her? I'd like to meet her."

Five tiny fingers curled around Vera's hand.

Dread wrapped its knuckles around Mick's heart and squeezed. "Would you care to sit first?" Despite the warm apartment, a cold spasm shot through him. He focused on Millie's face, forbidding his gaze to catch the rosebuds scattered all over her dress

Flowers. Just flowers.

Why did such a trivial thing awaken the oppressive monster? Mick tried to shove it back into the feeble cage of his mind, but the beast had outgrown it, feeding on the trail of fear leading to Mick's past.

The impending conversation involved a murder. Artie's, not Phyllis'. Mick had to detach himself from the swelling pain and focus on the present. His fingernails pressed into his clammy palm.

"Is this about Artie? Did he get in trouble?" Millie sank into the wingback chair. "He did something when he was drunk, didn't he? I don't … I don't have any money to bail him." She raised her palm to her forehead and slowly pulled it down to her cheek. "I have nothing."

"Vera said that you were Artie's sister." He shifted in his seat and sorted through his tangled mind, grappling to present routine questions. "Has anyone from the Cavenhalt family contacted you?"

"No. Not a word. But that doesn't mean anything." A weak smile hung below her worried eyes. "You see, I'm not his real sister. Not by blood. Not by marriage either." She fussed with the lace on the throw pillow beside her and released an embarrassed laugh. "His mother and my father weren't conventional about things."

Mick nodded. A polite way of saying they lived together. He'd figured as much.

"Artie was the only one who was kind to me. We kept in contact after our parents split." Her fingers abandoned their stranglehold on the pillow and pressed against her temple. "Sergeant, this is tearing me up. What did Artie do?"

Mick swallowed. Words he'd spoken countless times over the years now lodged in his throat—as if saying them would poke the beast, even though Mick seemed to have wrestled it into submission for the moment. Focus. On the present. "Artie was fatally shot."

The color drained from her cheeks.

"I'm sorry."

Millie buried her face in her palms. "Not Artie." She remained motionless for a moment, then sorrow took hold in silent sobs.

Mick lowered his head and gave the woman time to collect herself. He was glad Vera had taken the girl into the other room, but for some reason, he wished Vera by his side. When he'd grabbed her hand earlier, a tangible strength had roiled through him.

"Who did it?" Mille's raspy voice broke through the silence. "Why would anyone do this?"

"It's under investigation. Are you okay to answer questions, or would you like us to return later?"

"I don't think I can help." Millie's hands fell limp to her side. "That is … I don't really know. It's just so … I can't believe it."

"Do you know of anybody capable of this? Workers? Family? Did Mr. Cavenhalt relay anything to you?" Mick withdrew a notepad and awaited her response.

Her bottom lip quivered. "Can I ask when this happened?"

"About two weeks ago. May twenty-seventh. It happened early in the morning at the Kelly Club." He sounded like a newspaper clipping, for land's sake. Yet that was all the emotion he could permit. He trod carefully on the edges of his own sanity, so keeping hardened to this moment meant retaining a logical mind. "Artie's death was quick. The coroner said he had no suffering."

Her blue eyes pooled with fresh tears. "Nobody told me. I missed the funeral. Everything." Her pale fingers wrung the skirt of her dress, distorting those blamed flowers until the fabric hung in fixed creases.

Mick slid his eyes closed for a long blink. Just flowers.

"I can't believe it. I just can't believe George didn't call. Robert. No one."

"Understand your shock, ma'am."

"I don't know." She sniffled. "I don't know anyone who would do that to Art. He never said anything to me. Not one word."

"When was the last time you saw Mr. Cavenhalt?"

"Last month." Her brows pinched, then relaxed over widened brown eyes. "He needed to borrow my typewriter."

Mick leaned forward, detecting the shift in her expression. "Was that peculiar? Did he always borrow your typewriter?"

"No. That was the first time." She hooked a finger on her small chin. "But the strange thing was, after he typed the letter he replaced the ribbon. I know there was a lot of use left on it."

Mick flipped to a fresh page in his notepad and jotted that down. "What did he type? Did you happen to see?"

"He acted strange about it. Said it was a letter. But it must've been important because the next morning he left very early and returned after lunch. I found a bus ticket to Steubenville in the wastebasket."

Steubenville.

"Thank you, Miss Walters. We won't take up any more of your time."

Another tear slid from her face. She needed time to mourn. And he needed a moment to think.

"Abigail, have you ever had a tea party?"

"No." The child picked her doll from the bed and held her up so Vera could admire her. "She only likes coffee."

"Now, that's my kind of dolly." A cute one too. It was bigger than any doll Vera ever had, nearly two feet. Vera playfully tugged at the yellow yarn braid, then reached for the cotton-stuffed hand. "Nice to meet you. My name is Vera."

"Shhh." The little girl's blonde brows scrunched, and worry stole her smile away. "Is that Mama crying?"

Oh rats. Vera should've shut the door. Too late now. "Yes, little one. But she'll be okay." Hopefully.

"We don't like it when Mama cries." Abigail nuzzled her face into the doll's belly. "She cries lots 'bout daddy leaving. Don't like it."

She's too little to know anguish. "I don't like hearin' others cry either. It makes me sad." Vera smoothed her hand over the girl's corn-silk hair. "Do you know what I did when I was your age and felt sad?"

"Go like this?" Abigail plopped the doll on the bed behind her and clapped her hands over her ears. "I do this. I can't hear cries. Yells. Nuffin'."

"That's clever. But me, I used to sing. Singin' always took me to a different world."

"Like fairy tales?"

Bulls-eye. "Yeah." Vera clasped her hands together in exaggerated enthusiasm. "Let's make up a story about a princess who sings from the castle tower."

Abigail gave a skeptical look. "Mama says fairy tales are nothin' but pretty lies told to children."

Well, so much for that. "How about a song? Would you like to hear one?"

"You're going to sing?" The girl tilted her head to the side, her eyes round in wonder. "My dolly likes to listen to singing."

"Well, that's a pretty swell dolly."

A tiny smile graced her face. "Mr. Scruffy gave her to me for my birthday. I got to name her 'cause I'm her mother."

"That must have been a special birthday. Turning older and becoming a mother all in one day." Vera smiled. "I'm curious, who is Mr. Scruffy?"

"It's a secret. So you have to promise not to tell. Like this." She raised her finger. "Cross your heart." She drew an imaginary *X* over her heart.

Vera did the same. "Cross my heart."

The girl cupped her hand around her lips and stood on her tiptoes, trying to reach Vera's ear. Abigail wasn't even close, so Vera hunched over. "Uncle Artie is Mr. Scruffy, and he's smelly." Her high-pitched giggles bounced off the walls of the small bedroom. "Don't tell Mama I said that. I'll get in trouble."

Ah, Artie. "So Mr. Scruffy is your uncle?"

"Yeah. I call him that because he's got whiskers." Abigail traced her finger from her ear down to her chin and up to her other ear. Vera laughed. Whiskers meant stubble.

"Vera?" Mick's voice sounded from the other room.

"I'll be right there." Vera looked at her small new friend. "Thank you for sharin' secrets with me."

Abigail smiled and skipped out of the room, the doll bouncing off her leg.

"I'm sorry I couldn't help, Sergeant," Millie said as Vera joined them.

Millie, puffy-eyed and pink-nosed, held her daughter, rocking side to side as Vera had seen other mothers do. "If I think of anything, I will call you."

"Thank you." He acknowledged her with a tight smile and nod. "It was a pleasure meeting you and your daughter. I apologize for the sorrow this caused."

Vera eyed Mick. The quick rise and fall of his chest was visible through his shirt. His severe expression drained the strength from her heart.

"We'll be all right." Millie snuggled her cheek into her daughter's hair. "Nice to see you again, Vera."

"You too. You have a wonderful little girl." Abigail smiled at Vera's words, and Vera waved to the child. "Bye, sweetheart. Thank you for playin' with me."

"Bye." Abigail wiggled her fingers. "Betsy says goodbye too." She made her doll wave.

Vera slapped a hand over her mouth, her feet frozen to the splintered planks. "'It's a good thing Betsy got hungry.'" Three pairs of eyes fastened on Vera.

Mick looked at her sideways. "Ver, what are you talking about?"

CHAPTER 28

"Artie." Vera pointed at the cotton toy cradled in the child's arm. "He gave Abigail that doll." She waved Mick closer.

He stepped beside her, lowering his head, inclining his ear.

"Remember, I told you about what Artie said the night he died." She whispered, "*Good thing Betsy got hungry*. It's the doll."

Mick nodded, his face pensive.

"Abigail, sweetie." Vera crouched to her level. "Can I hold Betsy just for a minute?"

"Nope." The little girl shook her head, making her cheeks jiggle. She curled Betsy into her arms, putting the doll in a chokehold.

Vera sighed. Whoever coined the phrase *like taking candy from a baby* never met Abigail Walters.

"Abby, that's not kind." Millie gave her the Mama-look. "Remember what we discussed about sharing?"

Cue the crying tantrum. "But, Mama, she's mine." Tears poured in tiny rivulets down her porcelain-looking skin.

"Abigail." Vera put her hand on the child's shoulder. "What about a song? You said Betsy liked listening to singing. How about I sing to her before we leave? I have a special song my grandmother taught me when I was your age."

Abigail sniffed and wiped away the tears with the back of her hand. "You won't hurt her?" She made a face as her mother wiped her nose. "Promise?"

"I promise." Vera crossed her heart the same way Abigail had done earlier. "I know you love her very much because you're a good mother. I wish I had a mother like you."

Two small hands stretched toward Vera, handing over the precious toy.

Vera remembered her times at the club, singing while searching for dubious characters. This was one of those times, but instead of searching the club's crowded room, she'd be searching the cloth body of a doll.

Inhaling a steady breath, she settled in on the couch, Abigail to her left. She felt Mick's presence behind her. Embarrassment skittered about in her stomach. What if this turned out to be nothing? How could a toy solve a murder? A steady hand pressed on her shoulder. She glanced up and met Mick's dimple.

His confident nod bolstered her strength.

"Blessed assurance. Jesus is mine." Her eyes roamed the doll. *"Oh what a foretaste of glory divine."* She ran her fingers along the seams in the arms and legs. Nothing. *"Heir of Salvation. Purchased of God. Born of His Spirit. Washed in His blood."* Her fingers worked the buttons on the doll's back, loosening the snug dress. "*This is my story. This is my song*." She tugged off the tiny clothing and set it beside her. "*Praising my Savior all the day long*." Vera finished the verse and flipped the doll over, eyeing the cotton stomach. Ha. *Smart, Artie, real smart.*

Abigail reached for her doll.

"I have some sad news." Vera hugged the toy, pretending to console it. "Betsy has a tummy ache. Look right here." The little girl climbed onto her lap, and Vera smiled. "All the other thread is white. See this?" She pointed at the irregular stitching that spanned two inches of the doll's belly. "What color is this?"

"Black." Her eyes rounded. "What's it mean?"

"Betsy has something in her tummy that she shouldn't." Maybe. Hopefully. Vera smoothed away wisps of golden strands from Abigail's eyes. "I think we should get her fixed up right away. You're her mother. What do you think?"

"I know how she feels. I had tummy aches before." She hugged her stomach. "It's yucky. Mama fed me beef one time—"

Millie set a hand on Abigail's head. "Abby, dear, that's enough."

Mick's low laugh rumbled in Vera's ear. She angled her head back and smiled up at him.

Millie crouched to her daughter's eye level. "Abby, you can go to the kitchen and get a licorice. I want you to eat it in the bedroom while we work on your toy."

Abigail held up two fingers. "Please?"

"Yes. But stay in the room until I say so."

Blonde braids swung back and forth with each of Abigail's skipping steps.

"What do you think we'll find?" Millie craned her neck, making sure Abigail did as she was told.

"Not sure." Mick took the doll from Vera's hands. His eyes lingered on hers a moment, pools of green that Vera wished she could laze around in. He turned to Millie. "Do you have scissors?"

"Certainly." Millie scurried out of the room and returned with what resembled a man's tackle box. "Let's see. Let's see. Here's a pair of scissors." She handed the steel shears to Mick.

"Thank you." Mick focused on the doll and slit the black thread. "Here, Ver, your fingers are smaller than mine."

So true. His massive hands were ideal for enveloping hers but not so perfect for searching around a two-inch space of a doll's belly. She glanced over. The anguish she'd detected earlier in his eyes had lessened. Traces of hope brightened his features as he handed her the toy. She gently worked her fingers into Betsy's cottony innards. The thick fibers were coarse against her skin. Little by little, she pulled out the stuffing. And out something else came, landing on Vera's lap.

"It's film." Millie bent over the back of the couch. "A negative. How did—"

Mick took the brown strip from Vera's thigh and walked to the window, holding it up to the light.

Vera shot to her feet. "Don't be a hog. Let me see too." She wormed her way around him to catch a view.

Mick didn't shrug her away but lowered his arm so she could catch a better glimpse.

"What do you think?"

She saw something but couldn't identify what it was.

"It's a newspaper room." Millie's voice cut through both of them. "That's an engraver's machine."

"It is." Mick raised the film higher, the outside sun highlighting the image. "Didn't Kelly and Artie work at the *Pittsburgh Journal* together?"

"Sure," Millie said. "That's how they met. Art took the pictures, and Mr. Kelly cut the plates for the press."

And why hadn't Vera known this? She'd dated the man, for goodness' sake. And she didn't know his hat size from his shoe size. "So that's the *Journal*'s pressroom?" Her heart sank. Why would Artie stash that inside a doll? What was so important about it?

Mick wrapped the film in his handkerchief and dropped it in his front pocket. "Let's get going, Vera." He shifted his profile to face Millie. "Thanks for your patience. Got to head back to Pittsburgh. Thank you." He extended his hand to her. "You have been so obliging."

Obliging? Vera suppressed a laugh. He was all formal, like a tuxedo. Probably should get used to that side of Mick. Once they reached Pittsburgh, he'd surely return to the protocol-driven cop and regard Vera as though they were nothing more than strangers.

Ah, the outside air. Vera inhaled deeply. The light breeze carried summer on its airy wings, filling her senses with the fragrance of … well … oiled metal. The hardware store made its presence known in the alley where they stood. Still, refreshment stirred in Vera's heart. When she'd imparted encouragement to Millie, a good dose of it'd spilled into her own soul. She stretched her arms wide as if to embrace the sun. "Mick, I think we—"

Her words jammed in her throat as the sensation of Mick pulling her into his arms swirled through her.

"What you did in there was amazing. You're amazing." He motioned his head toward the apartment door.

His arms curled around her back, his touch igniting her pulse to soar. If the flecks in his eyes could be translated into letters, they'd spell—desperation. As if directing his stare any place but on her would be a waste of time.

"Ver." He dipped his chin in a painfully slow descent, his voice coarse. "May I?"

Her breath hitched in her chest. He'd asked. No one ever asked. They took. She nodded, her heart yearning.

He strengthened his hold, pressing her form to his. His lips brushed hers, gentle as if to be certain of their invitation. Oh, his touch had never been more welcome.

Vera threaded her fingers into his hair, exploring the nape of his neck.

Mick lowered his mouth to hers, strong and confident like everything else he did. His thumbs stroked her waist to a silent rhythm.

When he pulled away, he took her breath with him. She rested her head against his chest, his heartbeat a steady metronome in her ear. Vera'd never hungered for a man's affection. Never. But this wasn't any man. This was a man who would've given his life for her. Craving sprouted within her, growing stronger with each second, intensifying. Lips tingling, she moved in for another kiss, tangling her hands in his shirt.

But his lips stiffened under hers. His arms fell limp.

She lifted her gaze and was met with startled eyes.

"Ver." He stepped back. "I shouldn't have." Fists formed at his sides. "I shouldn't have done that. I was fighting it, and I gave in."

Her fingers touched her swollen lips. "You were fighting kissing me?"

"I shouldn't have done that."

"You said that already." And each time she felt it. Was she that vulgar to him? So repulsive he had to fight against kissing her, holding her? The grave look returned to his eyes. The same weighty stare she'd seen in Millie's apartment. The dumb case. "Is it the captain? Do you think he wouldn't approve?"

"No." His eyebrows drew together as if he was surprised by her question. "It has nothing to do with him. Listen, I—"

"Is it Phyllis?"

His head jerked back. "How do you know about her?" The lips that had been on hers only a moment ago were tightened at the corners in a scowl.

"You called her name that night I checked on you in your room."

He said nothing, his gaze harder than granite.

"So you do have a dame." The words swirled in her head, stinging the backs of her eyes. No, she would not let him see her cry. "You lied to me."

"No." He exhaled loudly, frustration coating his features. "Okay, yes. I did lie but that was—"

"Stop. Just stop. I thought you were different. Honorable, even." Fierce currents of emotion surged beneath her words. Could he hear the sob in her voice? Mick had done in less than two weeks what Carson hadn't accomplished in years—penetrated her defenses. Shame on her for allowing Mick to get that close. "When were you gonna confess about your woman? After you bed down with me?" She straightened her shoulders. "Sorry, Sarge, I'm through with men takin' advantage. Better luck on your next racket."

Despite his throbbing temple and definite rise and fall of his chest, the man stood stoic. As if he had no intention of denying her accusations.

"That whole protective charm had nothing to do with your work and everything to do with a primal nature that's disgusting.

Insulting. You're just like all the others. Nothing but a—"

"She's dead."

"What?"

His throat worked to swallow. "Phyllis. My former fiancée. She's dead."

Oh. Her heart shivered at the anguish in his tone.

Was that why he'd had nightmares? The reason he'd sworn off matrimony? His fiancée—someone he was to pledge the rest of his life to—had been ripped from his hands. A piece of her bruised heart ached for him. "What happened?"

The sun ducked behind the clouds, casting an ashen shadow on his taut face. "It's not something to discuss in the streets. I can't—"

"Then how about this one? You pretended to never have been involved with anyone. Why'd you lie?"

His hand cupped the back of his neck, eyes troubled as if talking of this woman pained him physically. Maybe it did. "I couldn't. Couldn't speak of it." His jaw tightened, then relaxed. "And, Ver, I'd never take advantage of you. If my goal was to seduce you, I wouldn't have pulled away from your kiss."

As if she needed the reminder. Okay, maybe he didn't have vulgar intentions. Perhaps the reasons for his actions stemmed from her not measuring up to his dead fiancée. The woman probably had more class in her pinky finger than Vera had in her entire being. "You didn't have to fib, you know." She caught the way he avoided her stare. "There's more to it, isn't there?"

A muscle ticked in his cheek. "Another time. Not here."

"Never mind." She struggled to keep her chin level in spite of the tug from her heavy heart. "I can't trust your words, anyway."

"I had to say what I did at the time. Because I didn't want you to …" He pulled a hand through his hair, tousling it. "I didn't want you to entertain, well … be interested in me. Last thing we needed—"

"Don't flatter yourself, Sarge." Her stomach soured. "I'm not interested." Not anymore. "Tell ya what, let's go back to the day at my apartment. Okay, Sergeant Dinelo? Go ahead and call me Miss Pembroke. I don't mind now."

"But I do. Listen, Vera—"

"Miss Pembroke."

"Vera." His tone emphatic. "Let me finish."

"I heard enough. Just drop me off at the nearest pawnshop, and we can part ways."

He reached for her but stopped, shoving his hands into his jacket pockets. "We're driving back to Pittsburgh, and I'm not letting you out of my sight. Your life is still in danger."

Her heart was in danger. A lump of beating mush around him. *No more.* "I'll do my part pertainin' to the case, but that's all."

A cold silence stretched between them as they walked back to the truck.

CHAPTER 29

Vera sank into Captain Harpshire's chair, eyes pricking with tears. She'd fallen in love. Fallen so hard her heart was black and blue.

She traced her bottom lip with her finger, his kiss still lingering in her mind, mocking her. It couldn't have been more than twenty seconds, but it branded her memory, unyielding. She released a frustrated laugh. Why torture herself? Mick didn't care about her. He was still in love with Phyllis.

A light knock sounded.

Her heart pounded. *Don't be Mick. Please don't be Mick.* She straightened, wiping the tears in one swift motion.

"Why, hello, Miss Pembroke." The captain backed into the office, his hands full of papers and folders. "Got to look over these later." He dropped them on top of a cluttered filing cabinet. "I hope you weren't waiting long?"

Mick had dumped her here ten minutes ago, and every second stung.

"I'm all right, Pops."

The older man pulled up a stool.

Oops. Probably shouldn't be parked on the head honcho's throne. "I'm sorry. This one's yours."

"No, that chair's reserved for pretty young women. Go right ahead and sit there." His smile matched Lacey's, the right side of his mouth hitching up slightly higher.

"So tell me, Miss Pembroke, what did you say to my sister to make her so enamored with you? I've talked to her three times in the past few days, and the conversation is centered around you."

"I miss her." Now more than ever.

The city hall's clock chimed from across the street. Five o'clock.

"She misses you too. You have to make a trip to visit her again." He glanced at the door and then to her. "Sergeant Dinelo told me some boys you knew arrived at the cabin yesterday."

Was that only yesterday? Seemed like forever ago. "Yeah, Angelo from the club."

The old man nodded. "Good thing you got away. There's a search out for him. Did you recognize anyone else?"

"No. I only saw Angelo. Mick might have seen others." But he hadn't mentioned it to her. Though she wouldn't be surprised. Mick'd had a habit of withholding valuable information. See, that was why she never trusted. Sooner or later, even the good ones failed you.

"I sent a few guys over there and, of course, relayed everything to the Kerrville police department. It's good to work together, especially since that occurred in their jurisdiction."

Vera filled the silence with the clicking of her nails against the wooden armrest. Chatting seemed more of a struggle during wounded moments like this.

"Got good news for you." Pops tilted his head. "My men brought your belongings back."

She perked up. Oh, to be in a fresh change of clothes. This dress was marked for the burn barrel. She was going to need a chisel to chip it off.

"What's left for me to do here?" Maybe she could escape before Mick came around again.

His gaze turned thoughtful. "Not much. The developers are processing that negative you found in that doll's belly. Ace told me the story. That was some great sleuthing."

"Thanks."

"What did you think of the negative?"

She shrugged. "Not much. It's the pressroom at the *Journal*. Doesn't solve anything."

"We'll see." The captain grabbed his mug off his desk and took a swig. "Ace should be here any minute to pick you up. You don't mind staying with him until this whole thing blows over? He's my best man. Trustworthy and honorable."

Staying with him? At his place? "I do mind."

His eyebrows spiked.

"I'd prefer to be on my own." She had no money. No place to stay. Wasn't looking fabulous, either, but her heart's survival depended on steering clear of Mick Dinelo.

He allowed a few seconds of silence before saying, "It's not a good idea, sugar."

Sugar. Now he definitely sounded like Lacey. She gathered all the self-assurance she could from her fatigued disposition. "I'm a big girl." Fail. Her voice shook, and it pulled his intent stare.

"Have you been crying? What's going on here?" He set his coffee on a stack of papers and pushed the door closed with his foot. "Did Ace try anything inappropriate?"

"No." Had the air thickened? She tugged her collar. "I just … I need to start thinkin' of how I'm goin' to get back into life."

"I see." He stretched the latter word to two syllables.

Didn't he believe her?

He slid his glasses further up the bridge of his nose, looking Vera square in the eye. "And it doesn't bother you that there are armed and dangerous men hunting you?"

His words sent shivers up her spine like a cold day in January. But still … "God's my protector." Never mind she only knew a few Bible verses and one hymn. Or the fact she'd hadn't stepped foot in a church since she was a kid. God would still look after her, right?

His nose twitched like a rabbit's. "I can't argue with God, but I can ask you to reconsider."

"No dice, Captain." Now for the kicker. "Not sure how to ask this, but—"

"You need some money?"

Was mind-reading a skill requirement for a police captain? Because this man had it down good. And as for Pops coming straight to the point, couldn't ask for more than that.

"Unless you want to buy this bracelet"—she wiggled her adorned wrist in front the captain—"for, say, a grand or so."

"That's more than I got on me." He laughed and put his hands on his chest. "Going to pawn it?"

"Yeah, but I don't know of any shops open this late. So I need to borrow only a little until I can get there. It would be a loan." She held up a finger. "One I'm goin' to pay back. I wouldn't dream of swindling a police captain." Aware her words could be taken absurdly wrong, she blinked with her most innocent expression. "Or swindle anyone, for that matter."

He pulled his billfold from his desk drawer. "No rush, Miss Pembroke." He pushed a wad of bills into her hand. "I'm still hoping you'll change your mind. That's a dangerous bunch out there."

Vera shook her head. "Thank you, Captain. You and your sister are tops." She had money and no Mick. Things were getting less complicated by the minute. "Now, where's my stuff?"

"Hold on for a moment." Pops stood when she did. "What are you planning for accommodations?"

"Well, I'm not goin' to the William Penn, if that's what you're askin'. I'm thinkin'—"

"Go to Willow Courts."

Her brows scrunched. "But those are apartments." Expensive ones too. "I ain't signing a lease." She'd only need a day or two of lodging. Serious decisions stretched before her. New York didn't seem as appealing anymore. Where else could she go?

"I know the landlady. She'll put you up for however long you need." He winked at her. "She owes me a favor."

She could see right through that. "Goin' to keep tabs on me, Pops?"

"It's nice over there. And going to extend those dollars in your hand." He shrugged. "As for the tabs, Miss Pembroke, I am relying on you to check in with—"

"You." She patted his shoulder like Lacey would. "I promise to keep in touch with you, Captain." Not Mick. Better start the withdrawal feelings now and get it over with.

"Fair enough." He held out his hand and Vera shook it. "Here's my direct line." He took a card from his pocket and scribbled on it. "*Pops* is trusting you."

"I promise." She gave a half-hearted smile.

"Your bags are at the dispatcher's desk."

With a tight nod, she marched out the door. Was it possible to snatch her stuff and sneak out before Mick saw her?

"Hundley just told me the Steubenville letter turned up missing?" The tightness which had huddled in Mick's chest only intensified since the somber ride back to Pittsburgh. "How could a critical piece of evidence disappear?" He felt like banging his head against the office doorframe.

The captain looked up from writing his reports. Frustration and something resembling concern bunched in his eyes. "I've been looking into it." The captain waved him in. "Shut the door behind you, Ace."

Mick took a step in and did as his superior said. "Arthur Cavenhalt typed that letter."

Aged, dull eyes brightened. "Any proof?"

"No. Just a hunch." Maybe more than that, but the vanishing of the letter couldn't have happened at a worse time. "Millie Walters told me that Cavenhalt borrowed her typewriter and then the next morning took a bus to Steubenville. Time frame coincides with our dates."

The captain bounced the end of his pen on his chin, gaze distant. "Why would Cavenhalt tip us off if he intended to weasel dough out of Kelly?"

Mick smirked at the captain's intentional choice of words. *Weasel dough*, a Vera expression. He pushed off the wall, restlessness inching through him. He had to talk to her soon. Get this all cleared up. "Maybe Cavenhalt tried to work both angles. Did anyone snap a photo of that letter?"

The captain's scowl deepened. "Yes, it's missing as well."

Mick couldn't control his darting glances. Papers stacked on the filing cabinet, on the captain's desk, and peeking out of drawers. It'd be too easy to lose a sheet of paper and a couple photos. "At least we know what it said." *May want to check into the Kelly Club. Overpriced gin isn't all they're selling.* Maybe he should've told Vera about what the letter said. She might have been able to help.

Someone rapped on the door.

Mick cracked it open. Officer Hundley stood on the other side, envelope in hand.

"From the development room?" Mick pulled the door open.

Officer Hundley nodded. "Sure is." He passed it to Mick and headed down the hall.

A slice of anticipation swirled in his chest. This could be the moment it all ended. He and Vera could put this case behind them and … then what? Nothing. Absolutely nothing. The eagerness he felt a moment ago slid into a groan. "Here they are, sir."

Mick pulled the prints from inside the envelope and placed them on top of the captain's desk. "Take a look. This is not the *Journal*'s pressroom." Mick was certain. He'd been there numerous times, and nothing matched with what he looked at here. The gazette had smooth white walls throughout, but this photograph depicted dark wood panels.

"That certainly is an engraving machine." The captain leaned in, eyes squinting. "What's this right here?" He pointed with his fountain pen.

"Looks like a metal door." Baffling. A plate-cutter and a metal door. Just like a puzzle, it had to piece together somehow.

"Does the Kelly Club have metal doors, Ace?"

"Not a one." He'd inspected that place after Cavenhalt's death. If that door was there, he'd have known it. "Let's show it to Vera. Maybe it's from Kelly's house."

Hopefully, she'd been given enough time to cool down. She hadn't spoken to him the entire drive back from East Liverpool, cuddling up to the shaky door of Hewitt's truck, her eyes glossy and complexion pale. And it'd been all his fault. His lips shouldn't have claimed hers. It had been brief, but so were earthquakes. And her kiss resembled one, his heart the epicenter, the tremors coursing through every part of him, causing shifts in him that he hadn't been prepared for.

"She's gone, son."

His heart bottomed out, collapsing. "What? Captain, did you just say—"

"Vera's gone."

"Excuse me, sir." His pulse sped and his legs soon matched pace. He jogged out the office, gaze scrutinizing each hall.

"You won't catch her." The captain's voice called from behind, halting Mick's steps. "She's been gone about thirty minutes."

His breath came in jagged, his heart raging against his ribs. A hand clapped on his shoulder.

"Back into my office. We're going to have a chat."

She'd left. All alone. He forced the steps into the boss' room, fighting the urge to chase after her trail. If she'd even left one. He stomped a foot on the metal stool. "Why? Did she say why?"

"I believe it has something to do with you." The captain reclined into his leather chair and kicked out his feet. "Now, my boy, fill me in on what's going on between you and Miss Pembroke."

He cleared his throat. "What makes you think that?"

"Don't let these cheaters on my face deceive you into thinking I can't see." The captain chuckled. "Because what I saw today was a beautiful young lady with a sore heart."

He'd been charged with protecting her, obsessed over keeping her safe, and ended up being the one injuring her. A sickening feeling twisted his gut. "I didn't mean to, sir."

"Didn't mean to *what*, Ace?" He pulled in his feet and leaned toward Mick, one brow spiked almost to his hairline.

"No sir. It's not what you're thinking. No foolish business of any kind." He held up both hands. "I didn't mean to give her reason to think that we, she and I, could have a future together." He eyed the door. Every fiber in his being pulled at him, demanded that he search for her. It took all his restraint to keep him stationary. Breathe. Pittsburgh was a big city.

"Glad to hear you were honorable. I trust you like a son."

"Thank you, sir." *Ver, where are you?* "If you don't mind me asking, why did you let her go?"

"She was determined. It's better for her to leave on my terms than to have her run away and not see her again."

Not see her again. The words wrapped like barbwire around his insides, twisting and slicing his hope into shreds. Why did she always run? Anytime conflict came, she took flight. "May I ask what your terms were?"

"I made an agreement with her."

Did the captain want to reduce him to begging? The way Mick's heart was feeling, it could happen.

"Don't sweat it, Ace. She'll be fine. Go home."

"Sir, if—"

"Go on home, Sergeant. Take a well-deserved rest."

How could he rest while Vera meandered the streets? Would she retreat to a former lover? His muscles tensed. "Captain, do you know where she is?" He tilted his face to the ceiling, fighting the sting in his eyes.

He stood and patted Mick's shoulder as though he was a good little boy who needed to obey. "She promised to check in with me. Go home."

"With all due respect—"

"Thank you, Ace, for all your hard work." The captain smirked and moseyed out of his office.

Mick cupped his neck with his hand, squeezing. Desperation clawed his soul. He had to find her.

CHAPTER 30

"There." Vera secured the last pin into her hair. She piled it atop her head, looking more like a housewife than a single, jobless nobody.

When Mrs. Elridge, the landlady, had opened the door, she'd regarded Vera as though she was a vacuum salesman. Then Vera mentioned Captain Harpshire, and the woman turned giddy like a flapper at a dance hall.

The salt-and-pepper-haired woman had placed Vera in the best room of the apartment building, one boasting a shower. Studio apartments had never been her favorite, but this one dripped with charm. The living area and tiny kitchenette were the main features of the space, the bed and shower toward the back. And to Vera, it was like staying at the Ritz-Carlton. This was the part of Pittsburgh she loved.

And never in her life had she thought she'd be so ecstatic to put on fresh undergarments. The boys in blue had done great collecting her stuff from the cabin.

Whispering Pines.

She sighed. Thoughts of Mick pestered her like mosquitos. You slap away one just to have another land in its place. It was best for her to find out now that Mick hadn't cared for her than to journey deeper into her feelings for him. She swallowed back what tasted more like hurt than pride.

No one had warned her that love came with pain.

Twirling around, she made certain her back buttons were even and her stocking seams straight. A little overdressed to remain indoors, but necessary for her mood.

She glanced at the money on the table. The thirty dollars Captain Harpshire gave her was a lot of dough but could go quickly if she wasn't wise. She had to think differently. She was on her own again.

No more canary life. No more finding men to secure a job or comfort. God would bring something her way.

Knock. Knock. Knock.

She glared at the door, agitation tightening her muscles. Something was being brought her way. Rather, someone. But it wasn't from God. Twenty minutes after she'd arrived, another boarder had introduced himself as Vernon Listeller. This was the third—no, fourth—time he'd rapped on her door.

The first had been to tell her she could order dinner from Mrs. Elridge, the landlady. The second to say what time dinner was because he'd forgotten to mention it before. The third to show her how to lock the windows because they were *tricky*. She'd assured him she'd be all right because she was on the third floor. When his face had flushed with embarrassment, she'd believed he'd leave her alone from then on. This was ridiculous.

She jerked the door open. "Mr. Listeller, you've got to stop disturbin' me—"

"Vernon?" Mick, with arms folded in front of him, leaned against the wall, looking like he'd been there all day. "Do I need to have a talk with him?"

Air evacuated her lungs. She stood, blinking. "Sergeant Dinelo." Did her heart just run down the fire escape? "Why are you here?"

He shoved his hands into his pockets and took a step forward. "I was going to ask the same thing about you."

"You … live here?"

He tipped his head in an annoyingly handsome way. "Down the hall on the left."

Captain Harpshire. The old billy goat. "He knew the whole time." Of all the shenanigans.

Mick let out a steady breath. "He didn't let me in on it. Not a word. Captain let me scour the streets of Pittsburgh looking for a lanky redhead."

Her brain caught up with her pulse. Mick Dinelo. The man who'd kissed her in the alley then had regarded her like garbage. "Goodnight, Sarge." She pushed the door, but Mick shoved his foot out, stopping it from closing.

The raw pleading in his eyes was the only thing keeping her from stomping on his foot with her heel. "Please, Ver?"

With a huff, she pulled the door open.

He breezed past her into the room, settling on her tiny sofa, looking like an elephant on a park bench. "Your place is nicer than mine." He stretched out his legs. "Do you mind? My feet are tired."

"I most certainly do. I—"

"So I search everywhere I know. Poking my head down alleys. Traipsing around the bus station. Rode the trolley several times. I'm tired, hungry, and in desperate need of a shower." He locked his fingers behind his head and emitted a masculine sigh. "I searched five hours for you."

"That long, huh? I'm touched."

"It gets better." He ignored her pert remark. "I take two steps into the complex and my aunt runs to me. Not to say, *Hello—where were you for the past two weeks?* But instead, *Guess what? We have the most beautiful new boarder with hair as red as autumn leaves*."

Her jaw slackened. Mrs. Elridge was his aunt?

"Then I understood why the captain kept telling me to *go home*. Crazy, isn't it?"

"I'm beginning to think Lacey taught the captain all her mischievous ways." Vera's emotional scale weighed between frustration and humor. "Is that all you wanted to say?"

"No." He stood and covered the distance between them in three strides. "My mind was in chaos all evening. I didn't know where you were. The danger you could have been in. A million thoughts flustered my mind. I was … a mess."

Was that supposed to give her a warm fuzzy feeling inside? "I'm keepin' the door open." She cocked a thumb toward it. "You can leave any time."

"I know you're angry." His tone lowered and his gaze fixed on her. "Hurt and confused. That wasn't my intention. Believe me."

Her heart begged for permission to sigh, but she scoffed instead. "Come on. It's after ten." She shuffled toward the door, grabbing the knob with one hand and waving him out with the other. "I think you can manage the walk home."

"Can we talk?" He gestured to her to follow him to the sofa. "It's serious."

"Ten minutes, buster." She pushed the door closed, wishing she could shut her heart to Mick as easily. The chair farthest away from him seemed safest. The longer he stayed, the more her strength ebbed. "You have ten minutes. That's all. I ain't fooling."

And neither was Mick, considering the solemnness shrouding his face.

A moment of awkwardness ensued. Did this little chat have to do with the case? They'd run in circles over the past days, grasping at the wind, finding only a shabby piece of film. Her shoulders slackened against the seat. "Are you going to talk, or am I supposed to read your mind?" Because unlike the captain, that skill came with a great degree of difficulty for her.

The skin bunched around his pained stare. "I killed my fiancée."

She clutched the chair's edges. "What?"

"I killed her." His voice raw, he wrung his hands, his knuckles turning white. "I was tasked with investigating the leading bootleggers. But it seemed every time I tried to get the drop on them, they were two steps ahead of me. I don't have to tell you how dangerous those men are."

Vera's throat squeezed tight. No, she'd witnessed firsthand the brutality of Pittsburgh's underworld. But how was this about

Phyllis? She took a steadying breath and waited for Mick to continue.

"When Phyllis and I got engaged, I wanted no secrets between us. It was important to me to convey how life would be, married to a policeman. For her to understand the risk in my line of work."

His words poked a tender spot in her heart. Mick viewed marriage as a partnership. Or at least he had at one time.

"I'd tell her about my day, tell her about the rumrunners I had my eye on. That way, she could pray for me." He let out a humorless laugh. "She took all that information and sold it to them."

A gasp escaped her lips. Oh, the betrayal Mick must've felt. No wonder the man held a passion for taking down bootleggers. His own fiancée had been tainted by their poison. "How did you find out?" And exactly how had that made him Phyllis' killer? The Mick she'd known was protective to a fault. He wouldn't harm anyone, let alone the woman he loved. Betrayal or not.

"All my intended missions failed. It happened too many times for it to be a coincidence. Then my notepad would go missing and turn up in random places. I hated to suspect my own fiancée, but she became too inquisitive. So I thought I'd try a little test." He shuddered and his chest heaved, tightening his features.

"What kind of test?"

"I fed her phony information. If she wasn't working with them, then nothing would come of it. But if she was, the knowledge I gave her would lead them right into my hands." He clenched his eyes shut as if reliving the dark moment. "It all went wrong."

The devastation marking his husky tone pulled her from her seat and to his side. He gave her room on the sofa, but it wasn't enough to keep their sides from touching.

"We met at Gino's on Fifth for dinner but never made it to the entrance. A black Ford came barreling down the road and stopped long enough for someone inside it to shoot her." Several heartbeats passed, Mick's strained breathing the only sound. "She died in my arms."

Woman, 22, Fatally Shot on Fifth Avenue.

The newspaper headline in Mick's Bible. It was about Phyllis. She'd been the one who'd been fatally shot. Vera's hand pressed over her heart, but she couldn't dull the ache for the man beside her.

His glassy stare turned from her to the floor. "I killed her."

"No, the goons did."

"But I set her up. I gave her false details." He dragged a hand across his face, settling it in a fist on his lap. "Her blood was everywhere. All over me. The sidewalk."

She placed her hand over his, but it didn't seem enough. How could she comfort him? "Mick, I'm sorry."

"Her dress. I'm forever haunted by the image of red-stained rosebuds."

Her eyes slid shut. It all made sense now. The way he'd responded when Lacey had handed him a rosebud-embroidered napkin. His haunted expression at Millie's apartment. The woman had worn a dress covered in those flowers. "Did you ever catch the men who shot her?"

"No." He tightened his hand into a fist, then unclenched it, slowly. "But even if we caught them, the memories would still torment me. I put her in that position."

"Phyllis put herself in that position. She had no business selling your police information to them."

He shifted, turning watery eyes to her. "I can't move on past the guilt."

And what was she supposed to say? Being a Christian only, what, a whole two days? But there was one thing she did know. "Maybe you need to forgive yourself."

"I …" His heavy exhale filled the room with anguish. "I can't."

"Couldn't you ask God to help you?" She swept a lock of hair off his forehead.

He grabbed her hand and pressed it to his cheek. "I'm sorry, Ver." He stood and regarded her, his eyes wearied and shoulders curled forward. "Sorry I can't give you what you deserve."

She rose and kissed his cheek. "You can always rely on me as a friend, Mick." The urge to kiss him again burned her lips. To caress away his pain through her touch and carry the burden in her arms as she'd hold him. But … she couldn't. The sigh rose, but she pushed it back. "A good friend."

Mick fell onto his bed, staring at the blank ceiling. "God." Tears. Finally, tears. For years, he hadn't been able to cry. Not for Phyllis. Not for him. He'd imprisoned the emotion inside, numbing his soul.

Vera's word struck. He couldn't forgive himself. Guilt grasped his heart and dug in with ugly roots. The all-too-familiar restlessness churned through him. He stood, shoving his hands through his hair, squeezing his scalp. Could he bear a lifetime of this? He kicked the empty trashcan, sending it across the room. He wanted Vera. He wanted a normal life with her. But he couldn't.

"God, I don't know how to get over this."

My grace is sufficient for you.

The still small voice. So quiet, yet so distinct, echoing off the walls of his soul. He dropped to his knees. Never before had he heard Him so clearly. Yes, he'd get impressions and *caution nudges*, as Lacey would call them, every once in a while, but never this. *My grace.* Over and over, resounding.

It was time for him to take the ax to the root. Could he do it? He breathed in a ragged breath. "God, I choose to forgive myself. I ask you to help me cope with the guilt. The pain. I'm saying this by faith because I don't feel a bit better." And he didn't.

It would be simpler to have an overwhelming rush of peace backing up his words, but … nothing. Not even a goose-bump. But he couldn't live in this state anymore. "I *won't* live in this state anymore." God's Word said he was to walk by faith, not by sight. If this wasn't walking by faith, he didn't know what was. "I believe

I'm free from the torment. Free from the anguish. And free ... from guilt."

The sorrow may last for a night, but joy comes in the morning. He had tasted the sorrow. Had plenty of it. It was time for the joy.

CHAPTER 31

Vera stretched and rolled to her side. Sunlight squeezed in from the closed drapes. Her weighted eyelids and soft sheets invited her to drift. A knocking sound startled her. Neighbor's door? She hoped.

"Ver, it's me. You decent?"

Mick.

Her heart responded with a twist. The man responsible for her late-night crying session now stood outside her door.

Shoving off the covers, she stood and blinked to clear her vision. "Give me just a second." She tightened her robe while walking, leaving her just enough time to run a hand over her wayward hair. Sighing, she opened the door.

Hello, Sergeant Swoon. Instant alertness. Mick all cleaned up. And boy, did he clean up well. A crisp, white-collared shirt beneath a charcoal sports jacket, matched with light-gray trousers. And then there was her … in a robe. Better than the nightgown, though. She rubbed her lower lash-line, swiping away any sleepy sand.

Ah, Mick. His most alluring feature was the black mug in his hand. "For me?"

"For you." He handed it to her, taking care so it wouldn't spill. "My aunt makes a pot of coffee every morning. Sometimes two."

Vera inhaled the soothing aroma. "So tell me, Sergeant Vogue, how early did you rise to look all handsome?"

"Vogue, huh?" He half smirked, stepping into the room. "I do keep a bar of soap around. And the shave? I can do that myself." He stuffed his hands in his pockets and rocked back on his heels. "I take it, it looks good?"

"I take it, you know it."

Mick chuckled low. "You keeping the door open?"

"Yeah. I'm a lady." One with morning breath and out-of-control hair, but still a lady.

The amusement in his eyes faded. "I forgot to ask you something last night, Ver."

Oh boy, this could be anything. She pressed her lips to the brim of the cup.

"The film from that doll. We enlarged it."

"And?"

His mouth pressed together, then relaxed with an exhale. "It's not any room at the *Journal*. I don't think it's a newspaper room of any sort."

"I don't get it." As much as she'd prompted herself not to get her hopes up about the film, she had. To have this wrapped up and solved would lessen the stress on her. And Mick.

"I don't either." He shrugged. "But there was a door in the back. It's a metal gate. Was there anything like that at Kelly's house?"

She slid her hand through her hair. Argh. Tangled. "A metal gate? No, not at Carson's house." She set the coffee cup on the tall dresser and reached for her hairbrush. "But I never been in his basement."

He watched her closely. "So it's possible?"

"Sure."

"What about Vinelli's house?"

"Angelo." She squeezed the brush handle, narrowing her eyes. "What kind of person do ya think I am? I don't make house calls to every man in town." So she'd been right when she'd deduced he still saw her as scum beneath his shoes.

"I didn't mean it that way."

She shot him a knowing look. What other way could he mean it?

"You mentioned before that he was your friend. All I asked is if you've seen his house."

"No." She turned toward the mirror. Ah, the comfort of the brush needles against the scalp. Like a massage.

"Might find it there." He scratched his cheek. "Better coordinate two searches today."

She hated to destroy a good theory, but steel gates and doors weren't something out of the ordinary. "This is a steel town. You'll have your work cut out for you." She grabbed a clump of hair and pulled the brush through to the ends.

"I'm aware of that. I thought if I got a warrant for Vinelli's house, I could … Will you stop?"

"What?" She talked to his reflection in the mirror. "I'm listening. Heard every word ya said."

"It's not that." Mick put his fist to his lips, hiding a smile. "You're distracting me. It's not nice of you to be so pretty when you wake up."

Vera spun on her heel, facing him. "Mick Dinelo." Her warning tone only fueled him to take a generous step toward her. She raised the hairbrush like a tomahawk. "So help me, I will launch this at your head."

"You don't scare me." His mischievous grin unleashed, and he advanced another stride. "I've seen your aim."

A laugh escaped faster than she could mash her lips together. She shuffled back a step and smacked her heel on the leg of the cheval mirror, sending a sharp ache up her leg. She winced. "The way we're going, it looks as though we both may end up hurt."

All the playfulness fled his features. "I never want to be the source of your pain." His Adam's apple bobbed, and Vera's heart stumbled. "Last night, I thought I'd lost you. Then to find you here safe? I may have hid it well, but—"

"You don't have to." Her heart couldn't bear another explanation as to why he could never be hers.

"I want to." A gentleness overtook his eyes, disarming and engaging.

She should tear her gaze from his, but something in her wouldn't allow it. No man had ever looked at her with such tenderness. And probably none other would. The ache stretched wider, the decision sealed—she'd leave today. It was best for them both.

Which meant this would be the last time she'd see him.

She cupped his face, taking in the feel of his strong jaw. She studied his likeness, committing to memory every plane and angle, the perfect slope of his nose, his inviting lips. She pressed a finger to that perfect dent in his cheek. His dimple. Sadness gathered in her chest. Now, his eyes. The vibrant greens shone with an intensity enclosed by a jade ring.

Mick's gaze fused to hers, and the moment lengthened. For sanity's sake, she withdrew her caress, but he caught her hand and pressed a lingering kiss to the inside of her wrist. He then entwined his fingers with hers, a union of touch but not hearts.

She tugged from his delicate grip and hugged her arms to her chest. The few inches between them might as well be a canyon. He was out of her reach.

"Vera." His breathless voice swirled about her. "Are you in love with me?"

"Doesn't matter." Her eyes burned to cry as much as her soul ached to be his. "I think you should get going." And so should she. The longer she stood in his presence, the weaker she became.

"Ver," He dipped his head.

She jolted back.

"I'm not going to kiss you. I want you to know that I—"

"Can't give me what I need. I remember."

He didn't move.

"Please." What more could he want from her? Hadn't he made things clear last night? She wouldn't prolong the inevitable. Hardening to the dull throb in her chest, she straightened her spine. "I've got to get dressed, Mick, and I don't want an audience."

"Can you listen for one minute?"

"There's nothing new to be said." Vera held up her hand, keeping Mick from moving closer, the fakeness glaring at her from her fourth finger. That dumb ring. Why hadn't she removed it last night? "Here." She yanked it off, almost skinning her knuckle. "Give this back to Lacey for me."

"Listen. Last night, after I talked to you, I—"

Vera wiggled the ring. "Will you please leave?"

He exhaled loudly and held out his hand. "If you want to act that way, I'll go for now. But we'll talk later."

No, they wouldn't. She dropped the ring in the center of his palm, careful not to touch him. "Goodbye, Sergeant Dinelo." She clipped her words, masking the rising emotion.

At the door, he stopped on the threshold. "Please stay here and don't venture out."

She folded her arms.

"I'm serious, Vera. I'm going to the office to check on something, but I'll be back. Lock the door behind me and don't answer it for anybody. And Ver." His tone softened. "Please don't push me away. You mean a lot to me."

The air swept out of the room along with Mick.

Wasn't he the one who'd pushed away first? Her heart twisted before shattering into a million shards. She meant a lot to him. Sure. So did Lacey. So did the captain. So did that ridiculous Lincoln.

A tear escaping down her flushed cheek, Vera curled a fist around the golden cross hanging from her neck. No other choice surfaced. She had three hours to get to the pawn shop, buy her ticket, and be on that train.

Mick dropped his pen onto the desk. Another dead end. What was so hard about locating a warrant? Kelly's residence had been searched the day he'd taken Vera to Kerrville. Not that long ago.

Paperwork couldn't vanish into thin air. Had the filing cabinet eaten it? He groaned, the tower of metal drawers challenging him. Why couldn't the captain be more organized? Mick pushed folders back, searching the floor of the drawer for loose papers. Nothing.

He eyed the phone, agitation tightening his shoulders. The officer who'd been in charge of Kelly's search was off duty and impossible to get a hold of. Should Mick call again? He thumped the desk with his fist. Nothing today was going as planned.

Why wouldn't Vera let him talk? When she'd framed his jaw in her soft hands and taken in his face with a soul-ripping, pensive look, Mick had known at that precise moment—she loved him.

He'd felt it in her touch, heard it in her voice. But then she hadn't let him speak his heart. Though how could he blame her after all he'd told her last night?

The pressure mounted in his chest, and he inhaled a steadying breath, forcing himself to focus on the task at hand. What if he could start new, as he was for Vinelli's search? Get another warrant. Call another search. This time he'd take command. He could bring over a late lunch and tell Vera about it after she had time to regain her composure. Maybe it was better this way.

He grabbed the phone. Things were looking up.

CHAPTER 32

Vera faltered off the trolley, almost dropping her bag onto the street. She strengthened her grip and trudged down Forbes Avenue. A group of women consumed in conversation shoved past, bumping her with their parcels. She huffed. If it wasn't for Gregory Pawn and Shop two blocks over, she'd never be spotted on Forbes on a busy Monday. At least the bustle kept her identity obscure. A policeman strolled by, his gaze bouncing from her eyes to her bag. She held her breath, her heart pounding in her throat.

Had he recognized her?

Temptation pressured her to glance back, but she quickened her pace, her fingers aching from the weighted bag. She spotted Craft Street and relaxed her shoulders, the pawnshop now in view.

Her train would leave in an hour and a half. She had to be quick. With a sigh, she yanked the door open, bells jingling above her head. Her gaze scanned the room. She'd met Patrick Gregory a few times, but not enough for him to—

"Hey there!"

Her head whipped to the right. A lean frame stood between a row of bicycles and a table of dusty books. So much for him not recognizing her.

"Haven't see ya 'round. Where ya been?" His crooked smile exposed a gold tooth. Couple that with his overgrown stubble, and he resembled a pirate.

She lifted a shoulder. "Around."

He adjusted a tag on a rusty percolator and strode toward her. "Have ya been down at the club lately? They got a new canary." He put a heavy hand on her shoulder, and she restrained from shrugging it off. "That shortcake got nothin' on you."

"Thanks, Pat." She stepped away from his touch and forced a smile. "Um … I came to pawn my bracelet." She let loose of her bag and held up her forearm, but the man didn't glance at the diamonds. He sucked his tongue between his teeth, staring at her with a hunger that shriveled her insides.

"Let me take a look. Let's go"—he jerked his head to the back of the store—"where the light's stronger."

The air in the room thinned and warmed. Maybe this wasn't a good idea. After all—

"Sure miss hearing you sing, Red."

Red.

She bit the inside of her cheek, forbidding a gasp to escape. *The notes.* The ones she'd received daily at the Kelly Club. The person had called her *Red*. She'd always assumed it was Stony Eyes who'd written them, but maybe she was wrong. Or maybe this was a strange coincidence.

"I knew someday you'd come to me." His grin stretched. "Just had to be patient."

Her joints iced over, paralyzing her. "It *was* you. You wrote those notes."

He rocked back on his heels with a devilish wink. "You think I paid fifty cents a slug because I enjoyed that diluted garbage?"

"Listen, Pat,"—she stooped to snatch her bag from the ground—"maybe now's not the right time. I need to catch—"

He grabbed her wrist, and her bag slammed against her knee, almost knocking her off balance. "Now's the perfect time." He glanced toward the backroom, his lips pulling back in a wicked snarl.

No way she'd be accosted by Pat the Pirate. She tugged her hand, but his grip strengthened. She couldn't even strike him with her bag because he clutched the arm that held it. Her gaze darted. Maybe she could—

He pulled her to him, and she smacked into his chest. With a caged breath, she snagged a metal flashlight from the table to her left and bopped him on the back of the head.

He cussed and released her, doubling over.

Vera took that opportunity to bolt. Energy surging through her, she bounded out the door and raced down the street without daring to glance behind her. She snaked through the traffic, holding tight to her belongings, only stopping when she realized where she was. About a block from the Kelly Club.

Despite her chest wrestling for oxygen, she couldn't control her fast and shallow breaths. The familiar anxiety returned. Her body was strained from running, her mind spastic from Pat's advances, and now the Kelly Club was in her line of vision. She remembered Mick's instructions and focused on evening out each gulp of air. Within minutes, her lungs were stable. The pulsing of blood in her ears hushed, and a recognizable sound swept in.

A cart's wheels.

"Grimby."

His hunched back faced her, but she'd know him anywhere, the shuffling of weathered boots, the squeaking of cart's wheels. The urge to scram was tangible in her trembling knees, but she had to at least say goodbye to him. This was her only chance.

Vera covered the several yards between them and placed a hand to his shoulder, the fabric coarse under her fingers. How could this man stand wearing a trench coat in the summer? "Hey, there, Grimby. It's me. Vera."

He mumbled something, his jaw flapping up and down. She took in the empty cart and frowned. "Where's Fred?"

"Always so nice to me. So nice to me." His muttering was quieter than usual. "I set food out, but he didn't come."

"I'm sorry, Grimby. Fred was a loyal dog." Now the poor man was all by himself. Did he feel the loneliness?

She listened for a handful of seconds to his mindless chatter, all the while keeping a watchful eye on the club. Sweat ran down Grimby's face and throat. She withdrew a handkerchief from the top of her bag, and, just like two weeks ago, wiped his face.

"The light's on. The boat comes." The old man latched his stare on the speakeasy.

She felt so far removed from that place, it was like she gazed upon her former life. From what she could see, no one was there. She could retreat with ease. *Legs, stop shaking*.

"I got to go, pal." Vera put a hand on his shoulder. "But I promise to pray for ya."

"The light's on. The boat comes." His hand lingered in the air, pointing.

She blinked. "What's that mean Grimby? Show me?" It was day out, no sign of any so-called light.

Grimby held his stance for one intriguing moment, then clutched the cart and hobbled onward.

Was he trying to show her something? She glanced in the direction he walked. Just the back of the Kelly Club and the polluted Monongahela River, the place as lifeless as a graveyard. But what was an extra minute? She shot a look toward Grimby, who shuffled down the road, leaving her behind. Breathing deep, she stepped onto Kelly Club soil.

The farther she walked, the more unkempt the property became, the tall grass swallowing her feet. Rusty trash cans and broken wooden crates lined the back wall of the club. Nothing suspicious. Disappointment stung, her hope of Grimby possessing any sense of intuition sinking like a stone in the murky water.

She gave the broadside of the back of the Kelly Club one last glance. Too bad. Never should have … she stilled. A pale white circle dominated her attention.

A light. Fixed on the back of the club, a solitary bulb rested about six feet high from the ground. How about that Grimby? He understood more than he'd been letting on.

But a light? Nothing around it. No door. No window. And of course it wasn't on. Vera scrunched her brow. There wasn't a switch. Must turn on from the inside. "What are ya here for, little bulb? A signal of some kind?"

"What are *you* here for?"

Thick fingers bit into her shoulder, and something hard dug into her side.

Angelo.

"Walk with me and I won't use force." Angelo jerked his head toward the river.

The river! Her ankles wobbled like a leaf floating on the current. His cold glare met hers, and something ignited within her. She stomped his foot with her heel, squirming to get away. His grip strengthened, and she elbowed his gut.

He grunted.

"Help!"

He yanked her arm, pulling her into his chest, and slapped his hand over her mouth. She bit his palm. Hard.

Angelo cursed.

"Help! Someone! Hel—"

One-armed, he picked her up by the waist and threw her over his shoulder, sprinting toward the river.

"Stop!" She smacked her jaw off his back, her teeth slicing her tongue.

"Shut your mouth!" He bypassed the river via a hidden wooden stairway to a water-level platform, ducking under the dock.

She kicked her feet, pummeling his abdomen. "Let go!"

He pulled her off his shoulder, pinning her back to a wall. "Step aside." He panted, spitting on her. Light lined his face from slits in the deck overhead. "And no funny business." He shoved her to the mud-caked ground.

Her vision grayed, but she didn't dare shut her eyes. If Angelo intended to kill her, she'd fight with every breath.

Angelo pointed his gun toward her while unlocking … a door?

Who'd put a door under the dock? And why?

Shuddering, she tucked her knees beneath her and managed to stand.

Angelo opened the door, a dark, musty passageway stretching before her. He motioned with his revolver. "Get movin'."

CHAPTER 33

Mick knocked for the third time on Vera's door. How on earth could she hear him with the radio blaring? He wedged the dozen roses under his arm and fished in his pocket for his aunt's skeleton key, a smile escaping his lips.

Today he'd tell her.

He turned the key and cracked the door.

"Ver, it's me." He waited, giving her a minute to get decent if necessary. Brass instruments flavored the air along with Vera's perfume. He slid inside and glanced around. The sight enflamed his chest, burning into his gut. All her stuff was gone. Like that day at the cabin. "She ran."

He squeezed the stems in his hand, welcoming pain from the thorns into his flesh. Anything to numb the ache searing through him. Played the fool again. And why the running game? For him to chase after her? He threw the flowers, petals scattering on the pale carpet. Not this time. The captain could deal with her now.

He scowled at the radio where a jazz tune blasted. With a ragged exhale, he turned off the music. A note sat under the dials in Vera's handwriting.

Mick,

Had to leave. It's better this way. Tell the captain I'll check in. I'm awful at writing notes. I do better with songs. But I want to thank you. You've helped me, protected me, and proved to me that gentlemen still

exist. Remember the question you asked me earlier? The answer is YES.
Vera

The question he'd asked? When? He worked his jaw, his mind replaying their last moments together. She'd been standing almost right where he stood now. Her eyes a watercolor green, her hair brushing over her cheekbone, calling for his fingers to swipe away the tendrils. *Are you in love with me?* His heart did an about-face.

She loved him.

He shoved the note in his pocket and strode out the door.

Vera blinked several times, allowing her eyes to adjust from dark to light. From the creepy tunnel to … to the basement of the Kelly Club? Whoa. She'd thought only a crawl space existed under the gin joint.

"I'm going to have to use this on ya." Angelo dangled a handkerchief. "Open wide."

A tremble stole through her, the musty air clogging her throat. She stared at the cloth sullied with dirt … and blood? Her heart forgot to beat. Whose blood was that? "Don't touch me with that thing." His arms matched the size of beer kegs. Was it smart to be sassy with him?

"Then I'll have to knock you unconscious." Lips peeling from his teeth, he tapped the butt of his gun. "I don't wanna do that. Sit down." He jerked his head to a wooden chair in the corner. "Going to tie ya up too."

Bound and gagged. Not how she wanted to spend her Monday. Angelo stood solid, like a brick wall, fixing a glare on her that chilled her blood. Her heels slowly clomped the soiled floor. She stilled, mouth dropping open.

The plating machine. The press.

The items from the picture were as large as life next to her. Why here? This room held secrets. A mystery Artie had discovered. And he'd paid for it with his life.

A steel circle dug into her side. "Into the chair."

God, help me.

A squealing sound shook the walls. Her gaze flicked upward. "What's that?"

Angelo motioned to the opposite side of the room. The steel gate. The one Mick was puzzled about. Only, it wasn't a gate.

An elevator shaft? Her brain clouded. How long had she worked here? Why hadn't she noticed it before? Angelo stepped beside her.

"Vera?" Carson stepped off the shaft, his deep-set eyes locked on her.

Fear pounded its ugly fist on her heart.

Ward Voss, the liar of a lawyer, trailed behind him.

The three men spoke in hushed tones. What were they discussing? Her death? A shiver coursed over her, extending its icy roots to her marrow. She prayed for someone, anyone, to rescue her. A someone with strong shoulders, whose kiss she could still taste.

Carson strode toward her, leaving the two men behind. His face donned an inscrutable mask, his eyes raking her from the ankles up.

A trickle of sweat ran down her back, and she tugged the collar of her dress.

"I don't know what to say to you, Vera." His deep voice was scratchy, his mouth a taut line.

She pressed her lips between her teeth, keeping them from quivering. Silence kept her confident. At least, that was what she hoped.

"You ran off without a word. Then you accused me of murder."

She shifted her weight from foot to foot, willing herself to remain tall under his glare. Was he mocking her? Was he expecting her to apologize, drop to her knees and beg for mercy? White-hot anger kindled behind his calm expression. She'd seen this before, but this time she'd receive more than a blow to the cheek.

Carson tipped his head back to the bouncer. "You got the orders ready for t'night?"

"Yes, boss-man. Parvis should be here any minute."

"Good." His look swung back to Vera. "We had something special. I wish this never happened." He took out a cigarette and anchored it in his mouth.

The strike of his match made her flinch. Carson saw it, his lips curling as he lit the cigarette. "What's done is done." He fanned out the match and tossed it to the floor.

His cryptic words pulsed with an underlying meaning. She stared at a clump of dirt by her shoe. How could she have let this happen? Why did she have to be so nosey? If curiosity killed the cat, she didn't want to know what it would do to her.

No. Dread wasn't going to overwhelm her. She lifted her gaze to him, knowing she wasn't just glaring down Carson but fear itself. "My life isn't yours to take. You can't kill me."

He furrowed a brow but then lifted his chin, eyes confident. "I'm not going to touch you."

Mick's words echoed in her mind—*He has a lot of friends who are willing to do his dirty work.*

"I'll take this back, though." He grabbed her wrist, his hostile grip burning. "This belongs to me." He unclasped the bracelet and slipped it in his pocket. "I have to run, Vera. I have another engagement." He glared at her, eyes darker than the blackest sky, jaw set. "Goodbye, baby. Sorry that it had to end this way."

A fire kindled in her core. "Tell the cops I'm down here when you meet them at the door."

Carson turned awkwardly toward her. "Cops?"

Pull the curtains, it was time for a stellar performance. "I was supposed to meet them here. Guess I got here first." She shrugged. "They have the goods on you, Cars. Have fun in the pen. Don't be sore if I forget to write."

Carson studied her face, doubt swimming in his eyes.

"That was a bunch of talk she just fed you, Kelly." Ward stepped in between Vera and Carson. "My informant told me she's not under police protection anymore. And even if she's still buddied up to them, no way they'd allow her to come here alone."

Carson clapped Ward's shoulder. "My voice of reason. Thanks, Voss." He wagged his finger at her, a wicked smile playing on his lips. "You should be careful telling stories. They get you in trouble." He turned on his heel and summoned Angelo. "Take the boat. Go at night. Make sure no one sees you. I want you back here by four."

"Got it, boss."

His boat! Vera's throat tightened, locking the air in her chest. There was only one reason for Angelo to go at night and keep out of sight. She scanned the room for an escape. Ward leaned by the elevator shaft. Carson and Angelo blocked the tunnel. No windows. No other doors. Trapped with murderers.

Angelo glanced back at the parcels by the door. "What about tonight's orders?"

"I'll handle them. It shouldn't—"

"But you never deal with customers."

Carson sent him a scathing look, as if he might pummel the brutish bouncer for questioning his authority. "Taking care of …" He cleared his throat. "Disposing of the garbage is your job tonight."

Garbage? Vera's hand curled into a fist.

"Voss will be here too." Carson eyed Ward, who answered him with a small dip of his chin. "Did you coordinate everything for me? I need things to go smoothly."

"Yeah." Angelo reached for his flask.

Another glower from Carson. "Keep dry, Vinelli."

Angelo gave a tight nod and shoved the liquor back into his pocket. "The client comes at two-thirty. He's new. But he knows what to do."

"Good. Like I said, no sneaking sips." Carson glanced at Vera, and she narrowed her eyes. He smiled. "You need to keep your wits about you."

Carson and Ward boarded the shaft and disappeared.

Angelo pushed down on her shoulders, shoving her into the chair.

Her tailbone smacked against the wood. "Umph." Throbs shot up her spine like flaming darts. Angelo's grip strangled her arm. He bound her, the coarseness of the rope slicing her skin. With one forceful yank, he tightened it around her wrists. She sucked in air through her teeth.

"Got company?" A gangly man emerged from the tunnel's entry, his arms loaded with packages.

Vera gasped. *Stony Eyes.* She clenched the sides of the chair, wooden slivers spearing underneath her fingernails. The cloaked man who'd pulled her out of the club.

"Hey, it's my girl." Stony Eyes set the parcels on the floor and ambled toward her, his gait uneven, his lips wickedly curved. "Remember me, toots?"

Her gaze darted to Angelo, then to Stony Eyes. She pressed her elbows into her sides, squeezing.

Stony Eyes laughed. "She don't know, does she, Vinelli?"

"Nah, don't think so." Angelo kneeled in front of her, holding the soiled handkerchief. "Vera, open your mouth or get conked on the head. Which is it?"

Escape was possible with a gagged mouth but not with her being knocked out. She slid her eyes closed and lowered her jaw enough for him to wrap the handkerchief around her mouth. The bitter taste pushed bile up her throat.

Angelo rose to his feet and stood beside Stony Eyes. Both men gawked at her, Angelo studying his tie job and the other studying her legs.

Stony Eyes licked his lips, like a wolf in a chicken coop. "The boss wanted to test your loyalty for this joint and hired me to ruffle you up a little. I got extra dough when Kelly gave me two shiners." He pointed to his eyes.

Her toes curled in her shoes. Carson had set it up? He'd hired this man to assault her? Her shoulders spiked with an inhale. Here she'd thought Carson had defended her, but it had all been staged. All part of Carson's scheme to get her to run into his arms. Look to him for safety and by that, give him control. Her stomach lurched, nausea striking.

"This all of them, Parvis?" Angelo motioned to the brown, paper-wrapped parcels on the floor.

So the animal had a name.

"All twenty thousand." Parvis rubbed his grease-stained hands together. "I counted it three times." He glanced again at Vera, baring his crooked teeth.

Twenty thousand what? Dollars? Grams? Carson had never taken drugs around her, but who was to say he didn't sell them? The gag tore into the sides of her mouth, a burning sensation spreading to her ears.

"That's what we need. A boat is coming after closing at two-thirty." Angelo pulled a flask out of his back pocket and took a swig. "Check the light and make sure the bulb works."

Parvis flipped the switch, then walked into the tunnel.

When the light's on, the boat comes. For months, she'd wondered at Grimby's phrase, but never in her life would she have imagined she'd discover the true meaning this way. She glanced at the press. Maybe Carson falsified documents. A story once went around the club claiming he sold identification papers to immigrants. Back then, she'd laughed it off.

The mildewed odor lingered in her nostrils, threatening to close them. In a few minutes, she'd be reduced to breathing only through her mouth. Taking in air through the soiled handkerchief increased nausea. If she threw up, she'd choke.

Lord, please.

Parvis appeared in the entryway, panting and wiping his brow. "It works." He flicked off the switch. "I'm getting too old for this."

Angelo chuckled. "You won't be sayin' that when payday

comes." His face turned serious. "I remind myself of the cut when I have hard jobs to do." He glanced over at her, and her stomach shrank.

"She sure is a delicious one." Parvis stepped behind her. "Smells pretty too." The man bent over and sniffed her hair.

Vera jerked her head back, knocking the bridge of his nose.

"Ouch!" He cupped his nose. "It's bleeding." Putting his sleeve to his crimson nostrils, he cussed. "You little wench."

She ignored the dull throb on her crown as her brain scrambled to come up with a plan to escape.

Angelo shook his head. "That's what ya get for messin' with her."

Parvis pinched his nose. "I'd like to mess with her more. Maybe I can finish what I started that night at the club." The familiar predatory look invaded his eyes. "Can we have some fun before we have to ditch her?"

Vera's chest pricked as if with the stabs of a thousand pins, her breath shallow and rapid.

No, no, no. Not another panic attack.

Her thoughts tangled as the dizziness set in, and her eyelids drooped. No, she had to keep them open. She popped her lids wide and focused on a rusty beam lining the ceiling.

Breathe in. Breathe out. In. Out.

"Don't touch her until it's time."

The suffocation subsided, but the pain in her chest remained. She shifted in her seat, trying to find a position where the ropes didn't pierce as bad. Her spirit prayed within her, cutting short when footsteps thumped overhead.

Parvis raised a brow. "Kelly still here?"

"No. He'd be gone by now." Angelo pulled his gun from its holster. "Lookin' like we got a visitor."

Parvis' hands shook, fumbling to pull a penknife from his pocket. "What do we do? The heat is on this place." He glanced at the packages by the tunnel door.

The heat? Vera's mind scrambled to put together the pieces, but they swirled around her head like a twister. She couldn't grab a rational thought.

"Parvis, go out the tunnel and spy it out." Angelo lowered his voice. "Check and see if there's a car and—"

"Not me. I ain't gettin' shot full of holes. You got two legs and a gun."

"It could be anyone," Angelo grumbled and moved closer to Parvis. "Listen, let's both leave and come back for the girl later. She ain't going anywhere. I can't do anything until nightfall."

They murmured back and forth, not regarding her.

Now or never. She squirmed, getting her foot in a better position, stretching against the bindings to reach the wall. The nubs of the rope stabbed her, but she … must … try. *Got it.* She took a deep breath and put her toes to work.

CHAPTER 34

Mick smacked the back of his flashlight with the palm of his hand. It flickered and then poured a steady golden beam on the Kelly Club's floor. His steps were deliberate, his movements controlled. His heart the exact opposite, jackhammering against his ribcage ever since he'd spied Vera's bag in the grass beside the building.

He pushed his lips together. Why had she come here? Of all places. She wouldn't run back to Carson, place herself within his realm of mercy, would she? Surely, she'd know what those men do to those who betray them.

He'd understood her visit to the pawnshop. That was the first place he'd searched. The weasel Pat had given him a tough time, but cooperated when Mick told him he'd been obstructing a legal investigation. The pawnshop owner said he'd been nursing a headache at the time and asked Vera to return later, to which she'd left in a hurry. Mick'd scoured the streets until he passed the Kelly Club. Vera's bag had been identifiable from the road.

He'd forced a side door open and now inspected the main hall. A cockroach skittered, escaping into a crack in the floor. The door to her dressing room, or what used to be her dressing room, stood open. Nothing there but a couple gowns and a vanity.

He stalked down the hall and slipped into the room next to the kitchen. His light skimmed over wire racks stuffed with bottles and boxes. A storage room. His stomach tangled in knots. *Vera, where are you?*

Tap.

A. He dropped to the ground, placing an ear to the crusty floor. Hoping against all hope that it wasn't just a random sound in an old building.

Tap. Tap. Tap.

C.

He didn't need to hear the rest. She was here. Beneath him.

Vera tapped again. *E.*

He pushed his ear harder against the splintery wood. Men's mumbles. The tapping stopped. *They caught her.* His breath died in his chest. *Lord, keep her alive.*

How could he get down there? He made his steps light. Could they hear his footfalls? His gaze bounced with the flashlight. There was no door leading to a stairwell. A trap door, maybe? He put the beam to the planks under his feet. No. The flow of the flooring made it impossible.

He circled the room again with the light, a numbness twisting his chest. Something glistened from behind racks piled with large boxes and cans. He grunted, forcing a rack away from the wall. But it wasn't a wall. The flashlight slipped in his sweaty hand. He tightened his grip.

Found it—the metal gate of an elevator shaft.

He'd known this building had once been owned by a wealthy socialite but had no idea they'd installed a lift.

Mick stepped inside and operated the controls, lowering the elevator into the pit of the Kelly Club. The conveyor's squeals nullified a surprise attack. But it didn't matter. He'd give his last breath for her. With his gun cocked and raised, he readied for anything. The elevator lowered to a stop. He flattened his back against the corner of the shaft, unsure if he'd avoid any oncoming shots, his heavy breaths the only noise. Were they waiting for him to step off and then ambush him? He took a cautious step, listening. Nothing. With a quick motion, he leapt out of the shaft.

No assailants.

He glanced to his right. The printing press. Next to it, an overturned chair with …

Vera!

He sprinted toward her, boiling at the sight of her bound, unconscious. "Vera?" He holstered his gun, then removed his pocketknife and cut off the gag, the white fabric stained red.

Blood.

Everywhere, soaking her hair, pooling under her head, streaming down her neck.

Oh God.

Not again. Not with Vera. Looking at her, it was almost as if his own blood drained from his veins, deadening.

"Talk to me, Ver." He gently brushed the clumped hair from her face, exposing her pale skin.

No wound there.

His fingers searched for the source of injury. He stilled, inhaling quick breath. The crown of her head. Split open. He wrapped the gag tightly around her head, praying it'd keep it from bleeding more. "Pulse." He tapped her wrist. "Come on. Beat." It faded with every second. He cupped her face with his hands. "Don't you die, Ver. Don't you dare die."

The way her head was positioned induced more bleeding. She needed to be moved, but one wrong jerk could kill her.

God, help me.

He smacked his hands off his thighs, removing any shakiness. The knot that bound her to the chair was tight. Pulling it loose would jostle her. He grabbed his knife. Holding the rope secure with one hand, he made precise slices with the other.

The rope fell to the ground, and he folded her into his arms. She didn't groan or move, just hung limp against his chest. The coloring had left her skin, the rise and fall of her chest less frequent. Tears squeezed from the corners of his eyes. At this rate, she had only minutes. He'd been helpless with Phyllis and now even more so with Vera. No time to take her to the patrol car. If he did, he couldn't keep her stable and drive at the same time.

He clenched his eyes. He couldn't watch her die.

"God." It came out a pathetic sob. "Touch her. Heal her."

Her blood stained his arms, and he could hardly bear it.

"Lord, I believe, with everything I know to believe." The seconds ticked away in his mind, but he couldn't leave the words unsaid. Words—conscious or not—she needed to hear. He forced his stare on her ashen face. "I love you, Vera Pembroke." Hot tears gathered in his eyes. "I love you so much it hurts." His gaze flicked to the ceiling. This couldn't be over.

"Fine time to tell a dame." Through slit eyes, she looked up. Her limbs sagged, and her breath staggered, but she was alive. Alive!

"Sweetheart, hang on." Glory to God! Mick wanted to roar a victory shout, but she wasn't in the clear yet. He needed to find a way to get her help.

"Lord, You kept her this long, I believe You can keep her a lifetime." He hoisted her up with him to a standing position, hope bolstering his soul.

"Mick ... the press." Her bloodied and cracked lips formed more words, but no voice was behind them.

"Saw it. I'm only concerned about you." He watched her drift off again. "Keep your strength."

A door yawned open from the other side of the room. Vinelli appeared in the shadowed opening. Mick's heart stalled. He was defenseless. No way he could fight with Vera in his arms.

"Vinelli." He narrowed his eyes. "I'm warning you."

A wiry man filed in behind Vinelli. The attacker from Vera's apartment. Mick's pulse jumped.

"Take it easy, Ace." The captain's voice called from the dark hallway. "My .38 is directed at them."

Mick glanced at their handcuffed wrists. Tension eased from his chest, and gratefulness slipped in that he'd informed the captain about his plan to visit the pawnshop. No doubt, his superior had spied the loaner car Mick had been driving.

The captain stepped into the room, a blazing fire in his eyes. “Brought these vagrants back in the way they came out. I thought they should explain themselves.” The captain’s gaze shifted to Vera resting in Mick’s arms, and his expression hardened. “Boys, you’re in a heap of trouble.”

CHAPTER 35

A pain sharper than a thousand knives stabbed from the top of Vera's head, stretching to her temples. Soreness chased away sleepiness, but her eyelids refused to budge. Mick better not want to go on a nature trek today. The idea of the short jaunt to the outdoor powder room made her groan. A new pounding jabbed at the base of her neck. Why did she feel this way? She shifted in her bed, wishing Mick wouldn't be too long at Lacey's.

"For heaven's sake, child, don't move." An unfamiliar voice stung her ears.

Vera's lids popped open. The room's brightness gouged at her vision. She covered her aching eyes with her hand, needing to block out all light, ease the hurt.

Cold fingertips tugged her arm down and pushed her head back against the pillow.

"Keep it right there." Her throaty lilt shoved into Vera's thoughts.

What happened to Mick? The cabin? A shiver tore through her. "Where … am I?" She braved squinting. Everything blurred, then came into focus. A hospital room? She gasped. "Did I have an accident?" She lifted her brows, and something shifted. A bandage. Why on earth was a bandage around her head?

"Allegheny General." The plump nurse lifted Vera's wrist. "Pulse is strong. You're a lucky lady."

She scowled. If she was so lucky, then how come her body

screamed for relief? "I need an aspirin."

"Gracious me, no aspirin." The nurse grabbed a compress cloth and placed it on Vera's forehead. "The last thing you need is a blood thinner. And don't touch your dressing. It's set perfect."

Blood. Her memory triggered. The Kelly Club. Angelo and Stony Eyes. Her pulse raced. Carson and the boat. Had she been thrown in the river, and someone had rescued her? "What happened? Why's it dark outside?" The sky's black sheen lingered between the white cotton curtains. "Is it stormin' out?"

"Mercy, you ask a lot of questions for someone who's been unconscious all day." The nurse tapped Vera's forehead, reminding her to keep her head back.

Ouch. Didn't she just tell the lady her head hurt?

"And, no, it's not storming. It's half past twelve."

"At night?" Her stomach growled, yelling at her for missing lunch and apparently dinner. But the famished sensation rolled into nausea. The throbbing intensified, making her eyes ache if she looked anywhere but straight ahead.

"Yes, yes, at night." She pinched her lips. "Actually, in the morning."

Why did the nurse have to dance around her questions? Frustration pierced as deep as the pain. "Why am I here?"

The nurse tossed a soiled towel into the basket. "Your head got cracked open." She cupped her hand and made a motion of cracking an egg.

Vera grimaced.

Angelo. The image flashed of the brute with his gun raised. Next thing, she'd felt a thud and then nothing.

"You better thank your lucky stars you're alive."

Not her lucky stars, her wonderful God.

"How'd I get the honor of this beautiful thing?" She grabbed a handful of the hospital gown. Way too big and way too white.

"We had to check you to make sure you weren't injured anywhere else." The nurse faced Vera and popped her fists on her hips. "Now, are you done asking questions? Because I have to fetch the doctor and let him know you're awake."

One more. "When can I leave?"

The nurse laughed. "Let's get through the night with no complications."

And that wasn't an answer. Why couldn't she get a nice nurse? One that fed her chocolate pudding and rubbed her feet? But then, Vera had no money to be here. And her dreams of leaving town were now non-existent. She filled her cheeks with air and huffed.

"I'll be back. Keep that head of yours still. And if that cop comes, tell him he has to wait until the doctor checks you before he can schmooze over you."

"What cop?" Her heart pounded as much as her head.

"The one whispering endearments as he gave you—" Her mouth clamped shut. "Never mind. It's not my place to say." She put Vera's chart down at the bottom of the bed and strutted out, leaving confusion in her wake.

Mick had been here? And what endearments? Oh, she wished she had been conscious for that. A searing pain wormed across the back of her head. She clenched her fists and prayed for alleviation. Of all the nasty words Vera knew, she couldn't bring herself to call the thugs any one of them. Instead, she smirked. "I told 'em they couldn't kill me."

"That's my girl." A husky voice pulled her gaze to the door.

"Captain." She covered her disappointment with a weak smile and tugged the hem of the hospital gown over her knees. The movement made her head swirl and clouded her sight. She groaned and settled back.

"How you feeling?" He straddled a stool beside the bed.

"Right now, I'm seein' gray dots." Floating around in her vision like smoky bubbles. Remaining perfectly still was her best pain reducer. How could the ache extend to the tips of her hair? For goodness' sake, the woman could have given her one crummy aspirin. "I feel like someone let loose a jackhammer on my head."

"More like the butt of a gun." The stool creaked as he shifted his weight. "A blow to the head with one of these is just as dangerous as a bullet." He motioned to the gun on his hip.

Vera winced.

"You've had a busy morning, little lady."

"Maybe you know this. How'd I get here?"

"Ace."

Mick, the hero. What was a girl to do? Sigh. "He found me at the club?"

"Yes, he found the elevator shaft, the printing press, and you." His warm smile heaped a dose of comfort on her heart. He removed his glasses and wiped them with a handkerchief. His cloth reminded her of that disgusting one Angelo had shoved in her mouth.

"What about those goons who conked me on the head? Angelo and …" *Stony Eyes … what was his name?*

"Dudley Parvis?" The captain slid the glasses onto his face, a smile spreading. "I apprehended them myself."

Relief swept over her. "Why, Pops. I'm impressed." She would've loved to have seen the old man in action. No doubt, he wasn't as soft and easy-going as he was now. "What about Carson?"

He glanced at his watch, scrunching his brow. "Listen, Vera. You have to rest. The doctor said you're going to experience headaches and dizziness. He said no stress of any kind."

As if on cue, a sharp pain beat against her temple.

"I'm having one of my men take you to my sister's when you're able to travel. She wants to take care of you."

The idea of soon seeing Lacey made Vera's heart lighter. "The nurse said Mick gave me something. Where is it?" She wouldn't dare whip her head about the room in search of it. Maybe the captain could find it for her. Whatever *it* was.

"He gave you his blood."

Mercy. Good thing she was in a hospital because she was two breaths away from fainting.

"You were weak and had lost a lot of blood." His serious tone bothered her. Had she really been that close to dying? "Turns out, you and Ace have the same blood type."

She couldn't shake the thought that Mick was now a part of her. Inside her. Sustaining her. "Where is he now?"

"He'd left earlier with the promise to rest before ..." The captain frowned. "Listen, darlin', when the doctor said no stress, that means emotional too." He stood. "That means no Ace."

The man who had a habit of saving her life. The man who'd enamored her beyond anything she'd ever known. The man who didn't love her. "Did you tell him what the doctor said?"

Pops nodded. "He agreed and promised not to see you."

The words threatened to swallow her whole.

The captain had given him an escape, and Mick had snatched it. She was right back to where they'd been the night he'd spilled his guts about Phyllis. Guess happy endings were only meant for the silver screen. He was not Gary Cooper, and she was not Clara Bow. The throbbing returned and brought its friend nausea to bully her around.

"I'll let you rest. Tomorrow, if you're cleared to leave, I'll arrange everything for you to go to Lacey's." He gave a reassuring smile. "It'll be alright, darlin'. Get some shut-eye."

"Captain, you didn't answer my question. What about Carson?"

"Don't you fret about him."

But the deep creases in Pop's forehead raised her suspicion.

What was going on?

The waves smacked against the boat, spraying Mick with river water. He scowled and glanced over his shoulder at Officer Hundley. "From here out, you need to stay down. Vinelli said the client was coming alone."

His jaw clenched. Vinelli had better not be deceiving them. That tank of a bouncer had been right on the description of this boat and the name of the man who had the appointment. After Mick had reported it to the waterfront patrol squad, they'd caught the man at the last fueling. Nigel Witker now occupied a retaining cell, and for the time being, his boat belonged to Mick.

He squeezed the steering wheel. What was a clever way to impersonate a moonshining goon from West Virginia? A weird sense of pity niggled in his chest. Witker was only a puppet. Like Angelo Vinelli. Where Vinelli had the real estate tycoon Kelly as his backbone, Witker had the illegal gambling syndicate leader Frank Johnson.

Mick exhaled a choppy breath. He'd sworn faithfully to the captain and to the doctor who'd performed the transfusion that he'd get the prescribed five-hour rest, even though it nearly had unraveled him to leave Vera. But he had to at least pretend he'd rested or the captain would've never agreed to let Mick work tonight. Mick had never been aggressively persistent when it came to assignments, but he'd refused to allow anyone but him to head up this one. To his mild disbelief, the captain had supported him. He couldn't mess this up. Men like Kelly needed justice so that women like Vera could live secure.

Vera.

When the captain had phoned two hours ago saying she was awake and acting like her usual feisty self, fierce emotion had pushed tears from his eyes. And when he'd been informed he couldn't contact her, his breath had ripped from his chest. Vera had become the pulse of his reality, but if he had to stay away so she could be healthy, he would. God help him.

The wind blew in his face, carrying mist from the murky water. Navigating in pitch-black conditions heightened his alertness. The last thing he needed was to crash into a buoy or floating dinghy.

He scratched his nose, the false mustache irritating his upper lip. "Almost there." He squinted at the dim glow in the distance. His heart quickened. "Kelly has the light on." Which was the signal to the boats they were open for business. "Okay, Hundley,

I'm driving to the dock." If he could find it. He slowed the boat, inching toward a shadow extending over the water. There. He cut the engine, tied up the boat, then grabbed his hat and satchel. "Stay low. Listen for trouble."

"Got it." Hundley's voice was muffled.

"Backup is around here somewhere." He peered out over the tall grass surrounding the club, hoping it camouflaged at least ten of the state of Pennsylvania's finest. The captain had resorted to the only means of bringing down this syndicate—by appealing to the governor.

Mick leapt out. Now to find the tunnel he'd carried Vera out of this morning. The image of her bloodied face smacked his mind. He'd been so close to losing her. He clenched his hands into fists, then uncurled his knuckles slowly. Vengeance couldn't rule him. He needed to keep his head clear.

He rolled up his flannel sleeves and unbuttoned his collar. Soil crunched under his feet as he slipped beneath the dock. With the air whipping his face, he said a final prayer. The night was quiet, but he was about to knock on death's door.

CHAPTER 36

Knock-slap.

Mick counted to ten and raised his fist for the rest of the code.

Knock-slap. Knock-knock-slap.

The waves lapped against the pier, a slow dirge contrasting his erratic heartbeat. He rolled his shoulders and stretched his neck. It was time to place his order. "Hamilton fired first." Hamilton was now on the ten-dollar bill, right? The Federal Reserve was always changing things. If Mick'd said that wrong, he'd be greeted with bullets. With one hand on his holster and the other clutching a satchel, he waited in darkness.

"But Burr shot him in the heart." Kelly's voice boomed from the other side of the door.

Fire pumped Mick's veins.

The deadbolt unlatched. The door creaked open. A dim lantern dangled from Kelly's fingers, illuminating his face, casting shadows. His other hand gripped a revolver. "How many grieved Hamilton's death?"

Now the fun begins. "Twenty-five hundred."

Kelly grunted. "It was four thousand."

"Let's agree on thirty-five hundred. Thirty-five hundred grieved Hamilton's death." He did the math in his head. He'd pay thirty-five hundred dollars for five thousand fakes.

"Come in."

"I do all my business in the open air, mister." Mick dropped the satchel on the ground.

"That's right, you're a new one."

Mick gritted his teeth at Kelly's condescending tone. The big ox oozed everything Mick despised—arrogance and greed.

"How am I going to count money in the dark? Besides, your counterfeits are through this passageway behind me."

"All right. Have it your way." Mick bent low, appearing to pick up the satchel, but knocked the gun out of Kelly's hand.

The ox hesitated, giving Mick time to throw a punch. Kelly jerked his head, and Mick's fist struck only air.

Mick reached for his gun, but Kelly lunged, tackling him to the ground. Mick squirmed under his weight.

Strong fingers bit into Mick's throat, squeezing.

Mick could only move his left arm. His holster was on his right. He launched a punch and only grazed Kelly's ear.

"Can't quite reach me." Kelly laughed through gritted teeth.

Where was Hundley? Flashes of light pricked his vision as he struggled to breathe against Kelly's grip.

His hand scraped the dirt, searching for something, anything. His thumb brushed metal.

Kelly pushed harder on his neck. Mick writhed, the movement giving him the inch he needed. Got it.

"Say goodnight." Kelly spit on him.

Mick swung the lantern, smacking Kelly in the back of the head. It shattered, pieces of glass dusting his face.

Kelly moaned and collapsed to the ground beside him, unconscious. Mick scurried to his knees and drew his gun.

"Drop it." A voice shot from inside the tunnel. Voss, no doubt.

Click.

"That sound is my gun pointed at your heart."

Mick strengthened his grip on his pistol. No way Voss could see him, let alone aim at his heart. But Mick wouldn't dare speak and give away his location.

A shot fired. He flattened to the ground. The sound came from behind him. Hundley must've heard the glass and let off the signal.

"It's over." Mick launched to his feet. "You're surrounded."

Voss retreated in the secret passage, his heavy footfalls betraying him. Mick sprinted after him. He caught up and shouldered him into the wall, trapping the wrist of his gun hand.

Voss grunted.

Mick pressed his gun into the man's chest. With his other hand, he snatched the weapon out of the man's clutch and holstered it.

Beams of light skittered across the tunnel, landing on Mick. Hundley and several others appeared. "Hundley, keep a gun on Kelly. And send an officer over here."

The officer strode beside him, his flashlight shining first on Mick then on …

"Shultz." Mick's voice betrayed his shock. He'd not been chasing down Ward Voss as he'd thought, but the man responsible for prosecuting those in Pittsburgh's underworld. "They got to you, too, I see." He shoved the gun harder into the D.A.'s chest, teeth grinding.

The man's chin quivered.

"You've been in on this the whole time." That's why Kelly had been released. That's how Kelly had known to send Angelo to the cabin. Shultz had told him. Mick fought the urge to sock him in the jaw.

"I made more in a month than you could in ten years. Let me go and I–I'll give you a cut." His pathetic gaze bobbed between Mick and the other officer. "I'll give you all a cut. I–I will."

Harsh words scorched the tip of Mick's tongue. He bit them back. "You really think—"

"He's stirring out here." Hundley's voice drifted in along with Kelly's groaning.

"Be right there." Mick motioned to the officer next to him. "Cuff Shultz and take him out."

The younger officer got right to the task.

Mick jogged over to Hundley. "Take a few men and head inside.

Ward Voss is in there somewhere."

Hundley nodded, handed Mick an extra flashlight along with cuffs, and led the backup, their footsteps echoing through the underpass.

Mick squatted and slapped cuffs on Kelly, pinching them shut. "Justice is a lady, Kelly. Cross her and she'll make you pay."

Kelly winced, and his face went rigid. "Wanna talk ladies?" The rasp in his voice chilled. "If you want to see Vera again, let me go. She's with my men, but I'd have to hurry. They've got orders to dispose of her."

First, Shultz had used money, and now Kelly tried to use Vera as a bargaining chip. Heat ripped across Mick's chest. He grabbed fistfuls of Kelly's lapel, pulling him to his knees.

Kelly returned Mick's glare. "So what is it? Send me to the chair or get your girlfriend back?"

"Nice racket." As his favorite girl would say. "But Vera's safe." He let go of the shirt with a shove and watched the realization hit Kelly like a blow to the gut. "And your men are in custody. If you come across Vinelli, thank him for me. All his information came in handy."

Kelly cussed.

Voices sounded from inside the tunnel. "Looks like my men are collecting Ward Voss. I'd hate for him to miss out on the party." Of all the assignments, this one was the most satisfying. One he'd have the privilege of telling his children and grandchildren. "Carson Kelly, you're under arrest for the suspicion of murder and for the fraudulent manufacturing of government notes."

CHAPTER 37

Morning sun danced over the emerald treetops. Dew hung from thick blades of grass, sparkling like crystals in the light. Vera pressed her finger to the page of Lacey's Bible, keeping the breeze from lifting it.

Three weeks at Lacey's and no news of anything. Just that Carson had been apprehended, but no savory details. No word about anyone, namely Mick.

"You're up early, sugar." Lacey shuffled onto the back porch, armed with a coffee pot. "Thought you might like some now that you're feeling better. It's freshly brewed."

"No, thanks." She stared at the steam twisting up from the pot, unable to suppress the remembrance curling around her heart. The morning Mick had handed her a mug of coffee, the last time she'd spoken to him—while she was coherent, anyway. She tried to throw the memory like a stone in the ocean of forgetfulness, but it kept resurfacing as though it was made of cork.

And her walking around with his blood in her surely hadn't helped any. It was a steady reminder, keeping as close as her heartbeat.

Had Mick moved on? Was he back in his routine, glad to be rid of her? "Thank you for letting me use your Bible." She closed the pages, letting the book rest in her lap. Someday, she'd get around to buying her own. Whenever she found a job. A place to live. An existence beyond Mick and memories. A thorny pain gathered in the back of her throat. "How were the fireworks last night?"

"Splendid." Lacey set the pot on the metal table and reclined in the chair next to Vera. "I had a great spot on the church lawn with my lady friends. Fourth of July is one of my favorite holidays." She tipped her head to the side, a smile brightening her aged face. "Wish you would've come."

Vera had experienced enough fireworks in her own life these past few weeks, making the idea of explosives for entertainment unappealing. She'd been pain-free for four days now, and nothing could persuade her to risk a relapse just to hear a few *kabooms* and gawk at a colorful sky.

"You doing okay?"

"Yeah. No dizziness or nausea." An excellent thing, considering the first week she'd contemplated ripping her head off. She ran a hand over the scab on the crown of her head where the stitches had been removed.

"That's not what I mean." Lacey scooted her chair closer. "I want to know if your heart is okay. I've seen with my own eyes the transformation between you and Mick. There's no denying what you two share. You shouldn't run from that, or from anything in life."

Who was running? And what did they share? Not the same feelings. He was the one who'd agreed not to see her at the hospital. And that silent treatment had continued after her release. Lacey's phone had been quieter than a mime convention. "I have run, Lace, but not this time." She'd run from every problem, ranging from severe hardships to trifling arguments. Her heart had beat to a retreating drum all her life. "This situation is different. I can't stop thinking of him. Especially here. Too many memories." There, she'd said it. Didn't help her feel any better, but at least Lacey could sympathize.

"Well, someone's coming that's gonna cheer you up." Her face puckered in a conspiratorial smile. "Should be here any minute. I actually expected him sooner."

"*Him?*" Was Lacey referring to Mick? Vera's heart did a fevered version of the foxtrot against her ribs.

"My brother's at his cabin this weekend. He arrived late last night." Her blue eyes brightened. "He promised to take us to lunch in town today if you're up for it."

"Sounds swell." She forced a chipper tone, hoping to mask her disappointment. As much as Vera adored Pops, the captain would only remind her of his sergeant. Maybe the time had come for Vera to move forward. Her health wasn't at risk anymore, and her help was no longer needed on the solved case. Perhaps the only way to emotionally heal was to remove herself from this place.

The muted roar of an engine broke into her thoughts.

Lacey stood and smoothed the creases in her apron. "That must be him."

Vera followed her friend around the house to the front yard.

A beige Model A Ford pulled up the lane, the sun bouncing off the windshield, forbidding her a glance at the driver. The automobile slowed to a stop, and a stout figure emerged.

"Andy!" Lacey shuffled to her brother's side and pecked a kiss to his aged cheek.

"Hiya, Pops." Vera shielded the sun from her eyes with one hand and waved with the other.

"Good to see you both." He offered a warm smile. "Lacey, could I trouble you for some of that tasty lemonade you always have chilled?" He patted his pocket—from which an envelope peeked out—and directed his attention to Vera. "I have something important to discuss with this young lady." His mouth turned down at the edges, and her heart squeezed in her chest.

A few minutes later, Pops was settled in the kitchen with Vera across from him. Lacey busied herself in the other room with her latest needlework.

The stark white envelope teased Vera from its spot on the table, daring her to snatch it up and get this over with.

"Open it." The captain sipped his lemonade as if he wasn't

aware that Vera's future was tucked inside a paper rectangle with bent corners.

The envelope no doubt contained a farewell message from Mick, probably written on the same letterhead as the note he'd given her on her birthday, his masculine scrawl telling her politely—but plainly—to have a nice life. Vera should be happy. This was exactly what she needed to help push her into the next phase.

"I want your opinion." Eyes half-lidded, the captain cupped his elbow with one hand and tapped his chin with the other.

She wet her lips and scooped it up. Surely, Pops wouldn't want to discuss Vera and Mick's non-existent love affair. Maybe the man was as nosey as his dear sister. Her foot jittering against the table leg, she untucked the flap. Abraham Lincoln stared at her from inside. "It's a five-spot." Her shoulders lowered with a shaky exhale. It wasn't a *Goodbye, Vera* letter.

"Take it out." He leaned back in his chair. "Examine it."

She withdrew the bill, turning it over and then tossing it onto the table. "Looks fine to me."

"Kelly does good work, doesn't he?"

She stiffened. "You mean that baby's a fake?"

"Uh-huh. A genuine phony." He smiled, the lines crinkling around his eyes. "Looks like Mr. Kelly had an operation bigger than we thought. With the club located on the river, he could disperse these *babies* across several states."

Vera blew out her cheeks. "The big boy's in some deep trouble. But why counterfeit five-dollar bills? You'd think he'd be rolling out the fifties and hundreds."

The captain leaned forward and stuffed the fake back into the envelope. "Fives and tens can circulate without drawing attention. Kelly printed larger bills, but those went to the underground gambling joints. The unsuspecting customers would play the tables with their money, and if they won, the card sharks would pay out fakes. Brilliant plan, really. Because even if anyone found out, they couldn't report it without getting themselves incriminated. You see?"

"To think, it's all been under my shoes for years." She clucked her tongue. "And you, my man, must have gotten a big slap on your back by your superiors."

"All except the D.A. He got slapped with handcuffs for being Kelly and Voss' silent third partner."

Her jaw about fell onto her lap. "The D.A.? He was in on it?"

"Yeah, we'd had suspicions for a while that a counterfeiting syndicate was running rampant." He grimaced, disappointment shadowing his eyes. "But when the letter went missing, I—"

"Letter?"

"Yes ma'am. We'd received a letter the week of the Kelly Club shooting, inferring some wrongdoings over there. It was anonymous, but the letter was postmarked from Steubenville."

His words triggered the trap door in Vera's memory. She shot straight in her seat. "He said that. He said that."

"Who? What?" The captain jolted from his chair—quite spry for a man over twice her age—and grabbed a notepad and pen from Lacey's drawer. He returned to his seat and poised his hand to write. "Go ahead, darlin', and say it slowly."

"Right before Artie got shot, Carson said *I know about Steubenville*."

The captain scribbled something, then looked up, his glasses lower on his nose. "Shultz must've told Kelly, and he put two and two together." He sighed. "Then put a bullet into Cavenhalt."

Poor Artie. The lump in her throat crumbled into her heart. Maybe Millie would have some closure now. Vera would be sure to include both mother and daughter in her nightly prayers.

"Well." He folded up the paper and slipped it into his front pocket. "Enough about this business. How about I take you and Lacey to an early lunch? My treat."

"As long as you're not paying with this Lincoln, then you're on." Vera gave him a cheeky smile.

Man, she was going to miss Pops. And Lacey. Her gaze strayed out the window at the tall pines. She could travel a million miles from this sap-laced forest, but it would never leave her.

CHAPTER 38

"Do you mind if we stop by my cabin for a minute?" The captain glanced at Vera in the rearview mirror.

She clutched her cross, her belly shrinking. She'd never been there without Mick.

"Won't be too much of a delay," Lacey put in. "Might be good for you, sugar, to see the place. Considering what you told me this morning."

Could she visit the Boone cabin? Face the hurt?

Vera tapped her fingernails on the dark seat cushion in a spastic rhythm. Why was she jittery? It was just a house. Wood and nails. Forget it was the place she'd fallen in love. Her breath burrowed in her lungs and stayed there. Well, since she was in the neighborhood, she could pick up the heart she'd left behind.

Every jostle on the uneven road shook out more remembrances of her car rides with Mick. The way the gentle wind had played in his wavy hair. How he'd hang his hand out the window between downshifts. She dabbed the corner of her eye, hoping Pops didn't catch her movement in the mirror.

The captain turned onto the drive leading up the hill. Everything looked the same except for the overgrown grass. The timbers stood tall, and their branches waved at her with the help of the summer breeze. Instead of driving farther to the cabin, Pops braked halfway up the incline.

"There it is, young lady. Just for you."

Vera leaned forward and followed Pops' gaze, directed at the line of pine trees. A wooden stool sat beneath the canopy of branches. A guitar—Mick's Gibson—propped against the leg of the stool, and her breath squeezed from her chest. "I don't understand."

"Just go on, Vera." Lacey's gaze toggled between Vera and the scene outside. "And see for yourself."

With a shaky hand, she opened the door and stepped out, her heels slightly sinking into the soft ground. The Gibson shouldn't be resting in the damp grass. She moved swifter to retrieve it when Mick emerged from behind one of the pines.

Her breath went thin and patchy, a feverish fluttering in her chest.

The look of longing in his jade eyes was enough to whittle the strength from her. A million questions surfaced, but she couldn't voice a single one.

A car rumbled behind her, and Vera glanced over her shoulder in time to see the sneaky duo of brother and sister make their escape down the hill.

She returned her attention to Mick, who now sat on the stool, his Gibson perched on his right thigh. With the tall pines as a backdrop, he locked her in his warm gaze and strummed.

"*Though worlds apart …*"

Oh mercy. She pressed a hand to her cheek. He was singing.

"*Two hearts met under heaven's stars*." His low baritone timbre filtered through her ears and seeped into her soul, luring her another step closer. "*And for a moment, you were mine. When we danced beneath the whispering pines.*"

The dance. He'd remembered. Tears beckoned, but she blinked them back. With each step, a chain around her heart snapped, falling to the wayside, allowing the gates to burst wide. Her pulse throbbing wildly, she stood exposed, but safe before the only man she'd loved.

"*Let me be the one to prove, real love won't run out on you.*" His eyes glossed, and she adored him more for it. "*Can I be the one to show, unending love is true?"*

Did he understand what he was singing? The commitment behind the lyrics?

"Vera, will you be mine for a lifetime? Starting now, beneath the whispering pines." He stopped, and Vera's lungs seemed incapable of expansion. Silence hovered between them, both precious and excruciating.

"You said you needed a song." The sides of his mouth hitched, but there was a vulnerability in his expression. "It's all yours. And so am I."

Her heart wobbled in her chest as every coherent thought vanished. She searched his face, as familiar as her own. "Mick, what are you saying?"

He stood and propped the guitar against the stool. "I'm saying the same thing I said in the pit of the Kelly Club." Two of his long strides closed the gap between them. "Do you remember?" His eyes were a beautiful blend of seriousness and tenderness.

"The captain said you'd rescued me."

"No, you rescued me." He stroked her cheek with his knuckle. His touch awakened her, creating a thirst for more. "You were right. I couldn't forgive myself. That's what I wanted to tell you that morning in your apartment, but I never got a chance. I almost never had that chance again." He moved closer, his breath fanning her cheek.

"I'm sorry I wouldn't let you talk that morning." She slid a lock of hair behind her ear. "I was certain you didn't feel the same way for me as I did for you. Then when you didn't contact me all these weeks, I—"

"The doctors insisted you needed to heal as calmly as possible. *Any* emotional upsets, good or bad, could delay your recovery. I'm sorry my silence hurt you." His wounded gaze confirmed his words. "I wanted what was best for you. But believe me, I felt every second of our separation."

She nodded and another tear escaped.

"When I was holding you in that gin joint basement, I felt myself dying with you, but God intervened." He cupped her face, his calluses rough—but oh so perfect—against her skin. "When He saved you from dying, He saved me from having to live every day without you by my side."

Her feet seemed to anchor into the ground. His presence so steady, so comfortable. She had no permanent residence, but he felt like … home. "You gave me your blood." The breathy whisper escaped her heart. "How many times can one man save a girl's life?"

A slow smile built. "If you'll stay close for the next eighty years, we can keep a record." He grabbed her hand, lacing his fingers in hers. "I love you."

The caverns of her soul stretched, and his words fell right in.

"I told you first in the Kelly Club basement, and I'll tell you every day of my life if you'll let me."

"It's true?" Vera slid her eyes shut, the realization opening like a flower after the rain.

"Oh, sweetheart. I know I lied before, but I need you to believe me."

She wiped the tear away from her cheek just for it to be replaced by another. "I remember, Mick." She buried her face in his shoulder. The quickened beat of his heart matched her own. "I thought I dreamt it. But it was true." She was loved. By God. By Mick Dinelo. "You told me you loved me so much it hurt."

"It still does." He lifted her chin with his thumb. "That is, until you tell me that you feel the same way."

"I love you too."

He lowered his head, his lips hovering over hers. "May I kiss you underneath the whispering pines?"

"Yes." If she didn't melt into a puddle first.

Their lips met, and she swayed under the influence of his touch, pulling her in, inviting a response. Her fingers splayed on his chest, and he curled his arms around her waist. Her hands slid to his neck, the corded masculinity strong beneath her fingertips. She nestled in his embrace, savoring his love.

After years of struggling to make it through the day, she'd never looked forward to the future. Hope had become an empty word. But here, wrapped in Mick's arms, her soul expanded to welcome tomorrow. Not only did she lean on Mick's love, but she rested in God's. Just like that verse said in Lacey's kitchen—*He rejoices over you with singing*. She may not have always heard it, but it had been there, beckoning.

From this day on, life was in her song.

The End

Author's Note

Dear Reader,

Thank you so much for reading *The Red Canary*. There are a gazillion stories out there, and so for you to give mine a chance is an honor I don't take lightly. These notes are always a joy for me to write because it's where I get to provide behind-the-scenes details of the book! So allow me to point out the factual from the fictional.

While Vera Pembroke is completely from my imagination, I stole elements of her personality from a Roaring Twenties jazz singer. Helen Morgan entertained crowds at a speakeasy hidden in the back of Nixon Theater in Pittsburgh. She's known for inventing the iconic pose of singing while sitting/lying atop the piano. So naturally, I had to incorporate that into the first scene of the novel. Also during those early chapters, you may have recognized a *noir* vibe. That was completely intentional as it is a nod to my love of classic movies.

The views displayed in this story concerning Prohibition in Pittsburgh are accurate. Pittsburgh was known as the "wettest city in the dry nation." Crime bosses and bootleggers unashamedly bribed city officials and police forces in order to run their empires. Sadly, because the law enforcement was heavily corrupt, honest officers were few and far between. Prohibition was only acknowledged on paper because there were over five hundred speakeasies threaded throughout the city. Procuring justice for lawlessness usually came by appealing to state government.

The Allegheny National Forest, where much of this story is set, was purchased by the government in 1923. The 513,175 acres in Northwestern Pennsylvania is the only national forest in the state. This region is particularly special to me because a lot of my youth was spent within its wooded boundaries. The swimming hole, the teaberry patch atop the hill, the open space where Mick taught Vera to shoot are all real places. By the time my family occupied the place, there was running water and indoor plumbing, but I remember playing with the rusty pump, and that weathered outhouse was often "home base" when we'd play hide-and-seek.

Thank you again for reading this story of my heart. If you're interested in more of my writing and latest news, please visit me at RachelScottMcDaniel.com or on any of the popular social media platforms.

Blessings,
Rachel

CPSIA information can be obtained
at www.ICGtesting.com
Printed in the USA
LVHW030838271220
675096LV00005B/763